I'm not going to lie.

This is for The Goose, with undying love.

And for Lorraine, who was first to hear the story when we were only twelve years old.

Meanwhile the wild geese, high in the clean blue air
are heading home again.
Whoever you are, no matter how lonely
the world offers itself to your imagination
calls to you like the wild geese, harsh and exciting —
over and over announcing your place
in the family of things.
- Mary Oliver

The Advice Bucket
By Heather Hill

First Printing: 2017

www.heatherhillauthor.com

Ordering Information:

For details on quantity purchases, contact the publisher/author, Heather Hill - Email: hell4heather@gmail.com

U.S. trade bookstores and wholesalers: Please contact Heather Hill

Cover photo: Barnacle geese at Caerlaverock Wetlands Centre taken by Mark Chambers

Foreword

The Barnacle Goose is Very Clever, And Was Once, Technically, a Fish.

Winging its way across a whole wide ocean, the barnacle goose family often zeros in on exactly the field (on Islay) where the parents wintered last year — and stays thereabouts for the whole winter. 'They don't even take a fly about to see the rest of the island,' a resident ornithologist, Malcolm Ogilvie, told me. He told me, too, why the bird is named after a crustacean. Many centuries ago, the feathery looking interior of what is now called the goose barnacle prompted an answer to the mystery of why tens of thousands of geese simply appeared in the Hebrides every autumn, apparently out of nowhere. They had hatched from barnacles, it was suggested. This made the bird, technically, a fish. 'Which could therefore be eaten by the God fearing, even on Fridays,' smiled Malcolm Ogilvie. 'This may explain why the theory was not exposed to the critical scrutiny it deserved.'

Only within most Spectator readers' lifetimes, and with Ogilvie's help, was Greenland identified as the provenance of the west coasting goose and Siberia as that of the east coasters.

Facts like these amuse and interest, but nothing could prepare me for the sight and sound of the geese gathering in their winter quarters.

Islay is not a spectacular island, but gentle, windy and wide, with low brown horizons and a high grey sky suffused with soft light. Everywhere is the buffet of the breeze and the whisper of the sea. Around the shore are littered a tangle of telegraph poles, the geometry of small straight tarmac strips going nowhere, and little cottages strewn over the landscape —like packing cases fallen off a pantechnicon, as D.H. Lawrence remarked of Western Australia in Kangaroo.

My producer, Jeremy Grange, met me at the airfield and we headed for the skyline on a ruler straight road. 'There's some!' Jeremy exclaimed. We stopped. I got quietly out of the car as Jeremy reached for his tape recorder.

A whole wide flat meadow was speckled grey and cream as thousands of barnacle geese pecked furiously at the grass. The air was full of their cry. The bird is smaller than a domestic goose and strikingly marked. The face looks like a pale painted war mask, the pate and neck are black, and the wings are a beautiful, partly striped grey.

Seeing us, the whole flock took flight. Their screech was everywhere. They filled the sky with a fluid swirl of black streaks, drifting and diving: a Hitchcockian nightmare.

And I don't know why — call me anthropomorphist — but it seemed to me that these birds were excited just to be there. The barnacles were on vacation. Each family included a member who had never visited before. Their winter holidays in Scotland were starting.'

- Matthew Paris, The Spectator, October 2003

*Matthew Parris is a columnist for The Times and The Spectator.

Chapter 1: Gladys (c 1670)

The figure twirled and danced before them. He was a blaze of grey, black and brown feathers, the light of the fire casting an even more imposing shadow on the wall. She wished it would stop, aware of how he would appear to all that didn't know him. Like evil personified: not human, not entirely birdlike. He fancied he was a phantom, Gladys thought; or the God of all beasts of the sky. The small boy cradled in her lap remained unresponsive; almost tranquil. Some that had passed before now beckoned to him from a place far beyond this one. A world away from the spinning figure of Merrick Anderson, of this she was certain.

Gladys pulled the boy closer to her, wiping beads of sweat from his forehead with her sleeve. Staring down at his hands, which were grey as a jackdaw's chest, she ached with the pain of conflict. There was little time to consider her problem. Which one to save?

'Am I dead?' the boy murmured.

She smoothed back the hair that hung limp and wet over his right ear and, fighting back tears, whispered, 'Not yet.'

Only minutes away, the lynch mob would be picking up speed. There would be a long procession of angry villagers, each directed by the light from her window. That and the word of a dying boys' best friend. The Cailleach's lair. Gladys knew they were coming, she could hear the angry cries now. There was no way out for all three of them, she thought, with grim realisation, as she listened to screams of, 'This way!' and 'Kill the witch!'

As the boy took his last breath, Gladys startled at the glare of torches that now pierced the blackness. Blinking back tears, she looked from the window to Merrick, the bird man, who still circled them. Only she knew that it would be for the final time. '*Fortantium. Barnacaleus.* Fly,' she whispered.

At the flutter of new wings, the hut door exploded - smashed by the angry mob in moments. The men piled in, stooping to make way for the goose as it hovered in mid-air, beating its wings and barking in alarm. Gladys watched with relief as it finally soared over their heads to freedom. A dozen men now paced the room, stabbing at the air with their torches, baying for Merrick's blood. She cowered, as a tall, broad figure stood before her. When at last she found the courage to look up, she saw ruddy, wild eyes glaring at the boy's lifeless body. 'Oh, dear God! My son! My poor, wee boy. We're too late! Too late!' he sobbed, falling to his knees in front of her.

'Where is the heathen?' someone demanded.

'Evil wench!' another barked. She stared at this man, who had been first to break into the room, but didn't speak. 'Where did he go, woman?' the man insisted. 'I saw him through the window, he was right here.' He turned back to the rest of the group. 'I saw him, I swear it!'

Gladys hugged the boy to her and kissed his forehead. 'He's gone,' she cried numbly. 'They're both gone.'

The boy's father gazed from his son to where Merrick had stood only moments earlier, and she saw him gasp. 'B..b..but, he was there,' he stammered. 'I saw him too. Through the window.'

'Gone where?' the first man asked her, his eyes flashing with venomous hatred.

Gladys put a hand on the shoulder of the boy's father, but he brushed it off. 'He was only trying to save your boy, I swear it,' she told him, her voice strangled by emotion.

'Liar,' he said, covering his face with his hands. 'The sorcerer killed my boy!'

'Give him to us, heathen woman,' the second man growled, signalling for another to take the boy from her. 'You'll burn for this and so will Merrick.'

Gladys held the boy in one last, tight hug before he was wrenched from her grasp. 'We didn't do it,' she told his father, who remained broken on his knees before her. 'It was the consumption!'

'Lying witch!' the man bawled, lifting his head to spit in her face.

She bowed her head to wipe away the saliva from her cheek. Then she spied it, on the ground where the boy had lain seconds before: a single, black feather. Merrick, her Merrick, was free. As the vengeful group dragged her to her feet, she felt a need to explain to the poor man on the ground. 'He thought he could save the wee boy's life,' she told him. 'But he had no more magic in him than you do. He's no sorcerer, don't you see?'

'He's a murderer and so are you, witch,' the second man roared. 'He can't have gotten far in these woods.' He dragging her away from the men to him, barking, 'Find him!'

As every man except the boy's father made for the door, he gripped harder on her wrists, turning her to face him. 'Where is he?' he sneered. 'Ye may as well give him up now because we'll find him anyway. He's going to burn with or without you.'

Shaking more from cold than fear, Gladys stretched up to meet his angry stare. 'There'll be no burning here today,' she replied. 'Or any other day, damn you. I'll tell you where he is. He's taken to the skies and he'll no be back.'

As he sent her sprawling to the ground with a shove and a hefty kick, the only pain she felt was the sting of loss. The deed was done, her decision made. All that remained of her beloved Merrick were two feathers which lay just beyond her grasp. He would fly the skies from this day on, while her destiny was to stay and walk the earth, forever.

Chapter 2: Lucy

'Lucy Pryce?'

Lucy blinked at the burly man in an eighties style bomber jacket. He held a brown-black folder aloft as she peered at the badge on his lapel and squinted to read the name: Brains. Hmmm. Some people loved *Thunderbirds* too, too much.

'It's Colwyn, these days, er… Brains,' she informed him. 'I changed it by deed poll about a month ago, now.'

The shorter, mousey-haired woman, standing on the doorstep with Brains smirked.

'It's Brian,' the man informed her solemnly. 'We're From FDG.' Opening the folder, he took a piece of paper from it and waved it at her. 'We have a warrant for entry to your property to fit prepayment meters.'

Lucy looked from him to the grinning woman. 'Ah,' she replied, adding a sigh. 'Not Brains, then. You'll have to excuse me, I left my glasses in my very cold lounge.' She turned to the woman, and added, 'You enjoy delivering bad news to people in fuel poverty, don't you? What do you do for relaxation, club baby seals?'

The woman's smile faded.

'We have a team of engineers to fit the meters. Can you show us where they are?' No-Brains continued, not looking at her, but down at his notes instead.

Lucy folded her arms. 'And what if I don't let you in?'

He glanced up at her, taking a deep, over-exaggerated breath. Raising his eyebrows, he gave Lucy a look that told her he had heard the question countless times before. He of course had a scripted answer ready: 'Then I'm afraid I will be forced to contact the police,' he said, turning his attention to back to his paperwork. He added a few ticks here and there, nodding to himself.

As she observed him, Lucy began to picture a scene in her mind. She was barricaded in her home, holding next door's cat at toy-gunpoint, shouting through the letterbox. 'You'll never take me alive!' It was a plausible plan. But she never could wheel herself fast enough to catch that blasted cat.

'Okay,' she agreed at last, leaning over to wave to the six men in two vans and a car sat waiting in her driveway. A meeker woman would be mortified as this entire scene played out in front of her neighbours. Lucy was not one of those women. This wasn't going to go the way Brian and his ruthless, money-grasping employers would like it to. She was no longer pervious.

'Both meters are outside, so you can go find them yourself,' she said. 'But, I'm sorry to tell you, I won't be here to feed them.'

She adjusted her head scarf and stroked the new growth that was beginning to form a fringe. Only last night she had treated it to a cheerful, brilliant-violet update.

'Can you tell me why not?' asked Brian, still not looking up from the page. He held his pen still, looming over the 'we've got another live one' box, no doubt.

'Because I'm going travelling.'

The pen went back to work, as Brian scribbled something in his notes. Lucy imagined it was, 'usual delaying tactics.' As if *she* could go travelling.

'When?' the woman asked her.

Lucy gave her a satisfied smile. 'Tomorrow,' she replied.

'In that case,' said Brian, without looking up, 'can we have a forwarding address?'

'No, you cannot.'

He stopped writing and stared up from his page at her. 'Why not?'

'Because, as I just said, I'm going travelling,' Lucy replied. 'There will be no fixed abode; no forwarding address. No, in fact, power bills again, ever.'

'Except the ones you already owe,' Brian responded stiffly. He turned a page in his folder and tapped the new one. 'We will be fitting the meter today, regardless,' he told her. 'That is what we're ordered to do.'

His accomplice turned to peer around at the front garden. 'I don't see a "For Sale" sign?' she said.

'I rent,' Lucy lied. 'And I leave tomorrow. So I'm sure my landlord will appreciate this new, not-in-any-way-requested-by-me addition to his property.'

Brian pursed his lips and poked his inside left cheek with his tongue. It looked to Lucy like he was actually stifling a compulsion to laugh at her. 'So, you're going away tomorrow?' he continued, after the briefest of silences.

Lucy nodded.

'By yourself?'

She nodded again, noting his disbelief and delighting in it.

'Okay, well, we will be fitting the meters today regardless.' He patted the paper in his folder again. 'And we do require a forwarding address.'

'I understand,' Lucy replied. 'But, as I have explained, I won't have a permanent place of residence. I'll be couch surfing.'

Brian glanced wearily at his colleague, who looked as though she didn't know where to put herself.

Lucy eyed the wheelie bin at the end of her path, thinking she might like to help the woman with that particular problem. 'I can give you a contact number, though?' she said to Brian.

'Well, that's something,' the woman replied, a little too brightly.

Brian scowled at her, but made his pen ready again, regardless.

13

'Okay, well it's a sort of travelling desk number, to be honest,' Lucy told him. 'I won't be anywhere permanent, like I said, but I will be working to pay off some of these debts of course. And I'm far too broke to own any kind of mobile phone that hasn't been cut off already.'

Brian started to write. The woman nodded enthusiastically, as Lucy gave him the number. 'Now,' she said finally, 'you can go back and tell Fecking Dear Gas that I have, perhaps, six weeks to live and work, if I'm lucky. So they may want to rethink planning more executive bonuses with the help of my five pounds a week. I'll be making my own heat where I'm going.'

'You're dying?' the woman said, the colour draining from her face.

As she retreated inside and closed the door on the pair, Lucy heard Brian cough, then mutter under his breath. It was a misguided, heartless assumption; but one that made her feel triumphant. It was a sweeter victory than the premium rate number she'd given him to contact her on. Death was to be her final, solitary strike for anti-capitalism.

'Ach, pay no mind,' she heard Brian utter. 'They all say that.'

Chapter 3: Merrick

The call to migrate had come again, carried in the wind. It enveloped him in its irresistible magnetism, the smell of home. As in all winters past, the food was fast disappearing, signalling that it was time. Time to lead them all back to where lush, green fields awaited them.

For three centuries Merrick had been taking his flock away each winter, back to Islay. In the early years it had been a journey he made to go in search of Gladys. This was unbeknownst to those geese that, driven by both hunger and curiosity, began to follow him year after year.

After leaving her to fly the earth alone, he had first found himself among the tree geese. He knew of these creatures, who started life as barnacle shells hanging from trees over the Atlantic. Those that had fallen into the sea had become geese, those that fell upon the land perished. He considered that it was because of this game of chance that the early barnacle goose groups had been so few. Later, it had been by man's hand, he remembered, with a pang of guilty regret. Once, oh so long ago now, Merrick himself had been a hunter of the birds and geese. Now he was the hunted, yet he had used his human experience to serve the flock well. In the beginning they had been a few hundred. Today, he observed with an innate sense of pride, they were thousands.

She had been watching him observing them. Now, he stood, side by side with her. They each looked in opposite directions and bowed their heads as they called. It was an age-old greeting of a long-standing pair, yet the triumph ceremony was brief. There was work to do. A long and arduous journey lay ahead of them all.

His bark now brought the entire flock to silence. Through the Bear Island mist he could see every black and white head had turned to the south. In his boyhood, Merrick could have shouted out, 'let's go!' As a mature goose, his call was like the yapping of a small dog. Yet its message is received and understood here. In a blanket of black and white, spirals of air beneath tipped wings lifted them over the cliff edge as one. To Scotland.

Chapter 4: Gladys

There was an aching in her bones the likes of which Gladys hadn't felt for over three centuries. 'Well, this is new,' she said, sliding her legs over to the edge of the bed and making to stand up. 'MacPhee!'

The dog awoke from his slumber and stared at her.

'This is the bit where you get up and come right tae ma side,' Gladys told him. She slapped her knees and then grimaced at the pain she'd caused herself.

Her faithful Labrador blinked, but didn't move.

'Aye,' she said, patting her knees again, albeit more gently this time. 'We are going oot in the rain to stretch oor aching legs and look at the sky. Are ye coming for a walk?'

The word 'walk' would have had him bounding at the door at lightning speed a few years earlier, bad weather or not. But MacPhee was old now. He seemed to prefer the warm, unhurriedness of the fireplace. Reading his 'are you serious?' face, Gladys called to him again.

'MacPhee! Come on, old boy. Let's go. Joe's boat will be in soon, weather permitting.'

He cocked his head at her, before stretching his front paws forwards. She knew what he was thinking: that he might make it to the door without lifting his belly from the ground. In an instant she walked over to where he lay, stooped down and grabbed his collar, yanking him upwards. 'I said, let's go.' He followed at last because, she realised, he would know he had little choice. It was that or clean the floor with his fluffy body as she dragged him to the door. Gladys paused, wondering whether to fetch her umbrella, before grabbing her coat instead. Trying but failing to keep one hand on MacPhee's collar, she eased it on, pulling the hood over her head. She scowled at the dog, who was backing away again, and tugged him out with her into the brisk, mid-morning air. Looking up at the grey sky, Gladys felt icy rain on her face and, for the first time in years, it stung. Releasing her grip on MacPhee, she turned back indoors. In a moment she was back out, armed with the wind and rain's only enemy in the woods: an umbrella. As she turned to grin in triumph at the dog her face fell as he yawned again.

'Right,' she said, stooping to grab his collar before taking a dog lead from her pocket and slipping it on him. As she bent over, it felt like all the bones of her spine creaked. 'Hmm,' she mused. 'That's new as well.' Smiling, Gladys kicked out one leg and then the other, catching raindrops on her pyjama-clad legs. As the freezing rain began soaking through the material, she felt like skipping. 'Let's get out on to the hill,' she said, rubbing her achy back with a grin. 'I'm in pain, MacPhee! Actual pain!' She jiggled the dog chain with a peel of laughter.

Straightening up again, Gladys remembered the note in her pocket. It was one she'd pulled out of the Advice Bucket the night before. Taking it out and unravelling it, she spied the reflection of her youthful, unlined face in the window. 'Not looking any older though,' she observed. 'Not a day.'

She glanced down at today's note, and read it again:

Never pass on the chance to stop and appreciate the skies. Each day is a rare and beautiful thing. The sunniest day to the most furious of storms let you know in equal measure that you're truly alive.'

'Humph,' she sniffed, folding the paper up and placing it back in her pocket. 'A rare thing? You were only here for a few days, Olive, my friend.' She looked back up to take in the view as instructed. Straining her neck to notice the third stormy sky she'd seen this week, the bones in her spine cracked again.

'Well, well, well. There's a change in the air,' she said into the freezing, Hebridean wind that battered her exposed features. 'And you know what, Olive? Thanks to you, I know I'm going tae like it.' She looked down at MacPhee and jangled his leash. 'Let's get on now,' she told him. 'There'll be dog biscuits on that boat.'

Chapter 5: Lucy

And so it began. The easiest, most difficult days of a woman's life, known as, 'the end'.

After Lucy typed these words into the final post of her blog, she paused, sitting back in her wheelchair. Stretching to look out of the window at the rain, which whipped against the rattling glass, she sighed. Everything was getting on with the business of a typical, Scottish summer's day. It was as though nothing was different about it or the world for that matter. Nothing in nature will have changed, she thought. Only I have. Even after you've received the worst news you think you could get, the rest of life keeps on being normal.

'I'm dying, haven't you heard?' she said to the rain, falling into temporary disparagement. Adjusting her vision to view her reflection in the glass, she saw a sad, pale version of her former self. This was as any dying person would be expected to be, wasn't it? Pushing back her headscarf, which was slipping down over her eyebrows, she glanced back at the incomplete blog post and tutted. 'Oh, I've got to get this done now,' she said. 'I have, what?' She glanced at her wristwatch as though it was a death clock, and frowned. 'Six weeks, maybe less, to say everything I have left to say to the outside world? Why can't I get what I want to say out?'

She tapped her aching forehead in annoyance. Her stomach turned over, performing a familiar, squelchful, triple salchow. In all her thousand-plus, alcohol-fuelled student days, she had never vomited so much. This past year had taken the trophy. She'd endured forty-three chemotherapy and radiotherapy sessions. She'd been on enough hospital visits to be on first name terms with at least one consultant. There'd been two invasive, life-altering surgeries. If only it was the hospital food that was to blame for the countless days she'd spent looking forward to death. But it was more than soggy toast that had driven her to the edge. Death might at least bring some relief. There would be no grieving relatives at her funeral. Lucy was an only child who had never known her father. At six she became motherless too. Then the death of her eighteen-year-old daughter added to her share of the bad luck handouts. Thank you, Lord. Next had come His magnificent finale: a new, incurable brain disease. And Lucy was one of only three percent of people in the world lucky enough to have it.

'Thanks for the terminal illness I still can't pronounce!'

She raised her glass and sighed, before knocking back the dregs of red wine.

The only person who could speak at Lucy's funeral was her husband of twenty-one years, Greg. He was the only person alive to know the real her. But Greg's podiatrist, Rosaleen, might disapprove. Any involvement from him would be too upsetting, now that their two-year affair was out. Affairs tend to get discovered when you're huffing away on the sofa. Especially while your wife is at home in bed nursing the world's biggest headache. Had Lucy stayed at work that day, she'd have suffered a worse one for a few more years yet.

She would have been devastated, but for one, little detail. She detested the man. Rosaleen was Lucy's hero, the excuse she'd needed to get shot of Greg forever at last. She supposed she had loved him once. It may have been half past five on a Bank Holiday Monday. It was on that day he'd introduced her to a cinnamon swirl, on one of a series of inexpensive dates he took her on. She had become hooked on cinnamon swirls before the sickness, that's for damn sure. And there was nothing like the gift of cake to make you succumb to a temporary bout of love-blindness. Funny, she missed the cake. But Greg? Meh!

Who feels no pain when the man they've lived with for twenty years walks out of their life for good? she wondered. Someone whose days had become so bare, a little more emptiness wasn't noticeable. A little girl abandoned by her mum. A mother who no longer had her funny, beautiful, Nicola. Who'd lost an only child ripped from their lives by a drunken bus driver.

Lucy Colwyn told everyone it was she who should have died in that accident, over three years ago now. Why take Nicola? A bright, gifted and assertive young woman who was studying to be a doctor? She should have her whole life ahead of her. Why did everyone in Lucy's life have to leave? Her diagnosis would have hit most people like a truck. But in truth, Lucy was looking forward to the end; it was long, overdue and eagerly anticipated. Nicola could have gone on to save lives, whereas Lucy had brought nothing to the world. Nicola would be unable to carry her legacy forward. And now, after first saving her, God had decided that she was to die too. What was the point? She couldn't wait to find death, because everything she loved and missed was there.

She returned her thoughts to the keyboard, wheeling herself forward again, and typed:

And so, my darling life, I'm on the outside looking in. At last. I'm swollen, sore and more beaten than the window panes of the entire, west coast of Scotland. What have I left to do and what have I done? What was my purpose here? To bring forward the next generation? Well, I did. And He snatched it away.

'My darling life,' she read aloud, baulking at the irony as she pushed her wheelchair back from the desk with her feet. It was fair to wallow in self-pity today of all days. So she let it in, and it came crashing and hissing, like freezing water poured over hot coals. Her mother had chosen to leave her; Nicola had not. Between them and her late grandmother, who had taken her in after her mother's death, she had dealt with so much loss. More than a person should have to suffer in a hundred years. She felt entitled to be angry and miserable.

She clipped down the footrests on her chair and wheeled through for a second glass of Malbec. A memory flooded in, following her to the kitchen. After her mother's funeral, her grandmother had moved them to live at the holiday cottage on Islay. 'For some happier, new beginnings,' the old lady had said. The memory began with an image of her grandmother, lifting Lucy up to let her stand on the kitchen window sill.

'Look out there,' the old woman said, as together they admired the garden of their new home. 'Do you see it?'

The little girl saw nothing; only lawn, a fence and miles and miles of pine trees beyond. 'What?' she asked, sensing excitement in the air but feeling perplexed by it.

'There, over the fence by the edge of the forest! It's a rare one, for sure. Never seen that in these parts before.'

'What?' Lucy repeated, staring harder into the mass of trees. 'What is it, grannie?'

The old lady rapped on the window with her knuckles. The sound sent a blurry, oval shape with flashes of black and white, fluttering up into the sky.

'A barnacle goose, would you believe?' her grandmother told her. She lifted Lucy back down and kissed her on the top of her head. 'What a beautiful thing she was,' the old lady said. 'As are you.'

Lucy smiled up at her. 'I couldn't see it, grannie,' she said, feeling sadder for the old lady than herself.

'Well, it'll come again, no doubt,' came the reply. 'It was here last week too, you know. Old Mr Toe next door told me. All by itself. Odd to see one of the barnacle geese going about alone.'

She placed the girl back down and eyed her, as if waiting for more questions, of which there came none. Satisfied, she made her way over to the sideboard, to where she kept the Advice Bucket. This, she told the little girl, was where she would put answers Lucy might need throughout her life. 'I can't be here to teach you things forever,' she would say. Only now Lucy knew the truth. How well she'd concealed the sadness that must have filled her eighty-year-old heart. 'You have to get on with it and that's that,' she said. 'But you'll always have the Advice Bucket. It was your mum's idea, you know.'

'Then why didn't she make me one?'

'She did. But there perhaps wasn't time to finish,' her grandmother replied. A brief sadness portrayed behind her twinkling eyes, as she added, 'But I know she meant to. I know she did.' Tearing a piece of paper from the notepad next to the bucket, she scribbled something on to it. 'We're making new memories for you. Seeing that elegant creature has made me think of another thing I want to say.'

She finished writing, scrunched up the paper and threw it in the bucket. 'When you're old enough to read it, you'll see what it says for yourself. I can tell you, though, this one is about geese. Because, do you know what, little Lucy Goosey? That one is coming to our garden to see you. I'm convinced of it.'

Lucy poured the wine, holding the glass between her knees. Wheeling herself back to the sitting room, she paused at her grandmother's Advice Bucket in the hall. It was a thing she rarely looked inside these days. Despite the old woman's best intentions in making it for her, the bucket held nothing she needed now. It only served to remind her of days almost darker than those she faced now. The sudden and inexplicable departure of her mother, by the woman's own hands, had left her with questions. But there was no one left to answer them.

'I wonder which note she wrote on that particular day?' she thought, deciding to dig inside the bucket after all. She picked out a note and read it aloud, before shaking her head. 'Utter nonsense,' she said, screwing it up and pushing it in to her pocket. She'd try to decipher that one again later.

She would never know what her grandmother wrote on that particular day. 'Why did it even matter?' she told herself. She had never needed any advice about geese.

Chapter 6: Merrick

Merrick shivered. But the searing, bitter cold was nothing compared to - was that pain in his wing? An incessant wailing filled the air. He opened one eye, then another, to see only blurry next-to-nothingness. Next he hunched his shoulders, trying to deaden the sound. But it was useless and only made his wing throb more. What was that noise? People?

No, God, please not people. He had to warn the others. Pulling himself up to, was this a sitting position? he opened his eyes wide and strained his neck, feeling more agonising stabs to both his head and wing. He had to fly; to get away. But how? His wing was… what? Broken? And why so cold? Why the pain? He never had pain. Was this death? Finally?

The sound continued. A long, mournful wailing. A cry of some sort - a human in pain. Shaking his head to clear his brain, Merrick blinked as things began to materialise in his line of vision. With a clearer view now, his eyes searched for the source of the sound, but found nothing but grass, stone and the sea. If only he could stop the noise, then the pain in his head might subside. Was it beneath him? Inside him? He looked down, and spied a man's legs dangling over the edge of the small hillock he had perched on.

Got. To. Fly.

He beat the air with his wings, heart pounding and the pain forgotten in his haste to escape. Not now, not after all this time. He couldn't let the hunters get them.

Letting out a warning honk to the others, he heard a human scream. Instead of the cushion of air beneath each wing that would carry him soaring skywards, he felt only a cold rush. And he hadn't left the ground. He was sitting on the hillock! What's more, there were no others. Still there was screaming. It's afraid of me.

He let out a sigh of relief as the screaming stopped. Wait… he sighed?

'Hello?' he croaked.

He could speak! He remembered this speech thing, from so, so long ago. What the…? He scratched his head, which was wet with blood. Owwwoohhh! His wing-arm-whatever-it-was-today hurt like hell. He hugged it close to him with his other one. Finding a coat around him, he pulled it tighter, before looking down for the legs he'd seen earlier.

'Ahhh, there they are,' he said. What?

Getting to his feet, Merrick stretched, opened the coat and peered down to get a full frontal view of his body. No webbed feet. No feathers. Two arms. Two legs. Hairy chest. A naked man, in someone's coat.

Merrick cried out in anguish. He staggered on the hillock in shock, but found his balance to steady himself.

'I have legs!' he said. 'I mean… what the… what am I talking about? I'm asleep aren't I? I'm dreaming this? Am I? No, I can't be. Oh, SHUT UP!'

He grimaced. Merrick hadn't spoken for hundreds of years. Now his first conversation was an argument between him and himself. He peered down again at the human male form he still recognised, and felt a duller pain somewhere in his loins. He needed to pee. This was his body from three hundred years before, and he felt sure he remembered how it worked. Then he spied the familiar but long forgotten instrument for urinating. That well and truly settled the argument. He was no longer a goose.

Merrick was back! As the rain came on, beating his head and body with icy droplets, he pulled the coat closed again. This was how it was to be cold. Real cold.

'Hey, you oe'er there!'

'A human!' Merrick's mind screamed as the stranger's voice rang out. The stabby-urgency of pain now extended to his teeth. He aimed for the sky and jumped.

'Whit are ye doing, man? Stay there!' the voice ordered. 'The ambulance is here!'

Merrick felt his feet hit the ground again, and he lurched forward, stumbling off the edge of the hillock. There was a sickening crack as his forehead met a thick branch overhanging a stone wall in front of him. His last thought before passing out was of her.

Chapter 7: Dr Britten

Lucy Colwyn. The name had been on Dr Britten's mind all morning. Even while making interested noises at students who had fought for his attention, she was in his head. For many years, he had loved and loathed this job in equal measures. He was a consultant specialist, a brain doctor; one who should preserve life. His calling was to offer professional, astute observations and swift, efficiently prescribed treatment. Yet here he was, giving terminal diagnoses day in, day out. Even harder was the fact that he never developed an immunity to the hopelessness; he felt it every time.

He picked up Lucy's letter and read it again:

Dear Dr Britten,

It is with regret that you have to inform me that I'm going to die. I'm not afraid. Many people have died before me, the way is well trodden and practised by now. I don't expect it's going to hurt too much. After all, what was only called my existence – because it couldn't be labelled 'a life' – already came to an end. It was on an autumn day two years ago, when my daughter's life ended and mine was adjourned. That day I stopped seeing all the colours the seasons bring: the blue, the green, the brown and the gold. I mislaid all sensation: the soft, the hard, the jagged and the smooth. I forgot what it was to taste: the sweet, bitter, salt, and yes, even the wine. I stopped feeling, the day I stopped knowing every moment where my beautiful, baby girl was.

Do not fear, I will avoid busy roads and high bridges. I have no intention of taking anybody with me. But I will go quickly, the way my own mother chose to go. Before there's no happy thing inside what's left of my mind. Before all memories of Nicola desert me. Nobody should have to leave this life without a single, happy memory to hold.

I'm denied an assisted death, thanks to the laws of this country. These were all made by people to whom the term 'death with dignity' means nothing.

Yet I want to die, and I want to do it on my own terms. I wouldn't ask you how one goes about achieving a gentle death. I know it's beyond your remit to offer me a helpful overdose. I wish you could. Please tell the world it needs to stop deciding how much life before undignified death people should bear.

I am sorry to have to stop participating in the trials, but we both knew these were never for me. I took them part in them for the people that matter. It was the children, the future doctors, the counsellors, the teachers, the herbalists. It was even for the artists who might go on to create beauty this world will always need more of. I wanted to take people's pain away, but I couldn't even begin to do that in the end. No one knows where this disease has sprung from but they will, in time. There's hope that somewhere in the future, they will find out with your own, very brilliant, help.

Why was I ever here?

But that's not a question for you. You've been a wonderful doctor and, actually, a true friend in these trying times. Which is why you are the only recipient of this, my last goodbye. Thank you for listening, for being there as my days turned from plain pointless to numbered. You can pray for me, if you still believe there's a place for prayers to be heard.

My affairs are in order, there's nothing to leave, no one to inform. I've had no one to frighten with my close-to-death pallor, and the bin is out. Not even the bin men will miss me and I've made provision for the power company to pay their own bills. I want it to end and I want it to end now, my way, in a place decided by me and at a time of my own choosing. Whilst I'm sure medical research is a wonderful thing, I'm afraid, like my mother, I have decided to leave my body to the sea.

Thank you, so very much, for everything. You did all that you could do.

Lucy Colwyn.

Dr Britten turned the letter over and over in his hands, feeling conflicted. Life was hard, cruel, beautiful and everything between. No individual not battling terminal illness could know how Lucy feels. What facing your own death is like. They couldn't know any more than all the anti-death-with-dignity campaigners combined. He, admittedly, didn't. Would he take matters into his own hands in Lucy's place? Would the campaigners?

The buzz of the phone on his desk interrupted his thoughts and he pressed the speaker.

'Dr Britten?'

'Are you still here, Sandra?' he said.

'Yes, I was doing some last minute filing before getting ready to go,' came the reply. There's an urgent call for you. It's Dr Owyang, from the laboratory in Japan.'

Feeling irritated, he muttered, 'Now?'

'Sorry, yes. I did tell her you'd be getting ready to leave, but she insisted on speaking to you.'

He paused, rubbing his temples with his free hand. 'Dr Owyang, you say?'

'That's right. But I can tell her -'

'No,' he sighed, 'if she says it's important then I suppose it must be. Put her through.'

There was a click as Sandra put the call through.

When the woman spoke, it was with an American accent. 'Hello, Dr Britten?'

'Hello there again,' he replied, twisting his chair around to face the clock on the wall. 'How can I help you this evening?'

'Dr Britten, oh I'm so glad I got you,' Dr Owyang replied. 'I have news. Amazing news! I was waiting for the tests – more tests,

33

I mean – we ran several, and we couldn't quite believe them, so we did them again. And again. It's a miracle, that's what this is. We've finally found it, after all this time.'

'They call it eureka,' he heard a voice in the background tell her.

'It's a eureka,' Dr Owyang repeated. 'I can hardly believe -'

'I'm sorry,' he interrupted, 'I don't wish to sound rude, but do you think you could tell me what it is you're talking about?'

'It's Lucy Colwyn. She's your patient, right? The rare Morsley's Pholblastoma case?'

Dr Britten sat up straight in his seat. 'Yes... that's right,' he said.

'We got her lab results back from the latest trials this afternoon. And as I said, we've checked and then checked again, but the results are conclusive. I had to call you straight away, Doctor.'

'Conclusive of what?'

'She's cured. The disease has reversed itself, she's clear! Nine unsuccessful trials and the tenth one was a winner. It's a... what do you call it?'

He heard some brief, excited chattering in fluent Japanese, before she came back.

'It's a bloody eureka!'

Chapter 8: Merrick

When it wasn't the wailing, it was the beeping. Too much noise.

'Sister Regis,' a voice shouted. 'He's coming round!'

Merrick opened an eye and found a muddy stain on the ceiling that looked like a snake. He closed that eye and opened the other one. The snake had inched across to the right by a fraction. Then a woman's face appeared over him before a searing, white light took over everything.

I'm dead. This is death, for certain.

The light went out and he felt his other eye inched open with someone's fingers as more light encompassed him.

'Mr.. err.. what's the patient's name, Nurse Michaels?'

'We don't know, Sister,' the voice from earlier replied.

'Well, Sir,' the woman continued. 'I'm happy to tell you that you are still in the land of the living.'

He frowned, before opening his eyes again. Strange purple spots danced over the ceiling, the walls, the woman's face.

'What is this?' he said, feeling terrified. He closed his eyes to the world again, only to find the purple spots invading the darkness there. 'Where am I?'

'You're in a hospital,' came the quick, matter-of-fact reply.

'You had a bad fall,' another, gentler voice informed him.

A hospital. Merrick knew those. He knew buildings, people, artificial lights, transport. Progress. He knew it all. But he'd never been inside one of these time-modernised, buzzing with human life places. He only knew they meant danger.

'Or was the naked jump from a tree about something else?' the woman uttered. 'We know he wasn't high. Was it some kind of bizarre suicide attempt?'

Merrick didn't feel as though the question was to him, but answered anyway. 'A what?'

'Did... you... want... to... die?' a softer, more sympathetic male voice asked.

Merrick rubbed his eyes, then winced as a searing pain travelled from his wrist up his arm. Turning his head he saw the woman for the first time. She was much softer of features than she sounded. A blonde, plumptious lady with light blue eyes that gave away more concern than her tone did. Yet all his instincts were still willing him to flee – to fly. But that was all gone now. He had to surrender to whatever this human world wanted to do to him, only this time, he might meet with death. Was that possible? There was pain, much pain. That, he had forgotten from before. Yes, there was, for the first time in three centuries, the real chance of death again. Merrick drew in breath and swallowed. I can't leave her, his mind screamed. She needs me.

'It's okay,' the woman said. 'You have severe bruising and a bump on the head. But, there's no breakage or irreversible damage, thankfully. You're a very lucky man. Suffering from shock, is my diagnosis.'

'I need to get back for the gathering,' Merrick said, sitting up.

A man racing forward, placed both hands on Merrick's shoulders and coaxed him gently back onto the pillow.

'You mustn't get up too fast,' the man told him. 'You may feel a bit -'

'Woah!' Merrick's surroundings began to swing up and down and side to side. It was like he was soaring through the skies, only faster and in a manner which was not within his control. Like flying into the wind. 'The skies!' he groaned, 'I need to get out!' He tried to lift both arms but they felt too powerless and tired. His wings were gone. He was back, and he couldn't fly.

'As you may be aware by now, you have a bruised arm and some bruising to your right buttock. On the bright side, though, your blood pressure has returned to normal.' She turned to nod to the male nurse. 'Let's have Nurse Michaels call Dr Thomson.'

Nurse Michaels headed away to do as instructed.

'Your heart rate was through the roof,' the Sister said. She stepped forward and leaned over him, and he flinched. 'It's okay,' she assured him, 'I'm just going to fluff up your pillows to make you more comfortable, if that's alright with you?'

'Pillows?'

She leaned in again, and tugged at the fluffy lumps he'd been resting his head on: pillows.

'Where am I?' Merrick asked, guessing that if her wish was to make him more comfortable, he wouldn't be getting shot at, yet.

'In a hospital.'

He began to relax, rubbing his sore and swollen wrist. Wrist. Of course, these people don't shoot their own kind, do they?

'I know that,' he said. 'I meant, where am I? Am I on Islay?'

She shook her head. 'No, back on the mainland, I'm afraid,' she replied. 'You missed what would have been a fantastic flight over the Irish Sea. No hospitals over there, you see. Not much in the way of actual people, either. You're lucky someone even called you in.'

'I flew here?' He winced as she guided him back against the rearranged pillows, the pain shooting up his arm again. It was a sensation he'd long forgotten, far removed from his memory of flight. He knew exactly what it felt like to fly over the Irish Sea – over many seas in fact - and that he had to do it again, somehow.

'You did indeed,' she said.

'How on earth did I -'

'Air ambulance, all for you. I'd love a ride on one of those, to tell the truth. Sad you won't remember any of it.'

'Air ambulance,' he repeated, not knowing what one was. Not caring either, he had to get back to her.

'Can I go now?' he asked.

'What's your name?' the Sister asked, ignoring the question.

Her tone was less threatening now. Perhaps, he thought, because she sensed his fear and confusion. For a moment he thought she knew about his change, told in a report from the person who had found him. Could people smell fear the way animals do? He tried to remember. As he pondered it all, the woman took a stick from her breast pocket and walked to the end of the bed. 'Well?' she said. 'Do you have a name?'

He remembered that name well, like it was yesterday. 'Merrick,' he replied.

'Merrick what?'

'No, Merrick Anderson.'

'Very good,' she said, scribbling into her notes. 'And your date of birth?'

He blinked. Recalling information such as that was a little harder. Telling her, even if he could remember – even to the nearest year – would no doubt have some sort of consequence. Merrick didn't have time for consequences. There was the hunt; he could never forget those. And now there was death to contend with. He thought of her again and a deep longing washed over him, taking fear down to the very bottom of his stomach. The need to be with her came first, always. Before everything.

'I have to get back to… to…' He tried to remember, but his memories from where he'd landed were vague. 'To where I was,' he finished. 'Please, release me. I beg of you.'

She laughed. 'Release you? Of course, there is no need to beg on that front. We need your bed back.' She scribbled something else on her notes, and then turned the page. 'Finlaggan, on Islay? Will this be the area you might have been staying in?' she asked.

He nodded. 'Alexander's grave,' he muttered. How could he have forgotten?

'Alexander?'

Merrick swallowed. 'He was a little boy... I... knew.'

She frowned. 'Mr Anderson, although Finlaggan is a magical place, you'd be hard pressed to have friends buried there.'

He wanted to say that he lived there once, but stopped himself. Of course, this would sound ridiculous to a mortal woman. Nothing remained on Finlaggan besides ancient ruins and graves. Including that of the little boy he'd once believed he could save.

'I need to get back to Islay,' he said.

'I don't think we can do that today, Mr Anderson.'

He swallowed. 'Where am I again? I mean, what town?'

Giving him look that held no sympathy, she snapped the pages of the parchment shut and hooked it over the end of the bed.

'Nurse Michaels!' she shouted. 'Mr Anderson needs a psychological assessment and a visit from the Consultant Neurologist. Can you arrange that now please?'

She looked back with a frown at Merrick, opening her mouth to speak. But her attention turned to the next bed, as a young woman appeared from behind its closed curtains. She was carrying a bottle full of liquid.

'Nurse Roberts!' Sister said. 'There are heart patients on this ward, for heaven's sake! See about getting the hem of that uniform taken down a few inches.'

'Oh, Nurse, erm... Roberts, is it?' Merrick said. 'Can I please have some of that?' He pointed to the bottle. 'I'm so thirsty.'

Nurse Roberts' mouth fell open and she threw a horrified glance at the woman at Merrick's bedside. Before he could repeat the question, she put her head down and hurried away.

'Fancy yourself as something of a comedian, do you?' the Sister asked him.

39

'I don't think so,' he replied, puzzled. 'Unless… are these comedians allowed plenty of drinks? As I said, I'm very, very thirsty.' He gave her a weak smile, which only seemed to make her scowl more.

'I'll have someone bring you a jug of water,' she said, before sweeping out of the room.

Lying back again, Merrick stared at the ceiling and sighed. He had sat on the rooves of hospitals before. He recalled eating a discarded sandwich outside the door marked, Accident and Emergency. All the while, he had been able to observe the comings and goings from a safer distance than now. But he'd never been inside one of these vast, busy buildings. He wondered what 'a heart patient' was and why Nurse Roberts' uniform might cause them to come to grief. There was so much he could learn about this new age of humanity while he was back. Before he could ponder this further, Nurse Michaels came sweeping back in to the room. He was grinning from ear to ear as he unhooked and picked up the parchment the woman had left at the bottom of the bed.

'So, your name is Merrick?' the nurse said, reading the notes. He looked up again. 'Is it okay for me to call you that, or do you prefer Mr Anderson?'

Merrick sighed, but didn't reply. 'What time is it?' he asked instead.

'Six thirty,' came the reply.

Nurse Michaels sat on the edge of the bed. Merrick felt stifled by the closeness of this strange, human contact. The urge to fly away remained strong. This new situation was going to take some getting used to.

'It says here that you didn't give your date of birth. Can you tell me it? Just for our records, you understand. It's not like we want to tease people about their age.' He laughed, but Merrick couldn't understand why.

Merrick frowned. 'I'm not altogether sure, but it could be about three hundred and twenty seven.'

The nurse chuckled. Merrick eyed him with suspicion. This man was too cheery and was asking too many unnecessary questions.

The nurse seemed to check himself before continuing with a serious expression. 'I suppose you must feel a bit out of sorts after your fall. How's your pain now?' He put a hand on Merrick's arm, which he drew away again.

'I'm sorry,' Nurse Michaels said, 'I don't like to badger you. My job is to make sure you're comfortable.' He laughed again, sounding more nervous now. 'Are you comfortable?' he asked, looking concerned.

Merrick didn't reply, still suspicious.

'Do you need a painkiller?'

'There's been too much killing,' Merrick found himself saying.

Nurse Michaels coughed. 'I mean, can I get you an aspirin or something?' he said.

Merrick shook his head, remembering this was how he used to say 'no.' It was all beginning to come back - human nature. 'Can I get out of here now?' he said.

'I don't know if we can do that yet, if I'm honest.'

Merrick sighed. How much more time did he have to waste in this place? He had to find a way to escape; there was so much to do and he had no idea how much time he had to do it in. He turned his face toward the window and the clear, free skies outside. All these years he'd tried to stay near, watching these people. At first wanting to come back, but then, knowing he couldn't, settling for spying on them. His need for conversation and stories was innate. He recalled talking, and that sometimes it was good to share

41

problems with a sympathetic ear. He thought Nurse Michaels might have one of those. The large, very abrupt woman certainly did not.

'Nurse,' he said, sitting up, grateful that the spinning sensation seemed to have abated. He leaned forward to be able to speak quieter. 'The thing is, I'm fine and, well, I have to get back to Islay, today, do you understand?'

The other man pursed his lips before raising his eyebrows and blowing out his cheeks. 'As I said already -'

'But you have to understand,' Merrick went on, putting a hand on the nurse's arm. 'This is a matter of utmost importance.'

Nurse Michaels looked down. 'Go on,' he said.

Merrick breathed an inward sigh of relief. This might work. 'I need to look for a very special someone I left behind a long time ago,' he said. 'And if I don't go now, there's every chance that I'll lose them all over again.'

The nurse placed a kind hand on top of Merrick's and eyed him with concern. 'You're not in any trouble, are you?' he asked.

'Not trouble, no. It's about...' Merrick paused. What could he say that the man would understand? What was less strange, or alarming, than the truth? He thought of human mannerisms, of lovers he'd seen, and acts of empathy he'd seen, both before and after. Looking Nurse Michael in the eye, he said, 'It's about love.'

Merrick was right about human feeling and empathy. Nurse Michaels was not only soft-hearted but a hopeless romantic. All professional stoicism that he had been trying to maintain, melted away to nothing.

'Aww, that's lovely,' the nurse said, taking back his hand and sweeping his fringe from his eyes. 'Have you known him... her, long?'

Relieved to be getting somewhere at last, Merrick replied, 'I think, I mean it feels like all my life. Please, Nurse Michaels, I... we need your help.'

The nurse smiled. 'Wow,' he said, giving him a cheery wink. 'Three hundred and twenty-seven years is a long time. I was in a relationship like that once. What can I do to help?'

'I need help to get back to Islay,' Merrick said. 'You see, I was on my way to do something very special.'

The nurse gasped. 'Propose?' he asked, his face brightening.

Merrick didn't know what that was, but judging the nurse's excited expression, nodded. It was surely a winning excuse. 'Can you help me?' he asked.

Nurse Michael's looked at the door and then back at Merrick, before nodding. 'Okay.'

'Oh thank you!' Merrick said. 'All I need is for you to point me in the right direction.' He pulled back the covers to get out of bed, before pulling them back over himself again. 'Oh,' he added. 'And a pair of trousers.'

Chapter 9: Lucy

By far the easiest part of Lucy's life so far was becoming wheelchair-bound at forty-one. She let very few people in to her problems. Which was why needing to make a detour to visit Roisin that morning had surprised ever her.

She had met Roisin in the only place she had for socialising since her diagnosis: The hospital. The pair had shared a two bed ward during an admission for chemotherapy treatment. Lucy had listened for hours to Roisin. She was a mother of four girls. They were twins of thirteen years, a fifteen-year-old and a seventeen-year-old. The girls' father had walked out on them, never to be heard from again, twelve years earlier. The pressure of finding himself with four children under five was too much. Roisin had been way more forgiving than Lucy could ever imagine herself being. And now Roisin, like Lucy, was dying too. Although she was also facing the unthinkable: who would care for her daughters? Where would they live? Would they even be able to stay together?

Lucy told nobody the intimate details of her private life, but she was a good listener. The people she worked with hadn't known of her diagnosis. She had simply handed in her notice and left when it all became too much.

If anything, a regime of treatments and clinic visits had become a welcome change to a bereft, hollow life. Hearing of Roisin's plight had at first kept her mind alive. Then, in time, it began to touch her heart in a way she hadn't bargained for. It was clear that Roisin was a kind person and Lucy had accepted her friendship and advice from the off. It was Roisin that was responsible for facilitating Lucy's return to semi-independence. She had informed her of the welfare benefits she was entitled to, and ways of making life that bit easier. She advised her to source adaptions that would allow her to lead as normal a life as possible. She even coaxed Lucy into buying an electric wheelchair which meant she could begin to get out more. Then later - much later - a disabled adapted car. That had given Lucy the freedom of the road again. Her fear of driving at last overcome. Helped by neuro-linguistic programming; all learned about from hours of chatting to Roisin. The woman was amazing, and very sick. And all while raising a family on her own.

Lucy accepted the friendship begrudgingly at first. But Roisin didn't know they were friends at all. At times, Lucy would casually ask about the girls: Susie, Hazel, Ruth and Rachel. She would nod and smile, trying not to look too interested but feeling it all the same. Roisin, as with every other person Lucy knew, had no idea about her history. She shared nothing of her real circumstances or the fact that she had nobody.

Making her way to the door of the flats, Lucy paused. Her eyes searched the graffiti-emblazoned, cigarette-burned door entry panel for something readable. Finding the button marked 'trade', she pressed it. Within moments, she heard the catch release buzzer and reached for the door. Finding the handle too hard to grasp, she fell back defeated. The buzzing stopped. Before she could think of what to do next, someone appeared behind her and opened the door. A whiff of urine and cigarette smoke reached her throat before she had time to think of closing her mouth.

'Wait!' she said, making the man stop and turn around.

'Yeah?' he said to the nobody over her head. He was looking, she knew, for someone he felt must be accompanying the disabled person in the chair. As the most ignorant people always did.

Lucy coughed, and at last he looked down at her. 'I have a package for Roisin McKell,' she told him. As she looked down at her side and made a grab to get it, she heard him sigh.

'Yeah, so, ring her buzzer,' he said.

'She isn't in,' Lucy said flatly. 'Are there any -' she pointed to the door entry panel and added, 'services personnel in this building?'

The man guffawed. 'Sure, yeah,' he snapped back. 'We have a janitor, security staff and there's a personal trainer in the basement.'

'Oh, right,' she sighed. 'In that case, couldn't you just -'

As she held the package aloft, he barked, 'I'm not the bloody postman here. Or drug lord, for that matter.'

'Please,' she said, annoyed at having to beg this horrible little man for help. 'It's very important that she gets it. It's not drugs, it's... it's... the keys to her new house.' She bit her lip, wishing she'd been both a faster thinker and a better liar.

His angry, disinterested expression changed in an instant. 'She's moving out?' he said, looking surprised. A smile spread across his lips at last, and he accepted the package. 'You mean there'll be an empty flat?'

Lucy nodded, nervously fiddling with the tie of her headscarf.

'Well, hoo-bloody-ray!' he exclaimed, putting the envelope in his pocket and patting it. He grinned. 'You can leave it with me, I'll be happy to give it to her. My cousin has been after a place here for ages.'

'Is he even on the waiting list?' she asked, not interested in the slightest, but trying to sound like it. Did places like this have a waiting list?

'Yeah,' he sniffed, turning her parcel over in his hands.

Lucy paused, unsure whether leaving the keys and deeds to her house with this man was such a good idea after all. He wasn't the most trustworthy looking person she'd ever met. Why had she gone and told him what was in the envelope?

'You know, I'm wondering if she's in hospital again,' Lucy said, as the man had started into the building.

He paused.

'She hasn't been at all well,' Lucy went on. 'I'll try again, one more time.'

She leaned forward and pressed Roisin's buzzer. The man's astonishment at the move plain as the unlit cigarette he had in his mouth dropped to the floor. A young woman answered right away.

'Parcel for you downstairs,' Lucy shouted into the speaker, before turning back to the man. 'With... what's your name?'

'Tony,' he said.

'Tony,' Lucy finished, offering the open-mouthed man a wave and taking off towards her car.

It would be tight. But she felt sure she could make it away before Roisin's daughter descended from the sixteenth floor. She would never see the woman again, Lucy realised with a tinge of regret, as she headed away with only a bag and the clothes on her back. But, Roisin's eldest daughter, Susie, would be eighteen soon. She could only pray that the house would give the girls somewhere they could stay together. Or at least an income, something that would see them through after their mother's death. It was her way of saying thank you, to the woman who had, unbeknownst to her, been Lucy's only real friend.

Chapter 10: Dr Britten

'Sandra, I need you to get me every record we have on Lucy Colwyn, and I mean, everything!'

Leaning back in her chair, Sandra gave Dr Britten her best, you-are-putting-me-out, expression.

'I'm not being funny, doctor,' she said. 'But I should have gone home twenty minutes ago. The only reason I'm still here is to -'

She paused, as he leaned over her desk and reached for the computer mouse. The game of Patience she'd been playing appeared back on screen.

'- make sure there was nothing else you needed before I left. Lucy Colwyn, was it?'

She stood up and walked over to the filing cabinet.

'Yes indeed,' he replied. 'I need her address, her GP's details, and her phone number. I also need to know what information we have about how her mother died.'

'Suicide,' Sandra said, without turning round.

'You know about her mother?' Dr Britten said, surprised.

'Sure,' Sandra replied, still stooped with her back to him as she searched through the files. 'It was in all the papers at the time. Olive Fraser, poor woman.'

He caught his breath, feeling the hairs on the back of his neck bristle.

'She took a trip out to some obscure island in the Hebrides. Drowned herself, or so they believed. Her body was never found.' Sandra continued her search as she spoke. 'I can't remember the name of the place, but it was somewhere off the coast of Islay, I think. The Whisky Isle, yes, that's it! It was in *The Herald*. I haven't worked at this desk for seven years without taking an interest in -'

She turned around, alerted to the sound of a slamming door somewhere behind her. 'Dr Britten?' she said, to an empty room.

Chapter 11: Gladys

'Have ye brung ma paper?' Gladys asked the wiry-haired seaman, as he dragged his dinghy to dry land.

'Aye,' he replied, stretching up to meet her scrutinising gaze. 'It's last Tuesday's though. That's all they had left at the wee shoppe 'till the ferry comes o'er fae Islay. There's more bad weather aboot, ye ken. That's why I couldna get ma boat in here the day. The waves are murder.'

'So I hear on the wireless,' she said. 'You'll be rushing to get back today, then?'

'Aye.' He nodded, before turning to bend down and pick up a cardboard box full of groceries. Gladys stepped forward, keen to take them from him. 'I can carry them up to the hoose for ye?' he offered, knowing full well she'd refuse as she always did.

'Ach, away with ye, Joe,' she said, taking the box and turning on her heels. MacPhee, now free of his leash, ambled along behind her. 'I'll see you next week, if the 'Vrecken disnae eat ye,' she shouted.

'You will that,' she heard him chuckle, as she took off back up the hillside and out of sight.

Setting the cardboard box down on the kitchen table, Gladys stared out of the window. She rubbed her wrist, which, she thought with a tinge of regret, wasn't aching at all today. Neither was her back. Something wasn't going the way she hoped it was. She wiggled her fingers, praying for some restriction of movement. But there was none. She found again the nimble, pain-free digits of a healthy thirty-something woman. Some major change had happened, most likely in the last twenty-four hours, but what, she didn't know. Three hundred years of waiting. Now, as a little light had shone through, the long, bleak, hopelessness was back. Not for the first time she hoped he was happier than she, having the freedom of the air. Knowing he was out there, somewhere, was enough to keep her happy, at least, for him.

Every now and again, triggered by some random event, those memories of long ago would crop back up. It was as though three years instead of three hundred had passed. She could seldom bear to think of it all. Like Merrick's fate, held by the bronze coin that she'd given Joe long ago. His orders were to hammer it into the old wishing tree at Finlaggan. Stuffed behind the coin was one of the two spells Angus had given her to protect, scribbled on a piece of paper. Try as she might she could never remember the words, which was a good thing. And nobody, but nobody would be fool enough to remove coins from a wishing tree. You put them in there, passing whatever ails you to the tree. Whoever takes the coin out gets someone else's disease. Everyone with an ounce of sense knew that.

But Gladys only needed to hide a spell. The very incantation stuck behind the coin was what could bring Merrick back. But it was there for a reason, she couldn't keep him, no matter what, and that was why she would never try to find it. She should have burned the thing, but Gladys was charged with protecting it. If it got destroyed, then her destiny would be in tatters too. She was cursed, and she didn't know what would bring these long, lonely days to an end, only that one day they would.

'Pah!' She spat into the open fire, which fizzled in answer. 'It's all so bloody hopeless,' she told the sleeping dog, who now had his nose resting on her old socks. 'Why can naebody tell me why ahm still here? I done whit he telt me. Hundreds of years o' sittin' in this bothy, and for whit?'

She shook her head and sighed. She couldn't have love, or more company than that of a dog and the occasional chat with Joe MacNeish; this was her fate. The pains from yesterday had disappeared as fast as they'd appeared and now she knew she wasn't dying for sure. 'Is this yer wee joke, is it, Angus? Getting my hopes up that I was gonnae be put in that grave wae my name on it. Like I could get peace at last,' she said, to the empty silence of her tiny home.

Chapter 12: Merrick

'Could you run that by me again?' The ticket master stared, unbelieving, at Merrick. He stepped back, trying to hide behind Nurse Michaels.

'I said,' the young nurse replied, clearing his throat, 'this man is dying and his last wish is to visit Islay. He doesn't have anything but the clothes on his back.'

The ticket master looked Merrick up and down. The clothes the nurse had found for him him were ill-fitting to say the least. Nurse Michaels, or Jeremy as he now knew him, was a good few inches shorter than him. But he was so determined to help Merrick reunite with the love of his life, he hadn't had the heart to complain. Merrick smiled at him. Despite this overbearing scrutiny from the older man, he felt so grateful to Jeremy. He was going home.

'Are ye joshing me?' The grumpy ticket master looked so furious now that Merrick feared he might turn him away. His smile dissolved and he wondered why Jeremy wouldn't just give him the ticket fare. He could have wandered onto the ferry without all this angry fuss then. It wasn't long before he had his answer.

'Dad, please.'

Merrick didn't see the exchange that occurred next. His vision was obscured by the sun's rays bouncing off the silver anchor chain. It rattled over the sound of the ferry engines as they lifted it from the sea. With a hand over his eyes to act as a visor, he watched as the last few passengers walked aboard the ship. Then, he felt a firm grip on his arm, yanking him forwards.

'On ye come,' the senior Mr Michaels barked. 'Get ye up to the feckin' front where nae'body can see ye and make it fast. I could lose ma job daein' this.' He turned back to his son. 'How the hell's he gonnae go aboot with nae money?'

Jeremy reached into his pocket and pressed a wad of papers into Merrick's hand. 'When you get to Port Askaig, ask for wee Frankie,' he said with a smile. 'He's a very, very good friend of mine.'

The older man tutted, grumbling something under his breath that Merrick didn't catch.

There was no time to thank him, or Jeremy, who only had time to pat him on the back as Merrick was dragged away by his father.

'Good luck, Merrick,' the nurse called out. 'I hope it all goes well with your lady friend. And give my love to Frankie.'

As the old man swore under his breath, the roar of engines became louder, a signal they were ready to leave. Again Merrick's instinct at sudden loud noises was to take to the sky. But the dulling pain in his arm reminded him that he was tired, still weak and, more crucially, unable to fly. Uttering a quick thanks to Mr Michaels, he continued away into the ship's bowels as instructed. He'd ridden a ferry before, but this would be nicer. This time, he could wander around inside, seeing what the people saw, doing what the people do. How he loved ships. And the food had always smelled glorious. Much better than grass; he had to get him some of that food.

'Excuse me!' A gang of two young men and two women crashed past as he made for the staircase. They were laughing and swearing as they went. He tapped the young woman at the back of the queue on the shoulder and she turned to look at him.

'How long will it be until we leave?' he asked her.

'Aboot five minutes now,' she said, with a smile. 'Plenty o' time for a wee swallae.' With that, the young girl skipped on up the stairs after her friends.

He had no clue what a 'wee swallae' was, but he felt a rush of elation. Merrick was going home, at last, to her. As he stepped through a door to an outdoor deck, he knew from the smell of the air exactly how far it was. If iron will and love could push the vast boat forward, he'd be stepping on Islay now. He was almost there; almost within reach of where she'd be waiting.

He breathed in, tasting wind and rain in the skies ahead, and thought of the gathering. Looking upward, he was about to offer thanks to Angus. But the voice over the tannoy interrupted him. 'We're very sorry to announce that there's been an unexpected bout of bad weather out at sea. Could all passengers please prepare to disembark.'

Chapter 13: Dr Britten

Dr Britten sat at his desk at home, typed 'ferries to Islay' and waited. 'No, no. Damn it!' he shouted at the screen.

His cleaner, Niamh, shouted out from the kitchen, 'Are you alright, Dr Britten?'

He swept his fringe from his forehead and frowned. In his rush to come in and switch on the computer, he'd forgotten she'd be there this afternoon. 'Sorry,' he called back, as she appeared at the doorway to see what he was doing. 'I need some information and I need it fast. But the internet's not playing today.'

The young woman walked over to where he sat, and peered over his shoulder. 'What are you looking for?' she asked, a bemused smile playing on her lips. 'You academics,' she added, 'you shouldn't be allowed near new technology.'

He scratched his head. 'Niamh, this is serious,' he said. 'I have to get a ticket for this ferry and it has to be this evening, if at all possible.'

'Well, if you don't mind my saying so, you're internet has been a little slow today.'

'I know,' he agreed, before wondering how on earth he knew this. She was a funny woman, who always brightened his day. But she also had a habit of taking advantage of his kindness.

She reached over his shoulder and began tapping some keys, fiddling around with his computer settings. 'Useless,' she announced at last, taking her mobile phone out of her pocket and switching it on. 'Let's do this the modern way, shall we. Don't you have one of these things on you at all times, Dr Britten?'

His serious expression brightened. 'Oh yes,' he said, taking his own phone out of his pocket and waving it at her. 'Remind me how you use it for anything other than to answer calls,' he added.

She scrolled and tapped at the screen on her mobile and paused to read. Then, her cheery face turned to a frown. 'Oh dear,' she remarked.

'What? What is it?'

'The last boat to Islay for the day would have been about to leave, you'd never make it up there in time anyway. But it just got cancelled because of bad weather.'

'Well that is good news,' he said, sighing with relief.

She looked puzzled.

'Because it buys me some more time for what I have to do,' he explained. 'Check on the one in the morning. Then buy me a ticket.'

She looked so surprised at this, he couldn't help but laugh. 'It's okay,' he told her. 'I'm paying. Just give me the number, would you?'

'Yes, Sir,' she said, adding a salute. She looked back down at her phone. 'That sailing's full though,' she said after a moment. 'I'd guess it would be because of people that were supposed to travel today.'

'In that case, I'll have to get myself on the next one,' he said. At least he could go up there in the morning and try to catch Lucy before she boarded, he thought.

It was perfect; a sign. All the dots were beginning to connect at last. He grabbed a pen from the desk.

'What's the number?'

Chapter 14: Gladys

The dog was foaming at the mouth and shaking violently, only the shaking had nothing to do with the thunder and lightning that was raging on outside. He was oblivious to the noises and flashes that would normally have had him whining and hiding under the table.

'MacPhee,' Gladys called, falling to her knees at his side and clasping his head in her arms. 'What is it, boy?'

Even though his eyes were half open, she knew he couldn't see her. How could this be happening so soon? He was only sixteen!

Gladys pressed her face close to his and at last the shaking subsided for a moment. A gentle, almost whispered whining began as he came to and he tried to sit up but she clung fast to his neck to keep him down. A tear slid over the bridge of her nose and dripped onto his. She was crying again. She hated that. And it was a grief that went further this time than the one she felt at knowing she was losing him; it was remembering that she thought she'd come so close to going too.

'It's okay, MacPhee,' she soothed, feeling his body relax again under her gentle restraint. 'It's just a bad dream. Did the big buzzards chase you again?'

She couldn't decide whether lying to a dog who understands very little human language would help calm him, but doing it seemed to calm *her*.

MacPhee would have no tomorrow. *Damn it.* She was heartbroken to lose him, but there was nothing that would make her hold on another day and prolong his suffering. One fit was enough. Her beloved MacPhee would go tonight. How she hated being so alone in the world.

Chapter 15: Merrick

'Get yae in there and dinnae be thinking aboot stealing ma girl,' Mr Michaels fumed. He bent over to open a box in the bough of his fishing boat, before flinging Merrick a blanket.

'Your girl?' Merrick asked, looking puzzled. He looked about, expecting to see a woman somewhere.

'This,' Mr Michaels said, tapping the soaking wet stern. 'My boat, Big Jessie.'

With no room to swing a cat, Merrick wondered why it should be called 'Big' anything. But he decided to keep that thought to himself, as all he needed right now was to get in out of the rain. The clothes Nurse Michaels had lent him felt even tighter, thanks to a ten minute wait in the rain. He was sodden from being left standing while the old man hunted in his car for the keys to this, his prized fishing boat.

'So, I can sleep in here?' Merrick asked, pointing to the cabin.

Mr Micheals opened the door to reveal a small cubby hole with some badly torn seating inside. 'Aye,' he sniffed. 'You can sleep in here. The next ferry to Islay will likely be at ten in the morning. But I'm no working until the afternoon one, so you'll need to be ready to be on that.'

Merrick stepped forward to look inside the boat. There was a place that looked like it was for washing, a table and a pot with a huge plant in it. His stomach growled, something he wasn't aware of ever having experienced before, yet he knew what it was telling him. He leaned forward and pecked at a leaf.

'Whit the feck are ye daein?' Mr Michaels bellowed, as Merrick started and sprung back to face him with the leaf still between his lips.

'I'm sorry?' he mumbled, not able to stop himself from chewing. It had been hours since he'd eaten.

'That's ma bloody Yucca!' the older man hollered, looking his familiar, furious self again. 'Whit in the name o' the wee man? Are ye hungry or something?'

Merrick swallowed, dropping the very tip of the leaf on the floor in between them. 'Yip,' he admitted. 'Do you have any more of these... err... Yuccas?'

Mr Michaels stood open-mouthed for a moment, but didn't speak.

'Or I can hop over there for some grass,' Merrick finished, sensing some disdain. He knew well that people didn't eat grass, or Yuccas. He knew people bought food, from supermarkets and cafeterias and caravans next to the sea, but he had no money for anything except his ferry ticket from Port Askaig to Jura, a donation from the old man's son. If he'd lived on grass and grains for three hundred years, he could manage, even as a man again, for a few days more.

The old man was scratching his head in bewilderment. 'Grass is it? Grass?' He tutted. 'Look, I'm no taking you to my hoose as I don't know who you are, but if Jeremy says you're dying, then, you obviously need some help.' He frowned and scratched some more before brightening again. 'Wait there!' he said, climbing back off the boat and making towards the car park, shouting over his shoulder, 'I've some pieces and a flask o' soup in the car ye can huv. Then ye can get yer head doon on that cabin bed for the night.'

Merrick watched him go, wondering what 'pieces' were. Soup he knew. Slurpy, burpy leftover pleasures often found up the side and on the floor round dustbins. He looked over at the fresh, damp grass between the sea and the car park and his stomach growled, now with pain. With Mr Michaels back turned he picked up the piece of Yucca he had dropped and ate it, deciding to go foraging in the grass once the old man had left him alone.

How he hated being alone. He cursed the weather, making him have to wait until tomorrow to get back to Islay. But still, he'd be seeing her again.

'Here's yer soup.'

Mr Michaels had reappeared, thrusting a silver container at him. He took it and turned it over, wondering where the soup was.

'How do I…?' he began.

'Oh, gae it here,' the old man grumbled, snatching it back before twisting off the cap. Steam floated out and under Merrick's nose and he breathed in its delicious scent. Ahh, food! He took the flask back and threw its contents straight out onto the deck before falling to his knees to slurp it hungrily up. He didn't see Mr Michaels surprise, but he heard it.

'Whit in the name o' Christ?'

Chapter 16: Lucy

Lucy held onto her headscarf as Scotland's early morning, chilly wind tried hard to whip it off. 'Perfect,' she complained. 'Perfect, perfect, day.'

She wheeled into the passenger lounge, along rows of people who were settling down to sleep on the seats. It was 5.40am, an unscheduled early sailing that she was very grateful for. A red hue on the horizon told her dawn's early light was waiting to transform everything at any second. She paused, taking a small bottle from her pocket and flipping off the top. As she drank wine for breakfast, Lucy wondered who would choose sleep over such a terrific view.

She recalled a twenty-something man she'd met during one torturous wait to be seen at the clinic. He'd explained to her how knowing you were dying was funny like that. He actually used that word: funny. As though all the terminally ill people of the world were in a sitcom called, 'Who's next?'

'The moment you know you're dying,' he'd gone on to say, 'it's like someone switches on the lights. At once you're aware of the intricate detail of every living, breathing thing in the universe. Colours intensify. Every light and sound comes to meet you with all the subtle, gradual velocity of an explosion.' And this from a young man wearing a shirt saying, 'Bite me.' Yet it was information he had felt moved to impart. This was what he claimed knowing you're going to die did to regular people. It made you stop and take notice of all the things you'd spent too many wasted years taking for granted. It was, he'd said, like opening all your Christmas presents as a child knowing you only had a week to play with them all. Only this was not the case for Lucy - death was the only gift she'd yearned to open every morning for the last two years. She'd decided against telling him this particular news.

She'd never discussed suicide with anyone, not least any other patients. She hadn't even mentioned it to Roisin. How could she? The woman had four beautiful, loving daughters and everything to live for. You never knew if mentioning it meant they'd put you on twenty-four hour watch or something worse. Some do-gooder with no idea what it was like to be her would wave leaflets and offer a listening ear. Lucy hated it when they said that. 'Can we offer you a listening ear?' Like it was something they could snap off and pop in a sweetie bag for her. Whenever she thought about dying, it would dive out and jump on her shoulder, asking, 'Do you want to talk about it?'

The listening ear: it was the answer to all ills. Like cups of tea, barley sugars and, if you're very anxious and on the edge, a soothing glass of brandy. But whilst food and drinks could fill one kind of hole, talking didn't help. It couldn't bring Nicola back. A listening ear worked as well as paracetamol for her skull chiselling headaches. They were excruciating, and all thanks to Chewbacca, as she had christened her tumour.

She took her mobile phone out of her pocket to have it ready for taking photos, and then checked herself. Who were they for? It's not like she was coming back to share them with anyone. Reminding herself how little time she had left for pleasures, Lucy drank from the wine bottle. Emptying it, she pressed ahead, smiling as a woman held open the door at the far end for her to get outside on deck. Her love of photographing and sharing her view of the world was ready for once last indulgence. Most of her recent pictures were of fields of flowers, shot between the palings of a fence. There were zoo animals captured through iron black railings. Once, she'd even photographed the top of her head in a lavatory mirror. Then she would Instagram them, where they might remain long, long after she was gone. Photos from my chair. Yes, she could do that today, even though it would be her last.

It was an ice cold morning, and it turned out she was the only passenger ready to brave the winds for a nice view. Yet, her thick overcoat, scarf and gloves provided good protection. She peered through the railings and looked out to sea, sipping on her second small bottle of Malbec. The day had broken now, the red hue of pre-dawn replaced by bright washes of turquoise and stormy blue. She longed to drag herself up for a closer look. If only. But the sun wouldn't be up after all. A storm was brewing, of course. This was to be her last day on earth, and she would have to have it without a sunrise. She cursed the sky, and not for the first time.

Tugging the bag off the back of her chair, Lucy opened the zip, threw in the empty wine bottle and took out a third. She had six single glass bottles to go. Whatever happened between now and Scarba, this would be the best, smoothest, last journey.

Chapter 17: Gladys

Gladys made her way up the hillside to a clearing, where there was a circle of small, flat stones, and knelt on the ground. The wicker basket she carried held a cross made from broken off tree branches, tied in the middle with rope. Across its centre, she had burned a name and date into the wood:

MACPHEE. 2012

Picking up the cross, she dug a hole in the soft, peaty ground and pushed it in before getting to her feet again. Eyes misted, she looked over all fourteen, identical crosses and sighed. Cold, wet, Scottish air filled her lungs. Yet it was more than that; it was salt, sea, sand, stone, heather and moss. It was blaeberries all the way up the hill behind her, sheep dung, frog spawn and bladder wrack. Even as the rain fell upon Scarba, her senses picked up hints of petrichor from several miles away. Gladys always knew when a storm was coming, when the sun would appear and when fog was due; she had a nose for it. Last night's weather had only been the beginning of the cocktail of rumbling delights that were to come.

And then there was the light that never seemed to leave. To Gladys, the marvels of the world were like pages in a pop-up book; everything was new and surprising. At least, it had begun to be, after Olive's Advice Bucket opened out the entire universe to her. The divine lucidity of thought, feeling and seeing often gifted too late to the dying. At last, it had been hers.

She took a screwed up note from her pocket and flattened it out over her knee. What did Olive have to say today? She squinted at the page. 'Death is for us all when we're done with living,' she read aloud. 'So, while you wait, live.' She shook her head, grinning in spite of herself. Olive's views were always short, always simple; ever philosophical. But this one, whilst profound

71

as always, made her laugh. What else did she have to do with her days but live?

She'd forgotten what the world looked like before Olive had come. This was peculiar in itself, because Gladys had lived for over three centuries until that day. She'd seen the astonishing, proverbial light ever since, and became humbled by it. Yet even after desiring it for so long, she'd grown tired. Through the notes she could prepare for looking death in the eye, yet she wasn't dying. All she wanted to do was go to sleep and never wake up, but she was needed. She had a purpose; the likes of which no other person would ever be able to claim again.

Gladys had to fulfil a destiny, which meant staying on until it was complete. Then the eventual meeting with her maker would come. She was prepared for death, but unable to realise it.

'Curse you, Angus,' she told the sky, the sea, the heather and all her eyes beheld forever. Because everything was because of Angus. It was Angus that had decided to take the pain and MacPhee away together. How she hated being alone in this light, too bright world.

Chapter 18: Dr Britten

Dr Britten's only hope was a hire car, on a wet miserable day, driving all the way to Kennacraig for the second ferry. Flights to Islay were cancelled due to high winds and unpredictable weather. As a consequence, the first ferry had left earlier than planned. Some of the day's sailings were also called off because of bad weather predictions for the afternoon. Whatever happened, he had to drive to the ferry regardless, and hope that the one he'd booked would be sailing today.

Waving goodbye to Naimh he thought of Lucy. She had left behind an empty house and an empty life with nobody to wave her off. Nobody would have wished her a fond farewell as she made what would be her final boat trip. The thought filled him with sadness.

Dr Britten had worked with terminally ill patients for many years. It was his life's work to tend to the dying and search for cures to the most destructive of diseases. He was not disaffected by the suffering of all his patients, yet Lucy's case had troubled him more than most. Hers was a recently recognised disease. Morsley's Pholblastoma was at first thought to be rare, but new cases had been identified in the last few years. It was beginning to spread at an alarming rate or previous cases had been misdiagnosed. New evidence had come to light, giving reason to suspect there might be a gene mutation involved. All things he had to get back to Japan to investigate further. But, first he needed to find Lucy and convince her to go with him. He needed to determine exactly why the latest treatment had worked on her and not the others. There was a greater task than running in and saving her though. Somehow, he had to make her want to save herself, and he had no idea how he was going to do that. He knew that even without the terminal diagnosis, Lucy may have reached the same decision day. She wanted to die; to be with her daughter at last. She was, as Naimh said, standing in a river with nothing to drink. How could he convince somebody who had nobody to want to turn their life around?

Chapter 19: Merrick

The bump on Merrick's head felt enormous. He would have to stop trying to take off every time loud noises startled him. Could he do that after three hundred years?

One minute he'd been sound asleep. The next, a coughing and rumbling had him trying to take to the air inside the tiny cabin on Mr Michaels' boat. Head against wooden ceiling, wooden ceiling lost. He stared at the dent the top of his skull had made and grimaced. This was worse than the chewed Yucca and way, way worse than the deck souping. This was permanent damage. He thought of Mr Michaels' angry expression, wondering how far the man's temper went. Before he could consider this any further, he noticed the time on the clock the old man had left him. He'd missed the early ferry!

The boat lurched forwards and he fell back down on to the couch again.

'Hey!' he called out, aware of a stinging and wetness on his forehead. He stood and reached for a piece of rag on a shelf. Holding it to his head, he opened the door to daylight. There he saw the reason for this sudden movement. Mr Michaels was steering the fishing boat away from shore.

'HEY!' Merrick yelled again. 'Did we miss the -'

Before he could finish, the man turned and, terror in his eyes, let go of the wheel. But it wasn't Mr Michaels, he realised with a jolt. It was a stranger. As the man staggered backwards, Merrick lunged to try and help him. Confused, he continued to back away, his eyes bulging at the sight of the bloodied rag Merrick held in his hand. Before he could stop him, the man had leapt overboard and into the sea.

'WAIT!' Merrick shouted after him. But the man thrashed through the water, swimming as far as he could away without looking back. 'In the name of…!' Merrick spluttered. The boat was travelling out of control now, with no one at the helm. He rubbed his bruised head again, the urgency of the immediate situation not quite sinking in yet. He'd better work out how to stop and turn the boat back around to shore before having to face Mr Michaels' fury once more. But could he steer a boat? And where had the old man got to anyway? Then he remembered another thing: the hole he'd made in the roof. The boat was humming further away from the wrath of Mr Michaels and towards her. He could be there this morning and never see the old man again! Sure, he could steer a boat. Sure he could. What was so hard? He recalled the scene he'd witnessed a moment earlier. The strange man, leaning over the steering wheel. Merrick raced over and grabbed on to it, sliding to the side as he went and feeling the boat jolt the same way. Ahh, so turning the wheel this way made it -

There was an almighty thud and a spray of freezing water washed over Merrick. With that, he felt himself and the boat momentarily lift into the air and fall back down again. He caught hold of the wheel again as he landed, preventing himself from falling overboard. Looking about, he realised the craft had crashed into a giant wave that had felt more like a brick wall than the sea.

'Holy hell!' he yelled, leaning over to the left and feeling the boat turn that way. He turned the wheel to the right, more gently this time. And to the right the hardy, little boat went. So this was how you steer. All he needed now was to be able to make it slow down. Glancing to the right of the wheel, he saw a handle and pulled it downwards. The boat slowed at last.

'Huzzah!' he yelled, pushing it back to the middle again. The boat obeyed his command, changing to a faster speed at the same time. He pushed it right back to the top, and again, there was an almighty jolt. The crash almost catapulted him off the boat, but he held the wheel fast. So, you slow down when faced with a big wave. He pulled the handle back down to the centre and left it there a while. Yes, he could drive a boat, even with these very new human hands. So he'd missed the ferry, which he could make out in the distance. He was a man again, and man commanded the ocean, didn't he? He could catch up with it.

Chapter 20: Lucy

The sunrise over the Sound of Jura was a resurgence of light and dark; a golden glow across a sky that sung of storms. Lucy fancied a more sentimental person might say they were witnessing a miracle. But to her, it was simply something that made a great photograph. An image observed through a secondary lens, the way she viewed all life in general these days. Nature was there for the alive, and it sure was spectacular, as all the things she read about it told her. But it held the same joy for her as a print would to an art lover. It was second place; non-representative of the artist's true talent. The artist in this case – who one might refer to as 'God' – had bigger plans. Adorning a canvas with glorious colour; all the while adding and subtracting. Giving then taking people away, especially the good, the great and the irreplaceable. Even leaving behind a shell of a woman when they could have taken her instead. Bastard. Bastard.

The sound of the door creaking and laughter made her turn her head. Three grey-haired women came pouring out onto the deck, each holding glasses of wine. One was much taller than the other two, and one was very short and stout, wearing her hair in a tight bun. The third woman, Lucy observed, looked a little younger. She wore full hiking gear - waterproof trousers, thick, heavy boots, and a pink, sporty raincoat. Not odd in itself, except that the other two were in more formal attire. The taller woman was perfectly made-up. She wore dark, glossy lipstick and sported a sleek, long, black overcoat and high heeled shoes. The shorter woman of the group had a purple rinse through her hair. She hobbled about on kitten heels that she could hardly walk in and a faux fur coat. Tripping and stumbling, she appeared to stop every so often to pull one of her heels out of a gap in the decking. Not ideal wear for a cool spring day in northern Scotland, Lucy thought. Noticing them eyeing her, she turned quickly away to look back out to sea. She had no desire to find herself in conversation with these very loud women. To her relief, she heard them usher over to the opposite side, in a series of snorts and whispers. Drunk. How great to live to your happy old age, she thought; and to go out with a bang. She wished she could feel more than tipsy right now. To be inebriated in her misery would be the best she could do for herself.

Lucy opened her bag to take out another bottle, eyeing the women's backs from the corner of her eye as she did so. To her relief she found them deep in conversation, oblivious to her. None of them wondering what the lone woman in the wheelchair was doing out on deck by herself. Good. There was nothing worse than the helpy-helpers. The strangers who took it upon themselves to ask if the poor disabled lady needed anything. Poor, disabled lady she was not. Lucy took a swig straight from the bottle, leaning over to discard the glass in the bin. She tried hard to remain disinterested. The group of women became louder, and Lucy couldn't help but turn around when they weren't looking. It was safe, she decided, observing them from a quiet distance.

'Do they have duty free on these ferries?' the shortest of the three women said.

'I don't know, Fleur,' the tallest, very well-spoken lady said. 'Why do you ahhsk?'

'Because I want some perfume for my trip,' Fleur replied. 'Do you know there's a really expensive perfume that smells of nothing?'

'Don't be daft!'

'There is! There is, I tell you! I need to get me some of that, and quick.'

The younger woman stood back to stare at Fleur, her face aghast. Lucy turned quickly back to watching the sea, and heard, 'Why on earth would you do that?'

'Because who knows what nothing smells like?' came the reply. 'We could be the first!'

Lucy let out a snort which she hastily disguised with a cough.

Trying hard to ignore them, she continued to stare steadfastly away. Louder, more excited chatter from the three old ladies made it much harder to do. She held fast on to the railing, not wishing to engage in conversation with anyone. Yet she couldn't help but smile, an unfamiliar sensation. It felt like she hadn't smiled in forever. She couldn't help but train her ears and keep listening in.

'Where?'

'There,' came the reply. 'Over there, see that fin in the water?'

'Well, where else would it be, Cathy? Flying over us? Look out, look out, there's a flying shark about.'

'Ooh, do they bite as they go?'

'I don't see any fin.'

'You don't see any *thing*,' the posh lady corrected.

There were more giggles, and then, 'THERE!' someone shouted out. 'Oh, it's gone under again.'

'Shit! Have we run it over?'

'That was a wave, not a bloody dolphin.'

'Maybe it was a dolphin waving.'

'Get out, you silly moo.'

'Oh, Fleur,' came the disappointed voice Lucy now recognised as Cathy's. 'You got me all excited then. I've always wanted to see a dolphin in the wild.'

'Talking of getting all excited -'

There were groans and the rattling of a bag.

'Well,' Fleur continued. 'It's what I am here for after all! Off to see a man with my bag of tricks.'

'Are you going to pull a rabbit out of a hat for him?'

'No, I'm going to pull a snake out of a pair of trou -'

'You can keep the gory details to yourself,' the posh lady interrupted her.

'Yes, we don't wish to know about your sex life,' Cathy added.

Lucy almost choked on her Malbec.

'Jealous are we, ladies?' Fleur asked.

'Not at all,' the well-spoken lady sounded indignant now. 'I am happily engaging in plenty of sex. I just don't rush to tell you all about it.'

'Getting a bit boring and samey, is it?'

There was an indignant splutter then a jangling noise, before Fleur continued. 'Do you want to borrow my handcuffs sometime, Joanna-Rose?'

Stop the boat, the woman had handcuffs in her bag. Lucy clung tighter to the railing and pressed her lips to her hands, stifling a desire to laugh out loud.

'Fleur,' came the curt reply. 'We don't all have to resort to using furry shackles to get a man to go all the way with us.'

'I don't need him to go all the way with me,' Fleur replied. 'Only to Leeds.'

'Why Leeds?'

There was more jangling as she said, 'Because I have some of those for him too. And a collar.'

Lucy positively needed the toilet now.

'Can we get back to the more tasteful subject of looking for that dolphin?'

As Cathy finished speaking, Lucy noticed a grey head pop out of the waves below, closely followed by another. She craned her neck, holding her breath. As the two dolphins began swimming in formation, a rare moment of delight overtook her. The pair followed alongside the ship, leaping in and out of the water in a game of chase. For a second she thought to call over to the now squabbling women, but decided against it. Reaching into her bag, she pulled out her camera and pointed it down towards the sea. If only she could get up out of this blasted chair to take a proper picture. But then, she'd pulled herself up before. Lucy was nothing if not independent and determined, chair or no chair. Placing the phone in her pocket she put both hands on the railings and started to drag her body up out of her seat.

'It was probably a porpoise,' Lucy heard one of the women say. 'They're quite common in these waters.'

'Yes, or a manky whale,' the Fleur woman piped up.

'Minke Whale,' the posh lady corrected her.

On her feet now, Lucy found she still couldn't quite see over the railings. She edged her body a little further out, until her toes began to leave the ground.

'That's what I said,' she heard Fleur scoff.

Lucy fumbled about in her pocket and stretched out an arm, aiming her mobile phone at the dolphin.

'There's a picture of a Minke Whale here in my book,' Cathy said, 'and that wasn't it.' Then, more uncertainly, 'was it?'

'Crikey,' she heard Fleur exclaim. 'It says here they are the second smallest of the Baleen Whales next to the Pygmy Right Whale. Was it next to a Pygmy White Whale, did you notice?'

'Well, I did see something -'

'Why does this make me think of you and your man in Jura?' the well-spoken lady said.

'I think I'm going to throw up,' said Cathy.

'Don't do that, you might hit the Minke Whales,' replied Fleur. 'There's nothing worse than swimming through wine and chicken mayonnaise sandwiches.'

'How would you know?'

'What, you think I haven't done it?'

'Come on, Cathy, let's go inside,' the well-spoken lady said with a tut. 'I need a drink.'

'Not wine though, eh?'

Lucy turned her head and watched two of the women disappearing back inside the lounge. Then, she heard Fleur shout after them: 'Make mine a large one!'

Lucy looked back down towards the sea. Giant waves crashed and splashed against the ship as the dolphins now swam a few meters away. She leaned further over, hoping to capture them before they submerged again. Her entire world wobbled. *This could be it. She could go now…*

'Hey, are you alright there?' she heard Fleur shout out, as the ferry horn boomed a loud warning. The deck seemed to rise up and Lucy felt her hands leave the safety of cold railings. As her body plunged downwards into icy, black water below, she thought of her mother.

Chapter 21: Gladys

Gladys needed a new dog and she had to be the one to choose it. It was time for her to travel to the mainland again. Some people were crazy about boat trips, especially when it was to buy a puppy. But she was not. Of particular annoyance were the very public passenger ferries. Once, she had obtained her own boat, a way to escape across the water to collect a pup without being noticed. But thanks to a navigational disaster, the Corryvrecken whirlpool had finished the boat. It hadn't been immortal like she was. Gladys had been sucked under by the tide and sucked back up by her own life force. Left bobbing up and under then up, then under again like a cork, she was lost for days. It might have taken her two weeks - maybe longer - to get back to the shore if some chap called Eric Blair hadn't spotted her. On that fateful day, in 1947, he and his son almost lost their lives because of her. Spotting her fight to remain afloat, he rushed to save her – all the while not knowing she was, in fact, unsinkable.

Joe MacNeish, and his father before him, and his father before him, had been her saviour. He was her only link to the mainland after she left to go into hiding. That single trip stopped her from ever making another sailing attempt alone.

In days long gone by, islanders had believed she was the hag goddess of winter, Cailleach Bheur. She was using the gulf to wash her great plaid, they said, and this ushered in the turn of the seasons. From autumn to winter they thought people were drowning because she was doing laundry in the sea. And they wanted to burn her for it. Merrick would have burned too, by association with her. But there was no such thing as Cailleach Bheur. No such person 'commanded' the Corryvreckan. It ate ships and spat others back out again indiscriminately. It stole and spared lives whenever the mood took it. But nobody was in charge of this, the world's largest whirlpool. There was no magic, only the force of nature at work.

Yet there was one thing the witch hunters had right about Gladys: she was immortal. She felt like she might be as old as time itself, maybe older. The truth was she couldn't remember how old she was. There was no one alive able to answer that question for her. One thing they'd forgotten to do when giving her the gift of eternal life was to give her the gift of eternal memory too.

'Och aye, Angus,' she said, on one of the many times she discussed her age with herself out here alone on Scarba. 'I'm aboot due a wee earth-sized birthday cake with all the stars for candles by now.'

If only she hadn't met him, the man who gave her the magic. Perhaps she wouldn't be so tired and old now. Perhaps she'd be long dead and with no duties to perform in the name of mankind. That would be nice, imagining a life with no responsibilities. No counting, no worrying no waiting, and no spells to guard. Death must be such a peaceful, uneventful thing, she thought.

She may have given the same burden of eternal life to Merrick, but without all her complications. All he had to do was live and breed, live and breed. Of course, she had wanted to follow him to the skies, but the spell hadn't worked on her. This had not been her destiny.

With a heavy heart, she picked up her skirts to make her way back to the bothy. A food delivery from Joe was imminent; at least she could catch a lift with him then. The only problem was this was October, the date of the barnacle goose gathering at Loch Gruinart. She would have to go in disguise.

Chapter 22: Dr Britten

Dr Britten knew he could ring the authorities and have the professionals chase Lucy all the way to Scarba. They'd have done it on his say so, for sure. Perhaps they'd even have caught up with her by now. Yet, he thought, there's a reason that somebody writes a suicide note to their doctor. It's because they have no one else to say goodbye to, meaning your options for talking them out of it are limited. Lucy Colwyn had nobody. Not a soul in the world was going to miss her when she was gone; she'd told him that countless times before. He'd offered more treatment, counselling and an introduction to other patients. Everything had fallen on deaf ears, she was doing this alone. He'd asked for names of people she might want to be informed of her condition, he knew that. There had been no one. She was an orphan. How could he not have known she was Olive's daughter? This information would have been pertinent to everything. They had the same disease. Why didn't she tell him this?

He wracked his brain for clues about what she'd told him of her family. A grandmother; a father she never knew and a late mother. The reason given for her death in initial consultations was unclear in his mind. Heart attack? No, it came to him now; it was suicide.

He recalled the air that became so heavy in-between them as she delivered her answer. It was given coldly, resentment clear from her pained expression.

Why would she resent Olive? A loving mother who would rather run away to die than have her little girl witness her slow, painful decline?

He inhaled deeply, carrying the ache of regret on his breath as he pondered it all. He should have stayed in touch with the family. He should have inquired about them each time Olive had turned up for her treatment alone. In retrospect, he could see that of course the two women were related. Olive had behaved as Lucy; keeping everything of her private life to herself. On the surface, both appeared as closed personalities. The truth was very, very different.

Discussing new treatments and the trials with Lucy had been fraught with difficulty. Only the idea that medical testing on her might save a child's life had won her over.

'Imagine if this was your child,' he'd said, hating himself for having to remind her again of the daughter she'd lost. In any case, the cure of Lucy's condition could be bigger than one child. Much, much bigger, he now knew, as more and more cases were beginning to come to light. This, had it been discovered ten years earlier, might have saved countless lives. But its future potential was even greater. Prevalence of the disease was changing, and Dr Britten didn't know why, but the death toll was increasing. Yet something, perhaps Lucy's genetic make-up, may be able to change that. It was terrifying to think how close he'd come to missing something so monumental; that between these two women, history was being made.

No, it was Dr Britten that had to go and get Lucy, only he could try to make her see sense. Illness or no illness, she wanted to end it all anyway. In such a remote place as Scarba or even on her way to the island, she might realise they were on to her. Then all she had to do was jump, and he knew that is what she would do. Lucy was one of the most determined people he had ever met. Yet he had so much to say; reasons for her to live that he must now impart. More than she could ever have imagined.

Hippocrates himself had predicted there was something in nature to cure every ill. Lucy Colwyn may be living, breathing proof of this at last. He hoped.

As his thoughts raced on, the rain began to fall faster, pattering its applause on the windscreen. He leaned forward, trying hard to concentrate on the road ahead. The wipers struggled to keep up, making his way look, at best, hazy. He thought about pulling over; perhaps make some of the notes he needed to write. A stupendous puzzle was click, click, clicking into place, and there was much to be recorded. It was almost too exhilarating for him to contain.

Yet all the while, as Lucy headed for Scarba, they were losing precious time. Her disappearance at this juncture might change the course of too many lives.

He pressed his foot down on the accelerator.

Chapter 23: Merrick

Somebody fell into the sea.

Heart pounding, Merrick wrenched the wheel over to the far right, steering away from the ferry. As he narrowly avoided a full on collision, a man on board the ship waved and shouted at him. But his attention was only removed from the place where he'd seen the woman fall. At least, he thought it was a woman. It was hard to know. Pulling the handle back to the middle, the boat slowed and he turned off its engine. The pull of the wake began drawing his boat back towards the ferry, and he thought they might collide after all. But the huge ship continued on course, unaware of its dropped cargo.

'Dammit,' Merrick cursed, searching the waters all around the area where he'd seen the body fall. He couldn't let her drown, or freeze. One thing Merrick knew for certain was that humans couldn't survive more than a few minutes in icy cold waters. Switching the engine back on, he edged the boat back towards the place where he thought she'd fallen. At last he saw a head appear above water.

'I'm coming!' he shouted out to the person, who was now splashing around. He pushed the handle to full speed ahead, hanging on tighter to the wheel. Hitting wall upon wall of waves, jolted to and fro from the impact, he held fast. With the ferry getting further away, Merrick battled in its wake to reach her. Finally he pulled back the lever to slow the engine and came to a halt beside the woman.

'I... I...' he heard her garble, as she fought to keep her head above water, her arms thrashing the surface.

'Can you swim to me?' Merrick shouted. He let go of the wheel and staggered across to lean over to the edge, holding out his arms to her. 'Swim to me!'

'It's my legs... I... can't...'

As her face disappeared under the water again, Merrick dived into the sea and swam for his life. It was ice-cold, colder than he could ever remember. Downy feathers would once have provided protection from a shot of chilly blood to the heart. Now, he had nothing. His body felt bare, human skin shielding his body with all the adequacy of wet paper. It felt as though his lungs were trying to retreat into his throat, constricting his airway. He paused, gasping for breath, his eyes searching the area where she had been only moments before. There was almost no time to lose. Pulling the sling from his injured wrist, he dived below, stretching the arms in front of him. If only they could be wings once more. Finding little strength to propel him downwards, he began to panic. As he fought against the water, the pain from his injury shot all the way up his arm to his jaw.

'Help me, God,' his mind screamed, as he screwed his eyes shut. Reaching out again, he continued to grasp blindly into the abyss. So much cold, so much darkness. For the first time, he realised he might die. Then, at last, he felt something. His arms entangled in sodden, floaty material. He grasped it with both hands, walking them along to its origins. Deftly, he caught the woman's body in his arms and, wincing in pain, pulled her back to the surface.

'I... don't... want -' she spluttered.

As Merrick breathed air into his lungs again, relief washed through his body. She was alive, but for how long?

'I have to get you back to the boat,' he told her, tearing the sodden bandage from his wrist. He put his weak arm around the woman's shoulders and started to swim with her.

'No,' she said.

To his astonishment, he felt her pushing him away from her. But even in pain, Merrick was too strong for it to make much of difference to their progress. In a matter of minutes they were at the boat.

'I'm going to have to leave you here while I climb in,' he said, pausing to wonder whether this was wise. He watched as she brushed her dark, wet hair from her face to look at him. 'Then I'll pull you out, okay?' he continued, noticing despondence in her eyes. He swallowed. 'Can you stay afloat? Will you?'

Shivering, she nodded wearily, much to his relief. As Merrick let her go to climb aboard the boat, he prayed she would still be above water when he reached for her again.

Chapter 24: Gladys

At the final day of reckoning, you'll discover it WAS all about love. Nothing else.

Gladys folded Olive's Advice Bucket note and pressed it to her heart.

'Once,' she said, with a sigh. 'Once I had love.'

She watched the boat draw nearer, anxious for it to be over. If there was one thing she couldn't stand it was going to the mainland. But it was a necessity; albeit one that only came about once every twelve to sixteen years, praise be to Angus. Only when her lonely existence required the acquisition of another dog. Although, to Gladys, 'acquisition' was far too cold and impersonal a word for the next MacPhee. She'd named all her faithful friends MacPhee, every one of them, for the last 300 years.

Yes, money would exchange hands for her Golden Retriever. At least, that was the way it had been in this century. It was the price she had to pay for puppy love; the only kind she could have in her life. The prize was far greater than the money. Dogs knew things humans couldn't. How the smell of the air changes with the seasons. How you could recognise family members by their scent. Knowing when someone was close by, well before any human sense could.

Dogs made Gladys feel safe in her solitude. But for the pain at the eventual loss of each one, she would call them the most perfect partners. To her long, ever-waiting-for-something-she-knew-not-what, life, they were essential. All that was missing in the painting of each day was yellow and gold. A faithful Labrador. A reason to get up each morning and face the day.

Joe MacNeish pursed his lips as she acknowledged his presence with a single grunt. Allowing him to help her step from the jetty, she walked across the gangplank and on to the boat.

'Nice day for it,' he said.

'Aye,' she replied, taking her usual seat at the helm and folding her arms. 'It's choppy alright.'

Joe passed her a life jacket, but she shook her head, keeping her arms tightly folded. He threw it back on the hook and frowned at her.

'Hmm,' he said, looking out towards the Isle of Jura. 'I'm not sure we should be going out today, you know.'

She thought the comment had been more to himself than to her. But she was going, whatever he said, so she ignored it anyway. He waited for her to speak. When she didn't, he shrugged, before leaning over the boat and reeling in the anchor. Cold water sprayed across her face when he lifted it out of the sea and threw it to the side of her. She felt sure she saw him smirk.

'Mind yourself there,' he mumbled, avoiding her steely stare and making his way back to the wheel.

'I hope yer sailing's better than yer manners,' she chided him.

'Och aye,' he said. 'I know these waters like the taste of a braw, Stornoway black pudding. But ye better hang on to your headscarf.'

The rain arrived as if from nowhere, on what had before seemed like a clear, blue sky day. She'd predicted its arrival of course, but never its consequences. From the stillness of the first ten minutes of sailing, came an untamed, unforgiving wind. The little fishing boat began rocking this way and that. She saw Joe struggling with the wheel, leaning to use all his weight to keep the vessel on course. This had not been on the forecast. He met Gladys's eyes for a brief moment, and she saw the unspoken question in his eyes:

'Did you know?'

She sat still, unfazed by all that was happening around her. Joe could manage this; he was an experiences sailor after all. As the storm intensified, she felt her body lift and fall with the helm of the boat. Yet it plundered on through crashing waves. She could imagine Joe thinking that maybe this was her work. Maybe she was the Cailleach after all, although countless times she'd told him she was not. Was she commanding the very seas around them to take revenge on him for soaking her with the anchor? But alas, no, that was ridiculous. And yet, as the Corryvreckan drew them to the left and won, his panicked terror was plain. While Gladys felt more annoyed than scared.

'I didn't know it would be like this!' she shouted.

Perhaps he heard, perhaps he didn't. But hers was the last face poor Joe MacNeish would ever see.

Chapter 25: Lucy

'I suppose I ought to thank you for saving me,' Lucy said. She hugged the jacket of silver foil he'd dug from the first aid box to put around her. It started to rain, and she shivered, adjusting her sopping wet headscarf as it started to slip down. Thank heavens she had held on to it. She looked out to see even darker clouds on the horizon.

'Here,' he said, lifting a blanket out of the cupboard on deck he'd been searching inside and handing it to her. 'You'll need this too. How a piece of paper can keep you warm, I don't know.'

'They're supposed to retain body heat,' she said. 'Although I suspect I've none to keep right now.' She shivered, accepting the blanket from him. 'What about you?' she asked.

'I'll live.'

It was true; he looked completely unharmed. Even as he stood soaking wet having braved the same icy temperatures she had herself. His face was flushed but he didn't so much as quiver with cold as he took to the wheel again and started the engine. If she hadn't been there to know better, she'd swear he'd been dipped in a warm bath.

'There's worse weather ahead,' he told her, his expression grim.

'Yes, it looks like a storm. Not good.'

'Well, we've tested the water already,' he replied. He turned his face up to the sky then looked ahead again and pursed his lips. 'How did you know about the thing?' he asked after a moment.

'What?'

'The thing.' He pointed to the first aid box under the steering wheel. 'Do you know about boats?'

She raised her eyebrows, surprised by the question. 'You mean, you don't?'

99

He pushed the throttle upwards and she felt the boat begin to edge forwards.

'Of course,' he replied, not looking at her. 'I don't know where everything is yet. It's not mine, you see. I've borrowed it; from a friend.'

'Borrowed it? Nice friends you have,' she said. 'I don't suppose there's a cup of hot tea anywhere on board is there?'

He looked so perplexed it unnerved her. 'Do you think there is?'

'You don't know?'

'Know what?'

'Whether there are drink-making facilities below deck?'

'He looked about him, before beaming a smile at her. 'There's water all around us,' he said. 'Would you like me to stop?'

A sudden realisation struck her. 'You stole it,' she snapped. 'You stole this boat!'

The last part of her sentence seemed lost, as the engine noise increased. She figured he'd only now worked out how to make the boat go faster.

'What?' he gasped. He wrestled with the wheel as the helm crashed into a large swell. It jolted the boat so hard, she saw that he was fighting to stop himself from being catapulted out.

'What makes you say that?' he asked, after he'd had a moment to collect himself.

'You don't know where anything is,' she said. 'Not even the bloody first aid kit, which is standard issue on every sea-faring vessel, I should think. And something any "friend" lending you their boat would want to make you aware of.'

'Oh, you're clever,' he said, his expression thoughtful, but his eyes firmly on course.

Lucy gasped, her mouth falling open.

'I mean -'

'Oh my God, I'm right?'

The man pursed his lips again and focussed on steering the boat, looking unsure what to say. When he finally spoke, it was a question that concerned her even more.

'Do you know the way to Islay?' he asked. She could tell that he was trying to sound casual; unconcerned.

'What? Please tell me you do actually know where we're headed?'

'Yes, of course! I do know these waters,' he retorted. 'I've been flying over them for years and years.'

'Well, perhaps it's time you slowed down a bit,' she said. 'Then have a better chance of getting where we're going with the boat and ourselves intact.'

'That's if the storm doesn't get us first.'

Feeling the biting wind on her face, she pulled the blanket tighter around her and grimaced. 'Do you think we will?'

He bit his lip. 'What do you care?' he asked her, after a significant length of silence between them had passed. 'A moment ago you didn't want me to save you.'

She shuffled in her seat and he looked at her. To her astonishment, she saw sorrow in his eyes. It was clear he'd felt instantly remorseful for bringing the subject out in the open. What business was it of his anyway?

'I had my reasons,' was her only response.

'Hey,' he said, a little too brightly, turning his attention back to the way ahead. 'How do people who drive boats know where they're going then?'

'They check a map.'

He looked at her again and blinked.

'It's probably in the storage space of one of these seats,' she said, raising her eyes skyward and shaking her head.

'Do you think you could -?'

'No.' Her reply was so quick and sharp, she saw his expression turn from blank to surprised.

'I can't drive and search,' he told her.

'Well, I can't look for you,' she retorted. 'My legs don't work.'

'Have you tried switching them on?' he asked, with a smirk.

'I mean, I'm unable to use them.'

He slowed the boat, making the engine noise change from a roar to a quieter whirr. 'What?' he asked.

'I said I'm unable to use my legs.'

'Look, if you're still cold then standing might -'

'I don't mean they're frozen,' she snapped. 'I mean they don't work, as in, they weren't working before I fell in the sea.'

Merrick rolled back his head and laughed, only to stop abruptly as he looked back down to see her glaring at him. 'I'm sorry,' he said, his cheeks reddening. 'It's just, you without your legs and me without my wings. Together... well... we're really something, aren't we?'

She shot him a look of cold indifference. 'Are you going to try telling me now you're a pilot?'

He shook his head, seeming to check himself. 'Your legs don't work,' he repeated. 'Well, this is going to be interesting to say the least. What on earth am I going to do with you when we get to Islay? Carry you?'

'We have to catch that ferry I toppled off,' she replied simply.

They both looked out to sea at the same time, where the ferry was just visible; far, far ahead and still going. 'I'm never catching up with that from here,' he said, scratching his head. 'This thing can move, but not that fast. I was doing okay trailing it until you, well, came tumbling down. Which was a mighty inconvenience for me, by the way.'

Ignoring the dig, she told him, 'Then you'd better get a move on and start now. I have a taxi booked at the other side,' she went on. 'And all my stuff's on that ship, including my wheelchair.'

'Can you see where it is?' he asked her. 'It's miles away! And there's weather occurring, as you already pointed out.'

'Yes, but you can still see it,' she said. 'And as long as you can see it, even in the distance, we can follow it. We can't be that far away.'

He stared at her, looking unsure.

'That is what you were doing up till now, isn't it? Following the ferry?' she said.

He nodded.

'So let's keep going. Or do you want to carry me around on your back when we get there? If we get there?'

He turned up the throttle again, and she felt her body pushed back in her seat.

'Okay,' he called out over the engine's hum. 'Let's go catch us a very big ship.'

Chapter 26: Dr Britten

'Yer too late, chum. Ye missed that last ferry by an hour.'

'But the timetable says four-thirty, look!'

'I don't think so, let me see.' The ferryman took the paper from Dr Britten's freezing hands and held it up to examine it. 'Ah, there ye go,' he said with a frown. He passed it back to him with a finger resting on some small print at the bottom corner of the page. 'It says "2014". You've gone and downloaded an old timetable from that interweb, haven't you?'

Dr Britten looked from the paper to the ferryman's weathered features and sighed. Arguing would be pointless. Even if things were desperate, there was nothing he could do if the ship had sailed.

The doctor turned to face out to sea, thinking of Lucy. She was out there now, knowing she was about to arrive on Islay at any moment. Almost certainly aiming to catch her connecting boat to Scarba this very evening. The place she was going to die. He turned back to face the old man, and cleared his throat before speaking. 'I wonder if there would be some way of contacting the crew?'

The ferryman stared blankly back at him.

'On the previous ferry, I mean,' he elaborated.

'Aye there is,' the man replied with a nod. 'But they'll no be coming back for ye the night, if that's whit yer thinking.'

'No, no, I understand that.' The doctor offered an affable smile that didn't betray the panic he felt in his gut.

Whatever he did now, he wasn't going to catch up with Lucy tonight. Not without drawing a huge amount of attention to her and himself. The sheer agony of the situation was almost strangling him.

'Look, I'm a doctor – a specialist in fact - and one of my very ill patients is on that ferry. I called ahead to make sure she was on the passenger list. But anyway, I need to get in contact with her as a matter of urgency. I mean, it is really urgent,' he stressed. 'Do you think that anybody could help me with that?'

The ferryman looked doubtful, blowing out his cheeks as he pondered the question.

'Sir,' Dr Britten went on, touching the old man's arm in earnest. 'It's literally a matter of life and death or I wouldn't ask.'

The ferryman looked down to where the doctor was holding his arm, and he instinctively let go. The man continued to eye him suspiciously. 'If ye go over to the office there,' he said. 'Sandra'll be able to help ye.' He pointed to a doorway in the building to the right which said Ticket Office.

Dr Britten nodded, thanked him and drove over to park in front of the building. Turning off the ignition, he reached into the back seat for his briefcase. Picking it up, he headed for the door of the building. He hoped there was something he would be able to do; some way of reaching Lucy tonight.

'The trouble is we need a little bit more than the fact you're her doctor.'

Dr Britten nodded at the middle-aged lady he guessed to be Sandra. 'Of course,' he said, reaching into his briefcase for some identification. 'But do you think you remember seeing her then? This lady is disabled so you might have noticed her getting on the ship. She's in a wheelchair.'

'Well,' she continued after a long pause. 'I dinnae mind seeing anyone like that come in here for a ticket, right enough. But there's definitely a Lucy Colbain on the passenger list for the last ferry.'

'Colwyn,' he corrected her. 'Is that the name you searched for?'

She looked back at her screen. 'Colwyn, aye,' she said. 'She's on that ferry, according to my list. Are you sure this cannae wait until morning, Doctor?'

'No, it can't,' he told her with a despondent shake of his head. 'I have to contact her tonight. What can I do? Is there some way of getting in touch with the crew on board?'

'Mobiles dinnae always work out there,' she replied, with a thoughtful expression. She tapped her lips with a finger. 'But they do have radios, for emergencies, like. But it would hae to be an extreme emergency.'

'Oh it is, I can assure you,' he said. 'You can call the hospital if you like, I am sure they'll be happy to verify my professional credentials.'

She nodded. 'Okay then,' she said, starting to type. 'What's the emergency?'

The banging of a door doctor made him start, and he turned to see a man and a woman entering the office. Dr Britten cleared his throat and leaned into Sandra's window to speak quietly. She leaned in to listen.

'This lady is vulnerable, scared and alone,' he told her. 'And as her doctor, I shouldn't really tell you this but I don't know what else to do in the circumstances.' He paused, clearing his throat. 'You see,' he said finally. 'She's heading to Scarba to commit suicide.'

Sandra's mouth fell open. Her cheeks flushed and her eyes darted back down to the keyboard as she began typing faster.

The doctor looked nervously back at the couple behind him. To his relief, he found they were deep in conversation, browsing the leaflet shelf. The guilt he felt at betraying Lucy's trust and privacy as his patient was matched only with his relief. Something was finally being done at last to save her. 'I had hoped to catch up with her here to change her mind, but now there's only one option left. We need to turn that ship around.'

Sandra stopped typing and looked him square in the eye. 'Then that's what we will do, Doc,' she said.

Chapter 27: Lucy

Lucy watched as the waters rolled and churned, the blustery wind becoming stronger. Their little fishing boat seemed to be veering off course; even as the man fought hard to steer ahead. Something wasn't right.

'It's turning around,' he said, sounding as surprised and confused as she was feeling. 'It's going to be coming right at us any moment now. What the -?'

'We shouldn't have followed this closely, didn't I say that?' she shouted, as her whole body was lifted from the seat. She gripped the railing and grimaced.

'Hold on tight,' he told her. 'I need to try and spin this thing about.'

'Spin?' she said. 'As in turnabout at high speed? Are you joking?'

He pulled the wheel to the left, leaning with it.

'Keep going ahead!' she shouted. 'It's hardly going to hit us, is it?'

'Who knows?' he shouted back, as the boat continued to turn so fast they were almost back where they started. 'He might not even see us down here.'

'Of course he can see us,' she snapped. 'It's a passenger ferry. They know what they're doing.'

For as much as she failed to value her own life right at this moment, Lucy wished she felt as confident as she sounded. This wasn't at all like the ending she had planned. Too panicked, no control, far too many witnesses. 'Look, stop the boat,' she ordered. 'Just stop it and wait. We can let the ferry go past.'

The engine slowed before coming to a stop and Lucy dared to breathe out her relief. In silence, they watched as the ferry full of people did as Lucy had predicted. Facing the way it had come before, it headed back to the mainland, rocking the fishing boat in its wake.

'See,' she told him, pointing at the ship. 'You panicked. That guy up there knows what he's doing.'

The man nodded. 'Alright, alright,' he said, sitting back and heaving a huge sigh. 'I did, I panicked. But you can't blame a man. I thought we might get sucked in with a big beast like that coming at us.' He continued to watch it, oblivious to them in the tiny fishing boat. 'I wonder why it's going back?' he said.

Lucy pulled the now soaking blanket over her head. Her headscarf now clung to her skull like a second skin. 'Now what?' she said, feeling miserable. 'Follow it back?'

'Oh no,' he told her firmly. 'I'm not going back, this is where I need to be and this is where you were going.' He pointed ahead.

Lucy followed his gaze to see an island. The relief she felt at seeing dry land was immense, she was soaked and freezing.

'Do you see it?' he said, as she nodded a response. 'I think you'll find that's our destination. Didn't I tell you I could sail a boat?'

'How can you be so sure?' she asked him. 'We've seen land from other sides too. How do you know that's it?'

'I've seen it from the air,' he replied. 'That is most definitely Islay.'

'From the air?' she said. 'So, you've flown here?'

He nodded, a look of whimsical pleasure washing over his face, which puzzled her. 'Ah yes,' he replied. 'Many, many times.'

'Well, that's great,' she said, glancing back over at the departing ferry. 'Except my bloody wheelchair is on that ship.'

His expression darkened. 'Oh,' he said, resting his hand on the ignition key. 'Well, in that case -'

'You're not planning to follow the ferry again, are you?'

'This wheelchair,' he said, leaning forward to rest his arms on the windscreen. 'That's a chair with wheels, right?'

She laughed. 'Yep, the clue's in the name.'

'Right,' he said, nodding. 'So you'll need this wheelchair thing to get about?'

'Ah ha,' she confirmed.

'That settles it then,' he said, getting back to the controls. 'You need that.'

'No, wait,' she said. 'I'm going to hazard a guess there's no way we are going to have enough fuel on this little boat to go back to where we came from. And I'm not willing to chance getting stuck, are you?'

The man shook his head as he started up the engine again. 'If you say so,' he said. And then, 'What's fuel?'

'Very funny.'

He scratched his head. 'Well, I could do with a laugh,' he said seriously. 'But how does this funny fuel prevent us from getting to the mainland and back?'

'It doesn't,' she said. 'Wow, you really are a natural sailor, aren't you?'

He stretched himself up, puffing out his chest. 'Yep,' he agreed with a proud grin.

She studied the man for a moment, not knowing what to make of him. His gangly legs, goofy grin and wild mop of copper-red hair. 'You're a strange egg, that's for sure,' she told him at last.

His brow furrowed. 'Oh no,' he said. 'I'm all grown up now.'

Lucy shook her head and groaned. 'Can we please continue now?'

He hesitated. 'Well, okay,' he replied. 'But I'm going to have to carry you ashore, if that's alright with you?'

Lucy stiffened, and then smiled through gritted teeth. Being carried by this stranger would be weird, but he had pulled her from the sea after all. And what option did she have this late in the day? 'I have a taxi booked to wait for me onshore,' she said. 'I'll ask the driver to do a quick detour. There will be somewhere over there I can hire a chair from, I'm sure. Oh, crap!'

'What?'

'Oh, it's nothing,' she replied. 'Well, okay, it's something. All my cash was on the ferry too. It was in my other bag.' She felt for her handbag, still hooked over her head and shoulder. It was still there, though sodden from her unplanned dip in the Irish Sea. She opened the zip. 'But I do have a bank card in here.'

'What is that?' he asked, as she hunted around inside it.

'A bank card?' she said, gasping with relief as she put her hand on the card inside a pocket in the bag. It was wet, but surely workable. 'Is this your way of telling me you're penniless and need a little help?'

'No, I mean what's a bank card?'

She wanted to laugh at him, but something told her he was being genuine. Either that or he'd lived on an island for all his days. 'It's a thing you get your money out of the bank with,' she replied. 'Are you telling me you've never heard of them?'

He threw her a puzzled look. 'No,' he said. 'I've never heard of them, but then, I'm very very old.'

'Sure you are,' she said, shaking her head. This man stole a boat and didn't seem to know what a bank card was. He was a tricky one alright, life-saver or not. Not that she wanted or needed a life-saver type on this trip.

The man pushed down the lever and the engine roared awake as they started to move again. Lucy sighed. It was drawing them ever closer to their destination – her second to last, she thought. Noticing the smallest pang of regret, she pushed it from her mind as soon as it arrived.

'I didn't catch your name,' she said to the man, realising he was her last companion on this final journey of her life. Even if he was, it would seem, a touch bonkers. But then, he wasn't dangerous or why would he have gone to such lengths to save her? And anyway, she no longer had anything to lose. 'I'm Lucy, by the way,' she added.

'Merrick,' he said, flashing her a toothy grin for the first time before signalling to the land ahead. He sighed. 'Welcome to beautiful, mystical and lovely Islay, Lucy Bytheway.'

'Is it beautiful?' she asked. 'I've forgotten.'

Merrick nodded. 'Beyond belief,' he told her. 'Why forgotten? Were you here before?'

Lucy felt a remembered pain. It was of desolation and longing; childhood happiness that was abruptly ended. The Advice Bucket she was promised but never received.

'I lived here once,' she told him. 'But it was a long time ago.'

'Really?' Why did you leave?'

'I grew up and went to university,' she said with a sniff of indifference. 'And I never came back.'

'Until now,' he said, his gaze fixed on the journey ahead.

'Until now,' she repeated.

Chapter 28: Gladys

With shaking fingers, Gladys took a note from the Advice Bucket. 'Tell me what it feels like again!' she shouted. 'Tell me about dying!'

Opening the note hastily, she read:

When I watch the ebb and flow of the waves, my spirit soars and I'm released. This is how it is with the sea. Go to it. Go often.

'Oh jings, yer timing's shite, Olive,' she sobbed, screwing it up before throwing it in the air and kicking it at the wall. Stumbling, she found a chair and sat down, put her head in her hands and broke her heart. Poor Joe was gone. Who on earth was going to take her to the mainland for a new dog now?

'Oh Angus,' she said into the emptiness of her stark and gloomy living space, 'Ye dinnae make this life an easy one, do ye?'

Joe was gone. Joe was gone. Joe was gone.

Would she ever have company in this long, ever-waiting-for-something life? And what was she waiting for anyway? What was it all about? All that she'd ever loved was gone; only somewhere in the skies above lived her darling Merrick. An old pain tore at her heart-strings as she remembered him now - tall, fair and trusting. He would have no idea why she'd sent him away and possibly no idea who, what or where she was now, it was all so long ago. Of course, as a barnacle goose, of all things, how could he remember her now anyway, after over three hundred years?

She thought she saw him once or twice over the years, but she could never be sure. The geese rarely travelled alone. There was the annual gathering on Islay, of course. This, she knew, bought twenty to forty thousand of them to Loch Gruinart. Yet even if he was there – and there was every chance and hope that he was – he couldn't and wouldn't forgive her. She'd hidden in shame from him for three centuries, knowing he would hate her. She had brought an evil upon him so great that he would never wanted to see her again. If Merrick could remember his former life as a man, his only conclusion would be that she'd betrayed him. She had shown herself as a witch to him; banished him. Turned him into a goose, of all things. He must surely despise her.

Love had never been fair, and it had stolen her own mortality long, long ago. She recalled the true Cailleach, who had not been a woman but a man. Not the witch that commanded the Corryvreckkan, but a medicine man. Angus, who had stood up and waited for mankind before it was her turn. It was a task she had unwittingly taken from him before he died, his destiny duly fulfilled.

'One spell is for immortality as a barnacle goose, one is for mortality as a person,' he had told her. He'd been her saviour at the end, breaking her out of the prison the witch hunters had thrown her into at Finlaggan. It had been months after the attempted burning. Unable to destroy her, the men had thrown her into a locked room. It had been months before Angus had come for her.

'I don't understand,' she'd said, frowning as he passed her the parchments for the second time. She'd thought the man was somewhat confused the first time, and as a result, she'd discarded them. On this occasion, she'd accepted them with the intention of keeping her word. It was because of the spells that the witch hunters had been unable to kill her. It was because of the spells that Merrick was still alive. Now she believed. 'Why would you need a spell to make someone mortal, the way we all are?' she'd said, trying not to sound sceptical.

'That is saved for the goose – mortal or immortal. It is for the goose of your choosing,' had been the answer.

'Ah,' she'd said, nodding and smiling. 'The goose, of course.'

Gladys had thought that she might never want to give that spell to anyone and she told him so. Many years after she'd realised the spells were real, she was still decided on that one. Which was why she had asked for it to be hidden in the wishing tree. Even if it was ever found and read out, it could never affect a person who was already mortal. Yes, she told Angus in her mind, I wis glad tae see the back o' that wan.

Was it okay to hide away the spell she was destined to keep? It could be found, but she'd be hard pressed to find out which coin it was hidden behind. At least it was safe. It had been a task she had allotted to poor old Joe years before. Although he had no idea the enormity of the simple piece of paper she'd asked him to conceal forever.

'I did as I was told, Angus,' she said aloud. 'Ahm the carer and protector o' all the spells. I don't know where wan o' them is.' She chuckled to herself, yet a familiar sense of foreboding followed her cheer. Angus had passed to her the task that he himself had carried for four centuries. It was to keep the spells, for the future good of mankind. Only, she had no clue what the future good would be. How could changing people into barnacle geese save the world? If that was what the future good of mankind meant.

She might never know, and there was only one chance for her to pass on this curse which Romney had labelled a gift. 'Pah, some gift!' She spat at the fireplace. 'The gift of living alone and unloved for three hundred years.'

She remembered his leaving her still, as thought it was yesterday. How he had thanked her for this chance to sleep at last. Good for him, she thought with cool indifference.

She was a formidable woman, who had lived what she considered to be a full life. With a will of titanium, she lived on the most unforgiving of lands. She'd weathered storms and climbed hills. She could hunt, build, slaughter chickens and gut fish. She could knit, sew, grow, mend, paint, bake, preserve, repair, renew, recycle and fight like a bull mastiff. But Gladys Anderson could not die, thanks for accepting two simple pieces of paper. And more and more, as the years progressed, she could not stand to live without love. It was what life was for, as Olive had said in her Advice Bucket note.

Gladys had loved only two things in her life: her many dogs, and Merrick. Yet hers was a strange and elusive destiny that might never allow her to meet with them again.

Chapter 29: Merrick

As she sat, face turned to the land ahead, Merrick studied the woman's slight frame. She was still wrapped in the wet blanket, still shivering. The rain was heavier than ever, but she had refused to let him carry her to the lower deck for shelter. Not for the first time since he saved her, he wondered what it was that made her care so little about herself. What made her want to fight him off and drown?

'So,' he said to her at last. 'What business have you on Islay? Family is it?'

Without turning around, she replied, 'no, there's no one I know there.'

'A holiday then?' he asked, doubting it.

'My grandmother had a house on there where I lived for a short while,' she said.

'Oh, that's nice,' he replied. 'So you'll be going to see the old place then?'

She shook her head. 'She died a long time ago, which was the reason why I left. I haven't thought of it in a long time and I'm not going there anyway. I have other plans.'

'Oh?'

She didn't reply, only looked out to sea, hugging the foil blanket closer to her.

'I'm sorry,' he said. 'You must be freezing. There's an old coat down below. I could get it for you?'

'That would be great,' she said, looking back at him with a weak smile through chattering teeth. 'Would you?'

As she turned back around to face ahead, Merrick pursed his lips. He wondered whether it was safe to leave her alone as he scrambled about below looking for the coat. As if reading his mind, she said, 'It's alright, I won't try to jump off or anything. My plan is to see Scarba.'

'Scarba?' he said, turning off the boat's engine and moving towards the steps to below deck. 'I don't think I've ever heard of it.'

'It's a tiny island off Jura,' she told him. 'Not many people have, but it's there. It's pretty much uninhabited.'

Ah, Scarba. Merrick knew and remembered the island, but not its name. Deciding to say no more about it, he tripped down the stairs, not convinced she wouldn't try to jump. Finding the old coat on the seat where he'd left it the night before after using it as a blanket. He picked it up and raced back up to give it to her.

'So why go?' he asked, taking the wet blanket from her and placing the coat around her shoulders. She put her arms in the sleeves and thanked him.

'Because it was the last place my mother went before she died,' she said, fastening the buttons of the coat. 'I wanted to see it, that's all.'

'And you plan to stay on this pretty much uninhabited island?'

She looked away from the land ahead to lean over the edge of the boat and peer down into the water. Finally, she replied: 'Yes.'

He sighed, but not so that she could hear him. Something about her concerned him, even when he had a whole host of his own worries to deal with right now.

'Where are you heading?' she asked, without turning around.

'I'm going to Islay myself,' he told her. 'At least, to begin with. I was following your ferry, which is lucky for you.' He wanted her to agree with the last part, but a part of him expected that she wouldn't.

'Do you have someone there?'

'No. Well, I did once.'

'So you're looking for someone you left behind?'

Merrick thought of Gladys. She'd eluded him for three centuries, even on a small island like Islay. It wasn't like he hadn't tried many, many times before to find her. 'Yes,' he replied, 'That's exactly what I'm doing.' And he knew it to be true, yet a different reality had only just occurred to him. He didn't know where she was. As a man she would see him now, she would know it was him. The only trouble was he'd searched for her so many times before, from the land and from the air, with no success. Could do it now, when it mattered more than ever? Could he bring her out of hiding to see him? He felt certain she would never have gone far; he knew her too well. She had some kind of purpose and he knew it to be here around these waters. But with only man's mechanical inventions to aid him, he hadn't thought about where to begin looking. At least, not further than his arrival on Islay. From the air, he felt he could see everything. But never her. Where would she be? Three hundred years of searching hadn't helped him find her; what could he do to find her now?

'Penny for them?'

Lucy's voice brought him back into the moment. 'Huh?'

'Your thoughts,' she replied with a smile. 'You looked as though you were somewhere else for a moment there.'

'Yes, I suppose I was. How far would a penny get me on Islay?' he asked, his mind racing to think of some information to sell to her as requested.

She laughed. 'A penny won't get you much these days,' she told him. 'Not even penny chews are a penny now.'

His eyebrows knitted as he tried to understand this, but after a moment, shrugged it off. He put the key in the ignition and started the engine again. Merrick's mind was blown and something told him that admitting it would give too much away. 'So, what's the attraction to Scarba all about?' he asked, changing the subject as the boat began to move off.

'Why wouldn't you want to visit Scarba?' she replied. 'It's beautiful, out of the way and steeped in history and legend. In fact, despite its size, it's not entirely uninhabited, you know.'

'It isn't?' he said.

'No,' she replied. 'There's someone living there, so they say.'

Merrick was only half listening, as a sudden gust of wind threatened to knock the boat off course. He held the wheel fast; his mind fixed on the task of steering it back.

'There's a huge whirlpool between it and Jura, called the Corryvrecken,' Lucy continued. He noticed she seemed oblivious to his struggle. 'Have you heard of it? It's the world's biggest whirlpool.'

'I don't think so, no.'

'It's swallowed many boats over the years,' she went on. 'Remarkable how few people have heard of the Corryvrecken. It's quite an incredible sight, from what I've read. It's sometimes referred to as the Witches Cauldron, because of the mistress who governs it. She's the one who calls it to awaken and devour ships.'

She stopped, as if waiting for a reply, but Merrick only grunted. He was oddly annoyed now that she was getting too talkative. Especially as he had to strain to hear her now as the wind and rain whipped his face.

'It's a great story, don't you think?' she said.

'I'm sorry, I'm struggling to hear you very well, what did you say?'

She offered him a wry smile, and shouted, 'I said, it's a great story, don't you think?'

'Ah ha,' he agreed, having not properly digested much of what she had said. Something about a witch on Scarba?

'I find the older I get, the more I want it to be true. The thought of some ancient, three-hundred-year-old woman living alone on a remote island.'

Above the growling and churning of the engine, Merrick felt his heart thud in his ears. He pulled back the lever and slowed the boat down to hear her better. 'A three-hundred-year-old woman, you say?'

She nodded. 'The Cailleach Bheur.'

'Christ!'

As he stopped the boat, the woman stared back at him, her expression apprehensive. 'What?' she asked.

Merrick turned off the engine, and the boat started to drift. 'Tell me more about this Cailleach Bheur, could you?' he said.

'Why?'

'Because... because it's interesting,' he replied, swallowing hard.

Lucy sighed. 'Is it so important?' she asked. 'It's only an old wives' tale. I was merely making conversation. I'm a little nervous, you see. And I ramble on when I'm -'

'Sorry,' he cut in, desperate to hear more. 'Please, ramble on, I want to hear it. It's just... I think this is a story I've heard before, that's all.'

'It is?'

He nodded. 'If I'm right, we might not be at such cross purposes after all,' he explained. He hoped this new information might make her help him. 'Please, tell me what you know of the old woman.'

'Witch.'

'Witch,' he agreed, with some difficulty.

'There isn't much more to tell,' she began, staring uncertainly back at him. 'And who said we were at cross purposes? You're going to Islay and so am I, at first. I can't get to Scarba without going there.'

'Why?'

'Because that's where the boat leaves from.'

'You have a boat ready to take you there?'

She nodded, eyeing him suspiciously. Merrick paused; all too aware he was making her feel wary of him. Yet his luck had just changed and he couldn't believe it. 'Cross purposes, you know,' he explained as warm and unhurriedly as he could. 'There I was diving into the sea to save you, and you didn't want to be saved -'

He bit his lip, as her gaze dropped so she was no longer meeting his eye.

'What made you think I didn't want to be saved?' she asked him almost inaudibly.

Slowly, he breathed in then out, gathering his thoughts. He had to make her trust him, one way or another. 'The way you tried to push me away when I was grabbing a hold of you out there.' He studied her face as he spoke. He was looking for some expression or sign that might tell him more than he knew she was going to be prepared to tell.

She stayed silent, not looking up. Merrick sighed, deciding to be direct. Whatever came out of this conversation he knew now he would be going with this woman to Scarba.

'Okay,' he said, trying his very best to sound sympathetic. 'Let's take it from the top. Did you jump from the ferry or were you pushed?'

'Neither!' she said, looking both shocked and, he noted, embarrassed. He'd failed on the sounding sympathetic part. 'I fell,' she insisted.

'But you wanted to drown,' he said, having no time in his day for faffing about. 'I know you did. I felt it then and I feel it now.'

'Oh, take us to Islay,' she thundered, staring away into the distance. 'I don't want to talk about this anymore. I don't even know anything about you, except for the fact you ask too many questions.'

'And I saved your life, even if you didn't want me to,' he reminded her. 'Lord, I even had to drag you from the steps to your seat, you weren't giving an inch!' he retorted. He took the keys out of the ignition and throwing them on the shelf in front of him with a clunk.

'I told you why,' she snapped. 'My legs don't work!'

He flushed. 'Of course, yes,' he agreed, feeling annoyed with himself. 'I didn't mean -'

'You are going to finish this trip, aren't you?' she snapped, spinning around to face him again. She eyed the keys he now held in his hand.

He watched her, taking in the soaked, cold and pale looking woman before him. She needed warmth, dry land; probably a hot meal. But much more than all this, she looked like someone who was hurting. Merrick had tried to be a healer in the earliest years of his human existence. He'd believed he could save lives, imagining he had a magical something but never knowing what. In three centuries as a barnacle goose, he had taken to the task of leading his new family. He'd worked to ensure the propagation and protection of the species. He led them to food, the best breeding grounds, and the safest nesting places. It went against all his natural, protective instincts to leave this woman so lost and alone. His goal was important, but here was a human being that needed... he wasn't sure what, but he decided perhaps it was a friend.

'I will,' he said at last. 'Once you've told me why you wanted to drown and what the real purpose of your trip to this Scarba place is.'

'I don't have to tell you anything,' she argued. 'We're almost there. I can scream for help when another boat passes and have you handed in to the authorities.'

'For what?'

'Kidnapping.'

'Kidnapping? But I saved your life!'

'What if I didn't want -' Lucy stopped, and he knew she was realising too late that she had almost slipped up. '...to go with you,' she finished.

He nodded, satisfied but saddened at the same time. The truth was out there now between them, and they'd both heard it. For a moment he cursed himself for pushing. But now he knew he was right, it made him care about her more. He couldn't abandon a woman with a death wish. There was something very, very wrong. Something that needed fixing, and it was his need to fix and to lead that had gotten him where he was now. He hung his head, remembering a small boy from many, many years ago. A boy he hadn't been there to hold as he breathed his last. As he looked at Lucy's expression, almost devoid of care or hope, he saw that boy from another lifetime. It wasn't in his nature to leave any living thing alone and desperate. Only he couldn't afford to fail this time.

'If it's Scarba you want,' he told her. 'Then why don't we head straight there now ourselves?'

She looked up in surprise. 'The whirlpool,' she said. 'Only the most experienced sailors can get around that. It's really dangerous. Are you experienced enough?'

He didn't reply, because they both knew the answer.

'I chartered a boat privately,' she went on.

'But I can get us there.'

'Us?'

He nodded. 'I want to go too,' he said. 'I've never been to Scarba.'

'Why?'

'To see the... er... the witch,' he said, hating himself for calling her that.

'She's not real,' Lucy scoffed. 'I told you. It's only a story.'

126

'And it's one I've heard before,' he explained. 'That's why I'm interested. It's why I stopped the boat to listen to you. I want to go to be able to see for myself.'

Lucy seemed to consider this for a moment, looking all about the bow of the tiny fishing boat. 'In this?'

He nodded.

It was her turn to look doubtful. 'It's the world's biggest whirlpool,' she said. 'You nearly shat when the ferry decided to change course in front of you.'

He grinned, then realised she wasn't joking.

'You have no idea how to steer this boat. You stole it, didn't you?'

He didn't answer.

'Or borrowed it,' she said. 'Don't think I don't know it isn't yours. You don't seem to know where anything is. Your steering leaves a little to be desired and, most obvious of all, you were following the ferry to Islay. So I don't think I'll be letting you try to navigate The Corryvrecken.'

He opened his mouth to protest, then changed tack. 'What does it matter if I kill us?' he said. 'You want to die anyway.'

She breathed in, holding his gaze with a steely determination that surprised him. 'When I die,' she told him, 'it will be my way, at my time of choosing and at my place of choosing.'

'Yet for a moment back there, you thought it was this sea?' He waved a hand out across the ocean, his expression grim. 'Why Scarba? You said it yourself, there's nothing and no one there.'

'Except the witch,' she snapped back, with a half laugh.

He swallowed hard. Merrick hated that word more than any other. A witch is evil; people burned witches. Gladys was special, perhaps not of this world. But she was not a witch.

Lucy stopped laughing and looked at him. 'Do you mean it?' she asked. 'You really want to try and find her?'

'Is that what you're going for?' he asked.

She raised her eyebrows before looking down. 'Perhaps,' she replied with a shrug.

'Then I want to find her too. So let's go together. What have we got to lose?'

'But I don't want to go to Scarba with you,' she snapped back, her sudden anger catching him off guard. 'I don't want to go to Scarba with anyone!'

Merrick blew out his cheeks, feeling an immense frustration. Sure, he could get to Scarba on his own. Yet, at the same time, he felt there was nothing to be gained from leaving Lucy alone. He had to make her change her mind about this death wish thing, whatever that was about. He knew it was there, he didn't know why and he didn't know how he was going to do it. But as he started the engine to take them finally into land, he had decided to do all he could to help her. Merrick had never been able to stop wanting to help. Nobody, under his wing, was ever left behind.

Chapter 30: Dr Britten

Dr Britten sat alone in the cabin hugging a hot cup of mint tea, trying hard not to breathe in cigarette smoke. Three ferrymen sat at the table in front, deep in conversation, all paying him no mind; all puffing on the death weed. Each oblivious to how close they were to a man who may be about to save thousands, if not millions of lives. The thought made him smile.

How often did people encounter the most significant of humans without realising it? He was not a boastful man, but there was no getting away from it: Dr Britten was about to go down in medical history. They would name the cure after him, as the doctor who had first discovered the disease had claimed it. He recalled the great Dr Morsley, his life dedicated to studying disease. It was important work that culminated in him finding a common link in a series of mystery illnesses. On his demise, another doctor had taken the research onward. Until, years later, Dr Britten had picked up where they left off.

'Are you okay, Dr Britten? Can I get you anything to eat?'

It was a young woman from the worker's kitchen that had interrupted his thoughts. He looked up to see her standing over him with a tray in her hand. 'No, thanks very much,' he replied, offering her a kind smile. 'I'm fine.'

'It might be a while yet before the ferry gets back,' she said, lowering the tray to show him a plate full of sweet treats. 'Are you sure I can't tempt ye with a wee cake?'

Sugar, Dr Britten knew, was a modern day demon; yet another destroyer of human health. There were others taking that cause on to eventually win. He hoped.

'No thank you,' he said. 'I don't eat cakes.'

'Aww,' she said, with a sympathetic expression. 'Are you diabetic?'

He shook his head. I don't want to *become* diabetic, he thought.

'Well, if I can get you anything at all, you come and see me,' she told him. 'Sandra said I was to look after you, on the house.'

She walked away into the kitchen with her cakes, and he sat in thoughtful silence again, chewing the inside of his cheek. Out of the room went the sugar, while he remained with the men and their nicotine. Why were people so relaxed with shortening their own existence? With the return of the ferry would come the key to changing and lengthening the lives of the victims of Morsley's Pholblastoma. He hoped at least *they* would treat themselves more kindly as a result of being given a second chance.

A sudden blast of cool air made him look up again, to see Sandra standing at the door.

'Dr Britten?' she said quietly, her expression serious. 'The boat's coming in.'

Chapter 31: Gladys

The Advice Bucket was full of end-of-life wisdom, but none that could have helped old Joe. Gladys stood watching the helicopters circling Joe's boat. It had been propelled towards Scarba in the end, but Gladys knew Joe's body wouldn't be found today. It would most likely be washed up somewhere obscure and far from here. Such was the hungry force of The Corryvrecken. Poor Joe. He had annoyed her on many a day, but she felt a heavy sadness for him and his poor wife, if he'd had one. He'd been the only MacNeish to tell her nothing about his life, something that told her he was the last in his line. Unfortunate, if true, for her. She'd relied on several generations of MacNeish men. They were her link to the outside world.

'Oh, Angus,' she said aloud. 'I hope there's no bairns left without a daddy tonight.'

The only woman Joe had ever brought to her attention had been Olive. Introduced as 'a good friend', it was Joe that had brought her to the island, begging Gladys to take her in. It was the only favour he'd asked of her in return for all he had done for her.

'These are her last days,' he'd said. 'Treat her well.'

She'd agreed, of course. Olive had been lost, alone and confused. Her memory beginning to desert her as the disease progressed. All she had with her was a tin bucket full of notes, yet she couldn't remember why she'd brought it. When, after several days Gladys finally managed to coax it out of her, the truth had been almost too tragic to bear. It was for Lucy, she'd said, the daughter Olive had left behind. Only she hadn't been able to recall where the child lived.

All Joe knew of his friend was that the family had been taking an extended holiday on Islay. Olive had him take her to the mainland in secret for her weekly hospital appointments. She was dying, but hadn't wanted anyone close to her to know.

'But what of the little girl?' Gladys had asked.

Joe divulged later that he'd seen her only once, finding her after the day he took Olive for her final journey to Scarba. The poor waif had been hiding in the back of his truck under a blanket. She'd followed her mother, hoping to find out where she was running away to each week.

'I wanted her to play with me,' the child had cried. With the little girl unable to tell him the address of their holiday cottage, Joe had taken pity on her. Learning she had only an elderly grandmother left now, he'd given her a day to remember. He took her to the beach, to the café for soup and ice-cream and to the play park before handing her to the authorities. It was a day the tiny daughter of a lost and dying woman would have been desperately in need of. The memory of it made Gladys's heart surge all over again. Poor, kindly, old Joe.

He'd been a heavy man; hard as she'd tried to save him the whirlpool had taken them under together. The last thing she'd felt of him were his fingers releasing her. He'd tried to save her too. His last, desperate moments spent helping someone who was immortal. Perhaps he hadn't believed that she couldn't drown; that she'd be back up at the surface like a cork within hours. And so it was. So it had always been and so it would be; this was her lot. Gladys had battled with The Corryvreckan herself over the centuries. Even though she would gladly succumb to the lost depths of the sea where it tried so hard to drag her, it failed. It always failed.

She looked back in the direction of her tiny bothy. High on the craggy hills, away from any of the few defined paths in Scarba, it was well hidden in the trees. Made from material collected from the woods, some of which had been provided by the MacNeish men. Lanterns, a sink, even a diesel powered generator had made life much easier. Power that allowed her to use the mobile phone she'd found on the seashore, dropped by a hiker. Not long afterwards Joe had introduced her to the World Wide Web. A modern miracle; the light in her dark, lonely world. Her home was a quaint and mysterious little place that had served her well. With the added conveniences of these latter years, the long drag of her life was more bearable. Only Gladys knew the exact location of the bothy. The building was so cleverly camouflaged, few people had stumbled upon it.

Turning her back on the helicopter search, she trudged onward. Her journey was to the sheltered eastern side of the island and her favourite place. Within the hour she reached it - the burial ground. It was here beside the chapel of Cille Mhoire an Caibel that she'd once lain under the ground waiting to be rescued. It was after Angus had masterminded her escape and the eventual faking of her death. After arranging a service and burial with the locals, he'd later returned to exhume her. Here was where she had accepted the cursed spells for the second and final time. The same cursed incantations that had kept her alive on Scarba for three centuries since.

'I need you to keep these so that I can pass,' Angus had told her. 'Please, please take them. Please, guard them. Can you do that for me?'

Finally believing him, she'd taken the spells. That day, assured that this time she would do as promised, he'd left Scarba to die. He was four hundred and forty-seven-years-old.

In turn, Gladys began to forget pain, constriction or breathlessness. That was until a few days ago, when she thought she might at last be making her way to the much awaited final sleep. It would be here in the grave of the one hundred and forty-year-old woman. Her last resting place; that which was already

133

her grave. Pain signified that the end was near, and this she could cope with. This she had looked forward to. Alas, the loss of that pain for reasons she couldn't understand seemed to suggest she was here to stay once more. Her task - her destiny - incomplete. Only now with the added problem of finding a new collaborator to her hiding place.

Money had once been a problem, as the coinage of the fortune she had left went out of circulation. Until she struck a bargain with Joe's great, great grandfather, Jamesy MacNeish. He was the original owner of the Craobh Haven boat company. Jamesy bought his first commercial vessel thanks to Gladys. He'd made a very handsome sum of money selling some very old items she had kept in her possession. In time his thriving business, and the existence of its benefactor, had been passed down, father to son. It continued through the generations until it came to Joe. Jamesy MacNeish had thanked the Lord for his own lost battle with The Corryvreckan. That fateful fishing trip that washed him onshore at Scarba, to be found and taken in by Gladys. Yet similarly, the MacNeish family had been pivotal to her survival. They'd helped her keep prying eyes away for years. Fate brought them together when they'd needed each other. She kept the secret of the origins of their good fortune. In turn, a long line of MacNeish's had kept good on their promises to tell nobody about her very existence. It was the bond between them, an unwritten sales agreement, and now the last MacNeish was lost to the sea. What would she do now?

She sat down among slate and shale, looking despondently at her grave. Then, she turned her attention to the ruined remains of the chapel, now cloaked in moss, heather and bracken. There were always seasonal bright colours in this area, from wild irises, bluebells and sea pinks. She loved this place. It was worthy of being the last resting place of a tired, old woman. A dark mass in the distance caught her eye and she looked up to the sky and sea beyond, scowling. A flock of geese; the reason she was here. Perhaps her beloved Merrick was there among them, still hating her. Oh, hadn't she sacrificed enough in this life? What did she have to do to be laid to rest? To finally forget her guilt at sending him off to somehow become part of a destiny she didn't understand. Why had this happened to them? What was it all for?

Bloody geese.

Sighing, she put her hand in her pocket and pulled out another of Olive's notes. She'd saved today's reading for this place, having no idea what it was going to tell her. The short, timely message brought long overdue tears to her eyes:

'Let more than one, trusted friend in. A life alone is not lived at all.'

Chapter 32: Lucy

It was as if the island had known she was coming home. As Merrick carried Lucy to land the rain had stopped and the clouds parted. Blinded by a sunbeam, she'd found herself thinking of her grandmother's Advice Bucket. Only now on this, the last part of her trip, did she wish she'd brought it along. She was ready to accept death. Yet it made her heart ache to think the old woman wouldn't be beside her, if only in letter form, in her final days. She couldn't afford to go back of course, because who knew how long she had left? How long before the decision for her own date of death was taken from her? And then there was Dr Britten, who knew of her plans. And there was Roisin. She must have made enquiries as to why someone she barely knew had left her a house and all her belongings. No, going back was out of the question.

The bucket had meant so much to her. Why was she only realising this now?

'What's the plan then, for your boat trip to Scarba?' Merrick asked her, breaking the silence between them. They were sat at a picnic table outside a fish restaurant at Port Askaig.

'He's picking me up at 6.30 from here,' she replied, shivering as she wiped a stray tear from her eye. 'The name's Joe MacNeish. I've to look out for a small fishing boat known as Mardy Sue.'

'Now?' he asked. 'Isn't it a bit late in the day?'

'It's not a long crossing,' she said, glancing at the clock on the wall of the restaurant as she sipped her tea. 'He should be here by now though.'

'Where was he coming from?'

'Craobh Haven. It's on the mainland.'

'The mainland? Well, why didn't you sail with him from there?'

'That was the original plan. But then he phoned to say he was coming over to Islay on some other business today. So we arranged for him to collect me from here.'

'Do you know this man, then?'

She shook her head, as another long pushed aside memory returned to the forefront of her mind. 'I don't think so, no,' she replied truthfully. 'Although I do recall spending a day with a boatman as a little girl.'

Merrick looked surprised. 'You spent a day with a boatman?'

'Yes.'

'Who you didn't know?'

'Well,' she replied. 'I know that my mother used to go out and about with him once a week. I used to wonder if he was a boyfriend. Now that I'm older, I'm inclined to think he probably was.'

'And where was your mum while you were spending the day with this man?'

She eyed him, wondering why he was so interested in her life. 'It wasn't something I'd planned to talk about to anyone,' she told him curtly.

'So humour me,' he replied. 'I'm interested in what little Lucy was doing running around Islay with a strange man.'

'He wasn't a strange man,' she told him with a frown. 'And I don't recall much of the day, I was only five years old. But it stands out, because -' She paused and her eyes misted over again. She brushed them with the back of her sleeve, hoping Merrick hadn't noticed. She turned in her mind to the last vision of her mother, walking away arm in arm with the man to his boat. 'Because it was the last time I saw my mother.'

'That's a shame.'

She nodded. 'I would say she was too, except that she left me without a word. Without any explanation.'

'Do you know what became of her?'

'She died.'

'How?'

Before she could reply, a man's voice made them both turn around.

'Lucy Colwyn?' The restaurant owner was walking their way, holding a piece of paper in his hand. 'We couldn't get you a wheelchair from the hospital, I'm afraid. There are few as it is and they generally don't let them out for hire. However, I've managed to beg for one from the airport, on the understanding that you'll have it back to them in two days. Would that be okay?'

Lucy nodded, feeling a huge sense of relief. 'Oh, I can't thank you enough,' she told him. 'And providing us with free teas too. You've been so very kind.'

'Well,' he replied with a look of concern. 'We can't have you stranded and cold. Not in this weather. I must tell you though, it's not an electric wheelchair as you requested, only a standard one. But I'm sure your husband will be happy to take some of the strain.' He grinned at Merrick, who looked puzzled.

'Yes,' she told the man quickly. 'I'm sure my husband will be happy to do that. Thank you so much for your trouble, you've been more than kind. How long will it take for it to get here? My charter should have been here half an hour ago.'

'Who is it?' the manager asked. 'I know most of the boatmen around here, perhaps I can see where he's got to.'

'Joe MacNeish.'

His smile faded. 'Oh dear me,' he said, 'I'm afraid there's been an awful business with Joe. I just heard about this, not twenty minutes ago from someone else. Oh dear, oh dear.'

'What is it?' she said, panic consuming her. Please, please, not more delays.

The man sighed, his expression grave. 'Joe's boat was found floating upturned in the sea last night,' he said. 'I'm afraid he's probably no longer with us, bless his lovely heart. Such a sad business. The whirlpool took him, no doubt. They haven't found him yet, but -' His voice trailed off and he turned to look out to sea. 'I fear they won't. Not for a wee while, anyway.'

Merrick and Lucy glanced at one another.

'Oh, that is absolutely awful,' she said. 'Was he a close friend?'

'Not really, no,' the manager admitted. 'But we all knew him. He was a regular face around the port and a very experienced sailor too, so it's a shock to us all. It's terribly sad.'

'Yes, it is,' Merrick said, adding, 'Do you know of anyone else who can take us to Scarba?'

Lucy flashed him an angry look, mortified by his lack of tact. 'What my... erm... husband means is, we are so sorry, but find ourselves – well - marooned now. We hadn't planned to stay in Islay and don't know of anyone else who could take us to where we're headed on such short notice. We don't mean to sound unconcerned over poor Joe, but needs must, you know?'

The manager nodded, not looking in the least bit offended. 'Naturally, and yes, there are one or two people you can charter a boat with to take you across. But I very much doubt you'll find anyone tonight at such short notice. I can get you a couple of numbers though.'

Lucy groaned. 'Is there a cash machine anywhere? I only have a bank card and no mobile phone. I'm afraid my luggage was delayed in transit with my chair unfortunately.'

'Yes,' the manager replied. 'Bad for business that ferry returning to the mainland on its way here. This weather wreaks havoc with the tourist season. Was there much else on there with your sister?'

140

'No, not really,' Merrick said. He turned to scowl at Lucy, before adding, 'I told her we should have travelled with her sister,' he added. 'But no, she wanted the little fishing boat trip.'

As he said the words 'fishing boat', Lucy saw him look over in the direction of where the boat was moored.

She followed his gaze, to see a policeman stood looking at it, before writing something on a notepad. Overwhelmed by panic, she turned back to the manager. He was watching them both with a bewildered expression. 'Everything okay?' he asked.

'Sure it is,' Merrick said. 'Except, how do we get this wheelchair? And a room for the night?'

The manager sucked in his breath, loudly. 'Ooh, that's going to be a tricky one,' he told them. 'There aren't many hotels and B&Bs on Islay and it's the busy season. They're booked up months in advance though. We don't get an awful lot of passing trade on this island.'

'No rooms?' Lucy said, unable to hide the anxiety in her voice. She may now be an accessory to a crime.

The restaurant manager shook his head. 'Definitely no rooms,' he told her grimly. 'There are quite a lot of holiday cottages, but I suspect there won't be many of those going for one night. Someone might know.' He looked over the road to the direction of the boat again and his face brightened. 'Oh, wait a minute!'

Lucy's heart hammered in her chest as she followed his gaze and realised he was looking at the policeman. She turned with a panicked look at Merrick as the man made to walk over to the officer. But a beeping horn from a minibus passing on the road between them and the boat stopped him in his tracks. A jolly looking grey-haired lady rolled down the driver's side window and beckoned to him.

'Hoi, Phil! I've got a wheelchair here in the boot for you!'

The manager looked back at Lucy and grinned. 'One problem solved!' he told her gleefully.

Lucy had never been so relieved to see anyone or anything in her entire life. Yet, she noted, Merrick seemed as calm as ever, which was puzzling. Didn't he see the policeman? The manager began waving the minibus driver over, before running off to greet her.

Lucy looked back at Merrick. 'We have got to get out of here, now!' she hissed.

'Why? What's the matter?' he said.

'The policeman?' she said under her breath. 'We came here on a stolen boat, remember?'

He looked confused, and she glared at him, hardly able to believe the level of his nonchalance.

'What?' he said.

'Policeman?' she repeated. 'The long arm of the law? In charge of throwing boat thieves into prison?'

'Oh,' he said, still looking perplexed.

Before either of them could say more, the restaurant manager was back. 'I've had a quick word with Sheila there for you,' he said breathily. He pointed to the bus driver who was waving and smiling at them. 'She says she can take you up to Myrtle's B&B and cottages. They might be full, but she says they sometimes let people camp on the beach. Would you be up for that?'

They both nodded, eager to leave as soon as possible.

'Right then,' Phil said, clapping his hands with glee before waving at Sheila, who started the bus again. 'So glad we've sorted you out. We won't see our much valued tourists stranded. Ooh, but wait a wee minute.' As the bus pulled up beside them, he disappeared inside the restaurant. When he returned, he handed a folded piece of paper to Merrick. 'There are two fellows I can

142

think of who should be able to get you across to Scarba tomorrow. These are their numbers. I'd try them tonight if I was you.'

'Thank you,' Merrick said, taking the paper and the offered handshake.

'I've never been there myself,' Phil told them, with a shake of his head. He looked doubtfully at Lucy, adding, 'The very best of luck to you both!'

As the bus carried the pair round winding, coastal roads to their bed for the night, Merrick nudged Lucy. She was staring out of the window, having been silent for quite some time. He wondered why she hadn't removed her soaking headscarf. Human's lost a lot of heat through the tops of their heads, he knew this. But decided not to remind her about it.

'How did your mum die?' he asked.

She turned and blinked at him, mulling the question over. It seemed such an easy thing to say now, yet Lucy hadn't spoken about her mother's death for several years. But this was the last road, the last journey. The last person she would ever speak to. She was going to need Merrick's help, whether she liked it or not. Finally, she replied:

'It was suicide.'

Chapter 33: Olive

It had been the coldest, wildest of days, when, brought to Scarba shores by Joe, Olive had arrived in flimsy clothes, the lightest of raincoats and plimsolls. It was October, she was sure of it. Or was it April? In her hand she held a tin bucket full of paper, but she couldn't remember why.

'Who told you to bring her here?' the woman that greeted them on the shore demanded.

'He said, "Take her to Gladys". I don't know who he was,' the man replied. He was Joe, she remembered now. He was her friend: Joe MacNeish.

'Who else knows I'm here?' the woman hissed. 'Who have you told?'

'No one, I swear it. The man rolled up at the quayside in a car and brought her to me that first time. I've never seen him in my life before, I mean it! Maybe it was my dad that told.'

Olive shivered. It felt as though the rain was seeping into her very bones.

'She looks ill,' the woman snapped, scowling at Joe.

'She is,' he agreed. 'I've been taking her to the mainland for treatment. Lately she's begun to get worse; much worse. And then the man called me.'

'Who was he?'

'I don't know who he was, I told you.'

The woman tutted, then took her by the arm and began leading her away.

'But... Joe... I -' Olive protested, sure there was something she had to say to him. Was it thank you? Goodbye?

Lucy.

She heard the word as if spoken in her mind. What was that word? What was it again?

She was in a small room now, wrapped in a thick blanket, sipping from a cup of warm, salty liquid. 'I… I… want to… find
-'

'Shhhhh,' the woman soothed, 'ye can tell me in a wee while. Let the broth do is magic, first.'

Olive looked around the dark, unfamiliar place and squinted. Then she spied a tin bucket in the corner of the room. I've left her notes, she thought. She should say that.

'I've left her notes.'

'Who?' the woman asked. 'Who are they for?'

'I… I can't,' she said, starting to cry. 'It's my mum. No, that's not it.' Olive shook her head, as a kaleidoscope of colours flashed in front of her eyes. 'It hurts,' she moaned. It really hurt.

She woke to find a kind, somewhat familiar woman watching over her. 'I wanted to give my bucket to Lucy,' Olive told her. 'Is she here?'

The woman nodded. 'She's coming, she'll be here.'

'I told her to brush her teeth and put on her pyjamas to be ready,' she said. 'I have a surprise for her.'

'How old is your little girl?' the woman asked.

It was five years, Olive thought.

The clock ticked in the corner, but it was so loud. Why was the clock so loud? Thunk, thunk, thunk.

'Where did you leave her?'

Olive looked up at the woman, surprised and angered by the question. 'Here!'

'Here?'

'Here. I told you!' she snapped. 'She has to be in bed for half past seven. I want her to have the bucket, before -' Olive's voice trailed away. She noticed a bucket in the corner. It made her feel sad, but why would it? It was a plain, metal bucket.

She opened her eyes again at the sound of a woman's voice.

'Olive, who said you were going to die?'

'I am,' she said, remembering. 'I'm dying.'

'Do Lucy and her grandmother know this?'

Olive covered her face with her hands. 'Lucy!' she cried. 'Lucy!'

'Where is Lucy?' the woman asked gently, cradling her in her arms.

Olive pulled violently away from the woman's grasp. 'I put notes in the bucket for her,' she said. 'I put them there for my baby girl. Will you give them to her?'

It was four-thirty in the morning. She could see the time on the wall in the candlelight, but it hurt to look at it. So much pain. She cried out and a person appeared.

'Olive, it's just a bad dream,' the woman said, cradling her in her arms.

'No, it's my head.' So many flashes of silver and purple in her line of vision, she couldn't see anything else. Pulling away from the woman's clutches, her eyes darted around the room, seeing the flashes of light everywhere. No clock; no bed, no room. Just light.

'It's time to go,' she heard the woman say. Or was it an angel? 'Olive,' the voice continued. 'I need you to help me find your daughter. Where is she? Where is Lucy?'

Olive cried out in pain again, holding her head in her hands. 'I don't -' she began, throwing back the covers and getting to her feet. She stumbled across the room as unseen objects crashed and tumbled all around her. She fell to her knees, feeling gentle arms around her shoulders again.

147

'Please, Olive,' the voice pleaded. 'Please try to remember. Where can I find Lucy?'

The agony was too much. It was all too much. Make it stop.

'I don't know Lucy!' she yelled.

Chapter 34: Merrick

Merrick and Lucy sat in front of two tents on a flat patch of sand, facing the sea. A small fire burned in front of them, with a pan of chicken stew and potatoes warming on it. Everything had been provided by Myrtle, the kindly owner of the B&B, which had been, as predicted, full. The community had taken pity on the pair; aware of the tragic accident that had befallen Joe MacNeish. Shelter, bedding, firewood, a meal and drinks had arrived from everywhere. Myrtle had even taken their clothes to wash and dry, offering alternative garments for them in the meantime. To Merrick's astonishment, Lucy had refused to let her take the wet headscarf. He couldn't understand why, yet Myrtle had seemed to brush over the matter. He thought perhaps it was a female thing.

The problem of mobility for Lucy had been solved in a less conventional way. There were ground sheets which she was going to have to roll along to get inside the tent or allow Merrick to carry her. She was fiercely independent, a trait Merrick admired. She appeared to have an incredible level of upper-body strength. He guessed her preferred method was going to be the rolling. It may have felt undignified to some, but Merrick could tell Lucy was not the type of woman to care for convention. He liked that about her.

Merrick had never visited Scarba, as far as he could recall. But Jura, being its closest neighbour, was familiar land. He could imagine what a rugged, wild and rarely visited place it would be. He'd settled on many similar islands in his three-hundred-year-old life.

'What are you planning to do there anyway?' he asked her, not for the first time.

She looked up and glowered at him. 'That's my business,' she snapped.

He sighed and stood up, turning his back to her. 'Do you suppose there's any chance after all that we've been through today, that you and I could become friends?' he asked.

'I'm visiting a place my mother once went to,' came the reply.

Putting one hand on his hip, Merrick took a sip from the paper cup of whisky the couple had also been given. He winced at the very strong, smoky taste and coughed. 'Lord above,' he said. 'People drink this?' He threw the rest of the contents of his cup at the water's edge and wiped his mouth with his sleeve. 'It makes my head feel funny,' he added. 'Sort of like -'

'Like you're flying?' she cut in, giggling.

'No,' he said seriously. 'It's definitely not that.'

Silence fell between the pair and he stood a while, watching the sun sink below the horizon. Light began to fade all around them.

'Merrick,' Lucy said suddenly. 'Do you think cows are friendly things?'

He turned to see that she was watching some cows grazing on the grassy bank to the left of them and grinned. 'Yes,' he told her. 'They are.'

'Good,' she replied, shifting uncomfortably in her seat. 'Are you going to put some of those peas in the stew?'

'Peas?'

She pointed to the bag of groceries they'd been supplied with. 'There's a tin of peas in there and a tin opener to get into them with,' she told him.

Merrick stared at the bag, his brow furrowed. 'A what?' he said.

'A tin opener,' she said. 'Oh, tell me you know what a tin opener is. Are you from the Dark Ages, or something?'

He bit his lip, resisting the temptation to confess all. He stepped forward to fill his cup again with whisky from the bottle at her feet. He didn't like the taste but the fuzzy head thing was pleasant enough. 'Let's try this stuff again,' he said. 'There must be something special, for so many folks to come here for it.'

She held out her cup. 'I'll have another too,' she said, with a smile. 'Then I'll show you how to open a bloody tin of peas.'

'Okay, but first let me tell you an important piece of truth,' he said, filling her cup as instructed.

She nodded a thanks, tipped her cup to his with a 'Cheers', and looked up at his face. 'Go on then,' she said, 'I'm all ears.'

He took a bigger mouthful this time, swallowed and felt his throat and eyes burn. 'Gah!' he spat, before coughing again. 'This is awful.'

Lucy threw back her whisky and laughed hard and loud at him. 'Wimp,' she said.

He took another drink, and felt his cheeks burn. 'Okay,' he said, screwing his eyes shut tight as another glug of the fiery liquid slid down his throat. He shook his head, his eyes streaming. But the light, pleasing fuzziness made him feel like he was floating on a cloud. 'I am from the Dark Ages,' he announced, much to his own surprise.

'And I don't know how to use a tin opener,' Lucy finished for him, grinning from ear to ear.

He nodded. 'And I don't know how to use a tin opener,' he repeated.

Placing her empty cup between her knees, Lucy held out her hands. 'Pass the bag over here to me,' she said.

As the pair finished off what was a very fine meal, Merrick became aware of the sound of footsteps. Someone was approaching them with a flashlight.

'Hullo!' a friendly voice said. As Merrick shielded his eyes from the dazzling light, he saw that it was Myrtle.

'I've had word that there's another boat going to Scarba tomorrow,' she said. 'So I've taken the liberty of booking you both on it.'

'Oh, that is so kind,' Lucy replied. 'I don't know how I can ever thank you.'

Merrick sighed with relief.

'No need,' Myrtle replied. 'Shirley will be back here to pick you up and take you across to the harbour at around ten o'clock in the morning. Course, you won't know when that is, so I've bought you an alarm clock.'

She handed the clock to Merrick, who took the thing and stared at it for a moment.

'Great,' said Lucy. 'If Shirley can run me to a cash machine I can get some money out to pay you back for all this generosity.'

'That'll be fine,' Myrtle replied. 'Although, we're not needing anything for the tents mind, they all came from the shed anyways.' She pointed to the half-empty bottle on the ground at Lucy's feet and grinned. 'Just for the food and whisky,' she added. 'Which I see you've been enjoying!'

'That's for sure,' Lucy replied. 'Although soft lad here can't handle it.' She looked to Merrick and both women laughed.

'We ladies have ayeways been able to out-drink the menfolk,' Myrtle said with a chuckle. 'Well, I'll be seeing you both in the morning. And don't mind the cows here, they won't bite you. Best get some rest now.'

'Aye, we will that,' Merrick said, raising his cup in a farewell gesture.

'Well then,' Merrick said, turning to regard Lucy, and noting she had stopped smiling. 'We'll be there tomorrow morning,' he finished.

'Oh no, we won't,' she replied, her sudden, shrill tone taking him by surprise. 'I want to go alone and that's what I'll do.'

152

'Why?'

She emptied the last remnants of whisky down her throat before answering. 'Because of reasons, that is all I will say on the matter.'

Merrick knelt on the ground, cup still in his hand, and looked her squarely in the eye. 'Do these reasons have anything to do with wanting to die?'

'We're all dying,' she snapped. 'It makes no difference.'

'No difference?' he said, engulfed by a deep sadness he didn't quite understand the reason for. 'Every life makes a difference. It's not yours to take, you know.'

Her eyes widened with shock. 'Who says I want to take it?' she asked, yet Merrick felt that between them, in the very air, was the unspoken truth. He knew it.

'Lucy, here's the thing,' he told her, more gently. He blew out his cheeks, preparing himself to deliver some truths. What could he have to lose, after all? 'I'm like you said - ancient. I am, in fact, over three-hundred-years-old by my reckoning.'

She scowled back at him, her expression loaded with scepticism. Of course she didn't believe him; he knew it sounded incredible.

Sighing, he went on regardless. 'There's one person in this world that I need to find right now,' he told her. 'And I haven't seen that person for a very, very long time. She's supremely important to me; you must understand that. I need to get to her. I didn't know a single, other soul on this earth until I met you. Whatever it is you have planned to do on Scarba, it's clear that in that chair you aren't going to be able to do it alone.'

'I can manage fine on my own,' she snapped. 'I'd been doing that for a long time before I met you.'

He frowned. 'Lucy, do you have any idea what the ground is like on Scarba? There's going to be some rough, wet terrain out there. You were never going to be able to get about by yourself.'

She glared at him, her cheeks flushed.

'Look, I can see that you're a determined, independent woman. Anyone can. I like that about you; it's an important and admirable trait. But at the same time you have to accept, at least some of the time, that you do have some limitations.'

'I have to go to Scarba,' she said firmly.

'I know and I promise you, if you let me come I will neither get in your way nor cause you any grief. I can help you. Now that we know a little more about each other I feel I can trust you. The truth is I think I need to go to Scarba too, and only you can help me get there.'

She started to speak, but stopped, pressing her lips firmly together and putting a hand on her chin. Then, she said, 'Merrick, you're clearly a bit crazy, but what on earth's there for you on Scarba? Because I think you only want to go to make sure I don't -'

'I think that the woman I need to see is living there,' he said.

'What makes you think that? Nobody lives on Scarba. Nobody.'

'Okay,' he said, frowning at her before grabbing the bottle of whisky and offering it to her. She held out her cup, listening as he spoke. 'So you think the story of my age is a crazy, made-up tale?'

She didn't disagree, but sipped again from the refilled cup. He marvelled at how she could throw the smoky liquid back so easily. To him it burned; an odd blend of bonfire and honey.

'Well, I can see that it would sound too fantastic to believe. So while I'm on that route, let me add another element of the incredible to the mix,' he went on. 'That Cailleach Bheur you talked about?'

'Oh, don't tell me,' she cut in. 'She's real, right?'

Merrick nodded.

'Of course she is,' Lucy laughed. She waved her cup at him. 'Boy, you're a fine story-teller; and a real hoot on this stuff. Drink some more, then we can talk about the pink elephants on the beach.'

'I don't like whisky,' he replied solemnly. 'Neither do I need it, because I am telling you the truth, Lucy. I, Merrick Anderson, was - until the day before yesterday - a barnacle goose.'

Lucy stopped laughing and stared at him, faltering for the briefest of seconds. 'A -?' she began. 'This is… is…'

He stared as the jolly, red colour drained from her cheeks and she swallowed. 'I know you don't believe me,' he said. 'And that's okay, it makes no difference to me, but the reason I was a goose was because of the Cailleach Bheur.'

'That… is… weird…,' she faltered, shaking her head.

'But true.'

Her mouth fell open, and Merrick waited for what might come next. It was worse - and more confusing - than he expected. Lucy fell about laughing.

'Did you… did you -' she began, her words interrupted by a huge burp. 'Oh heavens,' she said, giggling. 'Excuse me.'

He felt his cheeks burn. 'Did I what?'

'Did you used to visit me in my grannie's garden when I was little?'

'What?'

Lucy held her sides, laughing again, hardly able to contain herself. 'So now I'm in the middle of someone's fantasy,' she scoffed.

He stared at her, unsmiling, not knowing what to do or say next. Noticing his serious expression, she stopped laughing. Then asked, 'Merrick, are you getting any treatment for these delusions?'

He didn't reply, regarding this new, hysterical Lucy with concern.

'Alright, alright,' she conceded with a sigh. 'Maybe you're right and the land there will be tough for me to navigate myself, so we'll go together. You are right, it's clear I hadn't thought this through because of – well, let's just say reasons. Because even if you are a little strange, I do sort of like you. You did get me here, after all. And you do, at least, make me laugh.'

'And I did save your life.'

'And you did save my life,' she repeated, her expression grave. 'So there's not a lot left for me not to trust about you, I suppose. But if I agree to take you along, you have to promise me two things.'

Relieved, he nodded. 'Okay. And these are?'

'One is that you stop your stories of witches, long life and barnacle geese.'

'Even though it's the truth?'

'Even though... whatever,' she said, waving her hand dismissively. 'And then there's the second thing.'

'That I look the other way this time if you fall back into the sea?'

Lucy nodded. 'That you stop saving my life.'

She pursed her lips, and Merrick felt an icy air between them. He wondered again what had made this strong-minded woman in the middle years of her life want to end it. 'Is it because of the wheelchair?' he asked, before immediately regretting it.

'I want you to promise,' she said firmly, disregarding his comment altogether. 'That whatever happens, you let me go my own way when the time comes for me to ask you to do so.'

'And that's it?'

She nodded. 'That's it. No interpolation, no psychoanalysis and no offers of advice, no matter how well-intentioned.'

He swallowed and frowned. Merrick knew full well that the second thing was going to be way, way beyond the scope of his capabilities.

'Do we have a deal?' she asked him, her expression grim.

Whatever happened, he had to get to Scarba. A familiar pain stung his heart and he felt the weight of deep longing again. He had to get back to her, by whatever means. And Lucy was the quickest, easiest ticket. Even though she came with unimaginable complications.

'We have a deal,' Merrick agreed, very much aware that for the first time in his life, he'd told a lie.

Chapter 35: Dr Britten

Dr Britten had never managed to anger so many people, all at the same time and all in the same evening. Sure, he'd had to deliver some devastating news in the course of his work. This was the hardest part of it all, delivering the diagnosis to faces that begged him for hope. People were often angry when first receiving a terminal diagnosis. He expected sorrow, tears, desperation and a hollow state of disbelief. Yet anger was always a shock to him; it was never what he'd expected. He'd been staggered to find many people were – with Lucy being the angriest of them all.

'I wanted to die!' she'd yelled. 'I begged that it would be me. And now you're telling me that my daughter was taken and I was spared – albeit in this stupid chair - only to die anyway?'

There were stages of grief, he later learned. People experienced denial, anger, bargaining, depression and then acceptance. The anger was second; yet he had often seen it arrive before anything else. It was always a complicated process, never straightforward, never textbook. And the fury had been at its fiercest in Lucy.

Now it was his turn. The lifeguard and air rescue crew were tasked with searching for a body.

Lucy had not been on the ship, but her belongings were. Dr Britten had failed; she had jumped ship, somewhere in the middle of the vast, freezing ocean. Lucy had a life he had never gotten to tell her was not yet over, and now she was dead. None of the passengers knew why they had been brought back to shore. But judging by the attention the doctor had been getting from the crew, many assumed he was behind it all. They threw him angry glances as they headed back to their homes or to hotels, to await the morning ferry. But Dr Britten couldn't be moved by the furious passengers that walked past. He was too beside himself with grief and disappointment. He'd failed, both as a doctor and a human being, and all because of a stupid, out-of-date timetable.

'Dr Britten, is it?'

A young, red-headed woman in green overalls grabbed his arm, leading him to where Sandra stood. 'I need to ask you if you have a photograph of the lady the sea and air rescue team are trying to find.'

'Well, I expect she'll be the only woman out there in the sea, won't she?' Sandra snapped. 'Do you really think identification is going to be a problem?'

Dr Britten coughed nervously. 'I don't, I'm afraid,' he replied to the woman.

'Of course,' she said, choosing – wisely, Dr Britten thought - to ignore Sandra's angry outburst. 'It's a formality thing, you know? As it happens, we had a crew out that way already,' she went on.

'You do?' the doctor said, his eyes wide with surprise. 'What's happened?'

'A boat overturned between Jura and the Isle of Scarba,' the woman replied. 'Terrible business. We've found the boat but no skipper.'

Sandra gasped.

'How awful,' Dr Britten said. 'It's a sorry day out at sea today, that's for certain.'

The woman nodded. 'I don't suppose you have any way of getting a photo of Lucy? Perhaps sent to your phone by a colleague?'

He shook his head, his mind a blur. In truth, he didn't know. He wanted this woman and her crew up in the air, searching for Lucy. He couldn't understand why they weren't going already. 'She might be alive still,' he said suddenly, looking to the woman for some sign of hope. But her solemn expression told him it was useless.

'A person can only survive in these freezing waters for a matter of minutes,' she said. 'And plus, as you've told us, the lady intended to take her own life. I'm very sorry, doctor, but I have to suspect she will have succeeded some time before now.'

'I bet she jumped when she saw the ship turning back,' he said, the realisation making him feel sick. 'Oh my-!' He put a hand to his forehead. She was dead because of him. 'Shouldn't you be out there anyway, looking for her, NOW?' he pleaded.

'A helicopter has already left,' she assured him. 'I'm only here to gather some facts and offer back up.'

'Oh yes,' he replied. 'Of course.'

He felt numb. Dr Britten had been the judge, jury and deliverer of a death sentence. He should have been there to stop this. A woman was dead, needlessly. And all he could think of was what a terrible waste it all was.

'Dr Britten?' Sandra put a hand on his arm and held his gaze, concern in her eyes. 'There was nothing you could do.'

'Yes... Yes there was,' he said, his voice faltering with emotion that he couldn't hold back now. 'I could have been here in time to catch the ferry.'

'Look, it's going to be dark soon. You'll not be up to driving back to where you've come from this evening, not in this state,' Sandra told him, leading him away. She turned back to the woman. 'You'll have all you need now, am I right?' she asked.

'Yes, that is all we can do tonight,' the woman confirmed. 'I'll let the office know the minute we hear anything.'

'That's settled then,' Sandra said. 'Come with me,' she went on, leading Dr Britten back to the warmth of her office. 'I have a friend with a B&B near here. Let me sort you out a wee room for the night, okay? But we have to hurry,' she nodded to the crowds still making their way from the ferry into cars, taxis and buses. 'There'll be a few in the night.'

'I cannot believe you, Fleur Brookes!'

Dr Britten Britten rolled over in his bed and squinted at the illuminated alarm clock. It was one fifteen in the morning. He hadn't managed to sleep, but the whispered fracas outside his room door was irritating. Tonight he needed peace.

'Shhhhh!'

'Don't you shush me!' the first voice hissed. 'I can't belie… Joanna-Rose, are you hearing this?'

He heard someone wrestle with a key in a lock. Then, a third, more calm sounding woman's voice said, 'Yes, but keep your voices down.'

'She saw a WOMAN fall off the ship and she did nothing!'

Doctor Britten sat up, the hairs on the back of his neck prickling.

'I wouldn't say I did nothing! I ran over to try to do something but she was gone.'

'Why on earth didn't you tell someone?' he heard the calmer woman snap back. Throwing back the covers, he stood up, putting an ear to the door, not sure if he could believe what he was hearing.

'Because she didn't want them to stop and turn the boat around so she would miss her annual nookie fest.'

'What? Oh I can't get this damn key to work. Cathy, can you have a go?'

'I've never been so shocked - so ashamed - in all my life. No, wait a minute, I live with you, Fleur. I'm religiously shocked and ashamed.'

'Don't you blame me for your weird beliefs,' the first woman shot back.

'Oh, really!'

'Look, I only get it once a year. Me an' Dougal, we're like Kiera Knightly and Orlando Bloom in Pirates of the Caribbean. We only get to have a bit when our ships come in. He works all hours on that little ferry to Jura, you know. And I've brought a bag of things -'

The doctor clicked on the bedside lamp and reached for his glasses.

'Never mind your things,' he heard the other woman hiss. 'Lord knows, I don't need those mental pictures.'

'Cathy, you're only jealous. It's just because I get out and enjoy my life.'

He heard the rattle of some kind of chain. Then, the voice added, 'Do you want us to put you in my negligee and fishnets? Will we fasten you to the bed-post and order room service from the night-porter?'

'Uh, don't be so -'

'Joanna-Rose and I can leave the door unlocked and disappear downstairs for a dram or two.'

There was stifled laughter.

'How... even... could you?' the third, quieter voice stammered. 'I mean, why didn't you tell someone?' The woman's whispers were becoming louder.

'Because I saw someone save her.'

'WHAT?'

Doctor Britten threw back his covers and stood up, racing for the door.

'Lower your voices for heaven's sake,' the third woman cut in hastily, 'Let's get inside. There are people trying to sleep.'

'NO, DON'T!' the doctor called out, opening his door and spilling into the hallway. He was met with open-mouthed, shocked stares of three grey-haired, elderly women. One stood frozen with a key in her hand, as she had been about to open her

163

room door. He saw all eyes dart downwards, before remembering that he was only in a t-shirt and underpants.

Before he could apologise, the shorter, stouter of the three spoke. 'Of course, Dougal and I aren't exclusive or anything.'

'Boxer shorts,' said the taller, well-spoken woman. He recognised her as the quieter voice of reason from earlier. She waved a hand at him, before covering her eyes in an over-exaggerated way. 'Excellent for creating an, erm-' she pointed at the gap in his shorts, 'window of opportunity should we say?'

The third woman turned away, making a renewed, more desperate attempt to open their room door. Dr Britten cowered, crossing one knee over the other. He attempted to cover his modesty with both hands and began backing into his room again. 'Please, I'm so sorry about my outburst,' he said, his heart racing. 'But I couldn't help overhearing and I need to speak to you about the woman you saw. I'm her doctor... oh,' he made a grab for his dressing gown from the back of the door. 'Let me get some clothes on, I'm terribly, terribly sorry.'

There was a crash, as their room door finally swung open, hitting the wall inside. As sounds of scuttling ensued, he heard the short woman shout. 'We'll be waiting right here!'

His door started to swing shut as he wrapped his dressing gown around him. As it closed, he heard her add in a whisper: 'I'd happily climb in your window of opportunity anytime, Doctor.'

Opening the door back up, he appeared again, finding only the shortest of the three women still stood there. 'Did you say you saw the lady who fell from the ship being saved by someone, Fleur, was that your name?'

'She's not saying anything!' the well-spoken woman called out from inside their room.

'Of course,' Fleur replied. 'I wouldn't have kept my mouth shut and let the ferry carry on ahead if I'd thought she might drown. I saw a fella dive off a small fishing boat and save her, then I saw her pulled out of the water.'

'Are you absolutely certain of that?' he asked.

'Yes, I'm certain,' she replied, looking hurt. 'Look, Doctor, I'm not going to let a ship leave when there's a woman drowning in the sea. She was safe, I promise you. Don't get me wrong, my yearly love-in is important to me,' she added. 'But I'm not so terrible that I'd go to any extremes to get to them. What do you take me for?'

Chapter 36: Lucy

Rolling into the tent last night had been easy, but as Lucy looked out of the opening she noticed they were on a slope. She was either going to have to drag herself or call Merrick to help her get out. Neither was an attractive option. Particularly as she had an audience: two cows. They stood on the grass bank nearby, observing her with casual interest. Since her injury, she'd had to learn a lot of new, sometimes undignified ways of getting around. Almost always without help. This wasn't going to change now, not if she could help it.

Pulling herself out into the full light of day, she could see Merrick's tent door unzipped and flapping open. Beside the camp fire they'd made the night before lay a fresh pile of driftwood.

'Are you in there?' she called out.

When no response came she grabbed both arms of the chair and pulled herself up. Twisting her body, she sank her backside into the seat beside the fire. She looked at the pans still perched on top, pleased to find they'd been washed. Feeling hungry and a little light-headed, she poked at the fire. Finding that it still smouldering, she added some of the driftwood to get it going again. Then, she reached inside the bag of food Myrtle had left them. She dug out a tin of beans, tugged the ring pull to open it and spilled the contents out into the pan.

'Ahh, breakfast is on,' she heard Merrick announce as he appeared beside her with a carrier bag, making her jump.

'It's beans,' she replied quickly. 'And there are some eggs we can scramble.'

She looked up to see Merrick giving her a look of disgust.

'No, no,' he replied. 'I don't eat eggs.'

'Ah,' she said, nodding and trying to look serious. 'Of course not. Do you mind if I do? They're delicious with a little butter and cream. Don't tell the cows.'

Frowning, he put down the bag and took out a loaf of bread. 'I have butter,' he said, taking a gold foil packet out. 'You have the eggs, I'll have beans.'

'You can start the toast,' she replied. 'I need to use the bathroom.'

Merrick put the bread and butter back in the bag and stood over her with his hands on his hips. 'You'll need a push up the hill then?' he said.

Turning around, she looked at the sandy slope and then peered doubtfully back at him. 'I'm not even sure you'll get me up there through this sand,' she said.

'Aye, it will be tricky,' he agreed. 'Or I could take the wheelchair first, then come back and carry you.' He regarded her with a kind smile and waited.

Lucy thought of all the times before that she had let Merrick carry her. From dragging her to safety from the sea, to lifting her from the boat to dry land. 'Being carried by someone is such an intimate thing,' she found herself saying.

'Sure,' he agreed. 'But we're friends, aren't we? Lucy, I want to help you, that's all. I know you can do it yourself, but let a friend make things easier for you. Let someone else take the strain for a while. Can you do that?'

'Well, I erm…' She hesitated. 'I suppose it would be okay.'

Merrick knelt down on the ground to face her. 'I think in your position I'd feel the same. I'd want to do it all myself and why shouldn't you? But when it comes to going to the bathroom, I imagine speed is often of the essence. May I?' He held out his arms in offer of lifting her, and, despite herself Lucy found herself laughing.

'Okay, you're right there,' she told him, opening out her arms to accept his grasp. She placed them around his neck. 'And I have to tell you, it's probably best not to make me giggle too much while you're carrying me.'

'Huh?' he said, lifting her gently from the chair and starting up the slope with her.

'I might pee on the way there,' she said.

He came to a stop at the path and looked at her.

'Pee,' she repeated with a grin. 'That thing you do need to do in the toilet after having a drink?'

He sat her on the ground. 'I'm going back for the chair,' he said seriously. 'Don't go anywhere.'

As the pair sat quietly eating breakfast on the beach, Lucy watched the gentle waves. As they combed the shoreline, she saw a remembered vision of Nicola playing on the beach. She hadn't told Merrick that she'd brought her daughter here for holidays. It was too personal and not anything she felt the need to tell him about anyway. His mention of the barnacle goose had grabbed her attention though. It was such a strange coincidence. Lucy had memories of the lone goose that had watched her play as a child in her grandmother's garden. But then, much later, came the one that Nicola had seen in the same garden. Islay did have thousands of the geese flocking there every year, so it wasn't unusual to see them. Yet the geese, on both occasions, had been alone. They'd seemed to be watching her; observing. It couldn't possibly be the same one from her own childhood that Nicola saw, but it was very strange all the same. An apparently tame goose in her grandmother's garden, watching them. Lucy remembered too, the first time she saw the old lady place a note in the Advice Bucket. It had been moments after they'd been looking at the goose.

'Not yet, sweetie,' her grandmother had said, gently guiding Lucy's attention away. 'These are for you to read later. You'll have them with you when you grow up.'

A lump formed in Lucy's throat as she then recalled a later memory of the original bucket. It was of her hiding in the back of the boatman's truck under a blanket. She'd hoped to spend that day being close to her mum; they never played anymore.

For the first part of the journey, she'd watched as the pair stopped to visit the wishing tree at Finlaggan. Lucy knew about the tree; about how people would press coins into it, perhaps to make a wish. That day, she saw her mother place her wish in the tree.

But as she made the decision to come out and show herself at the next stop, she found no one around. Jumping up, she'd spied her mother and the man carrying the bucket full of paper on to a boat. Back then Lucy hadn't known what the bucket was for, only that it was very special. It was to be a gift to her from her mother.

'Mummy!' she'd called out, but it was too late for her to be heard; too far for her to run and catch her. Her eyes full of tears, she watched helplessly as her mum's boat left the island. A small child of five, not knowing it was the last time she'd see her.

She was left all alone, with no motherly wisdom to carry her through for the rest of her days. All she'd had was her grandmother's Advice Bucket. Now that was lost on a boat too. Still, she thought, she didn't need it where she was going. Lucy was leaving nobody behind.

Too embittered to return to it, Lucy had sold the house on Islay. It was after the accident that took Nicola's life and left her in a wheelchair. The memories of happier times had been too painful to endure. Now she was on the island again, only this time on a mission to be reunited with her little girl. She felt closer to Nicola here than at any time during those bereft, lost years after her death.

Lucy was going home now, she knew it. She felt it. There was no need for any Advice Bucket. No legacy required. No helpful hints to a future generation from a mother who never loved her enough to stay or even say goodbye.

'So, if I might be so bold as to ask, what happened to you?' Merrick said, interrupting her thoughts. He was - she realised - referring to her useless legs.

'I was in a car accident,' she replied. 'The other driver was drunk. I was thrown from the car, seconds before it burst into flames.'

She swallowed, the very use of the word 'flames' making her think of her daughter's last, terrible moments.

His eyes widened. 'That was lucky.'

'Lucky?' she said, her eyes flashing with anger. 'You might think that, I suppose.'

'You don't feel lucky to be alive?'

She shook her head. 'My back was broken and I injured my spinal cord. The result is my being stuck this chair,' she swept her arms over the wheels. 'I'm paralysed from the waist down. And you call that lucky.'

'It's terrible,' he agreed. 'But you're alive, Lucy. Living, breathing,' he pointed across to the ocean, 'taking in the views. That's something you have to feel grateful for.'

'I'm not grateful,' she snapped back, sorry for having let her emotions out in front of this virtual stranger. She bit her lip and fell silent. She hadn't planned to have anything like this conversation with Merrick. She had, in fact, resolutely planned not to.

She felt him watching her. As she stared down at her plate, feeling the colour rise in her cheeks, she fought back tears. Squeezing her eyes shut, she willed the anguish and the terrible memories away. She did not want to give in, did not want to tell him, or think about Nicola in that way.

'Somebody died, didn't they?' he asked her, making her prickle with surprise at his accuracy.

She didn't reply.

'Someone you loved?'

Lucy leaned over to put her plate down on the ground. 'I've had enough to eat, have you?' she said, looking up at him with eyes that implored him to change the subject.

He looked down at his own plate and nodded. 'Yes,' he said at last. 'I think I'm done. Who's washing up this time?'

'Ah,' she replied with a relieved sigh. She offered him a weak smile. 'Seeing as you did such a magnificent job cleaning last night's pans.' She grabbed her plate and held it out to him.

'What?'

'You can do it again.'

He stared blankly back at her. 'I didn't clean last night's pans,' he said.

'Oh yes, you did. They were wiped clean and I know I didn't do it.'

'Well, it wasn't me,' he said.

Lucy looked at the pans, wrinkling her nose in mystification. 'You must have,' she said. 'They were caked in casserole juice last night. But they were clean this morning.'

Merrick looked from her to over her shoulder, his brow furrowed as he sat deep in thought. Then, she saw his eyes widen in sudden apprehension. Turning to see what he was looking at, her eyes fell upon the pair of cows still grazing on the grassy bank nearby.

'You… don't think… that…?' she said, pointing at them as Merrick's grimace answered her question.

His face turned green and she saw his Adam's apple jog up and down as he swallowed hard. 'Cows do have very big tongues,' he said, jumping to his feet. He reached for the water bottle before taking off towards the guesthouse.

'Merrick!' Lucy shouted, not caring a damn about being carried anymore. 'Come back! I need to go too!'

Chapter 37: Gladys

Gladys looked at the Advice Bucket, the only thing she held dear and the last remaining memento of Olive. A wave of remembered sadness washed over her. It was for a little girl she'd never met: Lucy. She'd promised to find her and hadn't been able to fulfil that promise. There was no sense in denying how she'd failed her only friend, the only one she'd had in all her days. But Olive's confusion left room for no clues that might lead to the identity of the poor child. Gladys had tried hard to find them. Joe knew nothing more than that they'd been a family holidaying on Islay. He'd asked no questions – why would he? A fare was a fare. But Gladys had wondered at his lack of curiosity in the circumstances. Men could sometimes be unobservant, non-empathetic creatures, she concluded.

Yet in a short time her annoyance at being left caring for Olive had transformed. Gladys pitied her, of course, and had been happy to help this lost and lonely creature. Olive didn't have a friend in the world either, except for a daughter and elderly mother.

As far as Gladys could gather the little girl was loved and being well cared for. This was not a family that needed further intervention. They would mourn her loss. They missed the last, most difficult days with Olive, but that had been her wish. This was her driving force for heading to Scarba. She had decided, even with an addled brain, to wander away from home to die. To protect those she loved from the horrors. Did the family know she was dying? Gladys thought so, but she could never be sure. Joe MacNeish was to tell the world Olive had drowned. That way, the local news might take the details back to the family. And it had worked; stories had run on the local news and in the press. Little Lucy would at least know the fate and last resting place of her mother: The Irish Sea. But the ill-fated skipper, Joe, had never been able to find out where she lived. The child's identity had been a closely-guarded secret. Probably to protect her from the prying, news hungry outside world, no doubt.

But Olive's final days had not all been horrific or sad. The two women had been able to enjoy some good times together, between bad days. When Olive wasn't in horrendous pain or crying in brief moments of remembered loss. They'd enjoyed meals and even swum in the sea. They'd sat watching sunsets, barbecuing fish on the beach. They'd shared stories – Gladys had even revealed the full secrets of her long, long life. Olive never remembered everything the next morning and wouldn't be around to tell the tale. It was a tragedy this wonderful, caring woman had been dying. But Gladys had felt an immense comfort in spending those final days with Olive. Because death had eluded her for over three hundred years. There was some release from her long, laborious years to feel how it was to know your days were coming to an end. It was like she was dying vicariously through Olive. This was what dying was like; this was to experience living your last days on earth. Gladys had never known it before and had no idea whether she ever would.

The saddest memories came as the illness progressed to the point of the poor woman's delirium. The last days had been brutal; a time when it was obvious their parting was imminent.

Now she had only the Advice Bucket as a reminder. Gladys pored over the little notes in the years since Olive's departure. One note a day, the thoughts, hopes and dreams of a dying woman. Advice for a full and happy life, from one who knew her time was up when she was writing them. To a normal, mortal human, it would seem wrong to take pleasure from the thoughts and feelings of a dying woman. But to Gladys, who would remain forever without the luxury of a restful death, this was like oxygen. It was a few, brief insights a day. It was as close to death and dying as she might ever be. This was her penance.

She picked another note from the bucket and unravelled it to read:

We each have our own place in the Universe. Find yours, and never be tempted to give up your seat.

Smiling, she held it to her chest and thanked Olive again, as she did every day of every year.

'Thank you for this gift,' she told her long, lost friend. 'I'm only sorry I was never able to deliver it as you asked.'

Chapter 38: Dr Britten

Dr Britten walked out on to the deck of the Queen of the Hebrides, and into the morning sunshine. All that remained of last night's rain was a bank of mist that floated over the calm waters of the ocean. Sunbeams danced on gentle waves; it was the most serene view. He leaned over the railing, taking it all in. If there was a last journey at the end of life it would be like this, he decided. A peaceful, gentle sail over a sea of mist and diamonds.

But heaven could wait for one person. Lucy was alive; at least, for now.

The authorities had returned no news on finding a body, and the search had been called off at first light. Dr Britten had quickly passed on news of the positive sighting by the old woman, Fleur. Now, he hoped she was still on a course for Scarba; that whoever picked her up could be taking her there. In a worrying twist, a small fishing boat had been reported as stolen from Kennacraig a day earlier. It could be a coincidence, but if Lucy was travelling on the stolen boat, the thief had saved her life. The doctor doubted she was in any further danger, except by her own hands.

The last twenty-four hours had given the doctor so much food for thought. He'd stumbled upon an entire series of events that were riddled with coincidences. Like Olive Fraser - Lucy Colwyn's mother. Different surnames because, he imagined, Olive must have been an unmarried, single mother. Dr Britten had been the specialist in charge of Olive's care too. He could understand her wish to keep the terrible details of the disease from her little girl. This would explain why Lucy hadn't mentioned the link - she hadn't known, of course. Yet it was a pivotal discovery. Dr Britten knew everything there was to know about Morsley's Pholblastoma. And he knew that Lucy and Olive were the first related cases to ever come to light. This was a staggering development. Particularly as it was Lucy that carried the answer to a cure.

'Ooh look, it's Doctor Britten,' he heard a familiar voice behind him exclaim. He turned his face to see the women from the previous evening walking his way.

'Good morning, ladies,' he said, smiling at them each in turn. He hoped his fake grin didn't betray his annoyance at the interruption of his thoughts. 'And isn't it a beautiful one?' He turned back to admire the mist that still hovered over the waves and distant hills. 'The Sound of Jura looks like a little piece of heaven from here.'

'Oh, it certainly is a piece of heaven,' said Fleur, standing beside him to lean over the railing and look out to sea. 'Especially when you've got a bag of tricks to take over with you,' she added. He looked around to see her pointing to a large suitcase on wheels at her side.

He heard Cathy sigh. 'What are you telling the doctor that for?' she said to Fleur, with a scowl. She turned back to Dr Britten. 'She's got half the Ann Summers catalogue in there,' Cathy told him. 'And some more things you don't want to know about.'

Dr Britten half laughed, half coughed. 'Well, erm...' he said, 'I'm sure you and your friend will have a fine time when you get to Jura.' He smiled kindly at Fleur. 'It's a stunning place.' He turned his face back to the sea, before feeling a tug on his arm. It was Fleur.

'You can always talk me into a change of scenery, if you were up to it, Doctor?' she teased, with a mischievous grin. 'I've got a little nurses outfit in here,' she added, patting the bag.

'Fleur!' the tallest of the three women, Joanna-Rose, barked. 'Please would you tone it down, Dr Britten is a professor of medicine and a gentleman. Have some decorum.'

'It's quite alright,' Dr Britten said. 'I do also have a sense of humour. Even on this gravest of days.'

'I do hope you catch up with your patient, Doctor,' Cathy said.

'Yes,' Joanna-Rose agreed. 'We're all praying you find her quickly, I'm sure you will.'

''I'll be thinking of you,' Fleur added, patting her bag again with a wink. 'Although, not all the time, you understand.'

'Please forgive Fleur,' Joanna-Rose said, her cheeks flushing crimson. 'She always gets a little over-excited at this time of the year.'

'It's true, I do, Doc. I do,' Fleur said. 'But you know the saying, with my oats returneth my sanity.' She laughed at his blank expression. 'That means I'll be alright in the morning,' she added, with a grin.

'But we hope you find your lady and quickly,' said Cathy. She threw Fleur an unmissable look of disapproval.

Dr Britten nodded his thanks. 'I hope you're right,' he said. 'Now, if you'll all excuse me, I'm going to head back inside for a cup of coffee.'

Turning away from them, Dr Britten he made his way to the door. Before it closed behind him, he heard Cathy screech:

'I tell you, I'm going to bloody throw that suitcase full of kinky goodness-knows-what's over the side!'

The doctor sighed. There would be peace to think and normality indoors.

Settling down with his second cup of coffee, Dr Britten spread out the newspaper on the table. He flicked through the pages and frowned, scanning one depressing headline after another. Why did humankind seem so set on its own destruction? This was why he avoided reading the news as much as possible. It was too much for his highly-sensitive mind. He spent his life searching for answers to unlock a dreadful disease. Violence and terrorism was

181

a dreadful disease too. But he had chosen his particular path; he couldn't help everyone; couldn't heal the world.

He'd watched helplessly as death grew in people through no fault of their own. Destined for a painful and undignified death, he'd offered treatment and comforting words. But he had no answers.

Olive had been one of countless patients who'd been intent on taking an easier way out. Her little girl hadn't known why she left her without a word. At least now he could put that right. He could give Lucy something she needed to make her hang on to life: the truth about her mother. This and the news that with her help, thousands of lives could be changed forever. An experimental treatment had worked, and Lucy Colwyn carried many - if not all - of the clues about why. He wondered if Olive might have something to do with it too.

An announcement interrupted his thoughts:

'Ladies and gentlemen, we will be arriving at Port Askaig in approximately thirty minutes.'

Closing the paper, Dr Britten stood up and smoothed down his trousers. As people began in the café began rushing to finish their meals, he studied them all. Many would be heading for a holiday or to see family. Others, traveling for work. At least one of the ship's passengers would be pursuing a passionate need, he thought, with a wry smile.

No, there were no coincidences. The world turned with everyone at its helm. Everything and everyone was connected; bound together by an unseeable thread. This was Dr Britten's destiny unfolding; the eradication of a deadly disease.

Fleur had seen Lucy rescued from the sea and was, in her inimitable eccentricity, fated to tell him this. He prayed that he would reach Lucy in time, so that he could rescue her again.

'If there's a doctor on board, can you please report to a member of staff immediately?'

Hearing this new announcement, the doctor screwed his eyes tight shut. This cannot be happening; not now. He waited, but within minutes, there was a repeated call for help:

'If there are any qualified medical personnel on this ship, please report to a member of staff. Urgently.'

He looked about him, noting that there was no urgent movement from anyone. With a groan, Dr Britten headed toward the nearest crewman.

Chapter 39: Merrick

'I need to talk to you.'

Lucy had been waiting at the front door of the B&B for Merrick. She looked up at him as he spoke. 'What's wrong?' she said, her blank expression unchanged by his urgent tone.

'Is there a problem?'

Realising these called out words were coming from Myrtle, Merrick's heart sank into his shoes. He turned around to see her approaching them.

'I'm so glad I caught you,' the kindly woman went on, catching up at last. 'Shirley will be here in less than half an hour to take you to the boat. Here's your coat, Lucy. All dry and clean.' She beamed a huge smile at them both.

'No, no problem,' Merrick said, looking to Lucy as she took the coat and thanked Myrtle. 'I simply have to get us ready and quick. We have to clear everything up before we go.'

As Lucy threw him a puzzled look, he returned his gaze to Myrtle. He hoped he looked as unperturbed as he was trying to sound. 'Thirty minutes you say?' he asked her.

Merrick stepped behind Lucy's chair, ignoring her questioning expression. 'We'd better get a wriggle on then,' he said, taking both handles and starting to push her down the hill to the beach.

'Wait!' Myrtle shouted, running to catch them up. 'I forgot to give you this.' She held out a small, crumpled piece of paper and handed it to Lucy. 'It fell out of your coat pocket, right before I washed it,' she explained. 'I thought it might be something important so I rescued it.'

'Thanks,' Lucy replied, accepting the note and turning it over in her hands.

Merrick started to push her chair again. 'Right, must be off,' he told Myrtle. 'We won't be long.'

'What's the matter?' Lucy whispered as they reached the edge of the sand, out of earshot of the other woman. 'Why are you acting so weird, all of a sudden?'

Without looking back, Merrick lowered his head to whisper in her ear. 'A policeman called the B&B,' he told her. 'I overheard Myrtle's husband, Jim, speaking on the phone to him. I gather it was about asking everyone to be on the lookout for a very ill visitor to the island who's in a wheelchair.'

The colour drained from Lucy's face, but her expression remained unfazed.

'Like you,' he added, as though she needed the extra clue.

She looked at the piece of paper in her hand, seeming thoughtful. 'So, that's it then,' she said after a moment. Her shoulders rose then fell as she blew out a heavy, despondent breath. 'Journey over. There's no way we can get away from here by ourselves.'

'No,' he said quickly. 'Because while Jim was talking on the phone, I was making begging motions to him.'

'Eh?'

'I begged him not to say anything; to at least give me chance to explain.'

'And it worked?'

He nodded. 'I did have to reveal some of the fuller elements of your story to him, I'm afraid. Things I managed to fill in for myself.' He stopped, watching with baited breath.

Lucy chewed her lip before offering a reply.

'You did?'

'Yes, I did.'

'What exactly did you fill in for him?'

'What I overheard,' he replied. 'That you're dying.'

Lucy didn't say anything, only stared ahead.

'Jim knows the person looking for you is a doctor,' Merrick went on, feeling unbearably sad. 'So he doesn't think you're a murderer or anything.'

'Like I could be,' she said, not smiling and avoiding his eyes. 'The Wheelchair Strangler.' She laughed, and then asked, 'Are they coming for me?'

'Not at the moment,' he replied. 'Is it true? Are you sick, Lucy?'

He observed her face as she looked out to sea. He noticed again her unmistakable air of hopelessness and desolation. Everything was beginning to make sense. Lucy was a wise, fiercely independent lady, that he was certain of. Intelligent too. Yet behind her eyes was a sorrow that had tugged at every empathetic notion Merrick had in his entire body. It was true; she was dying. Overcome by an overwhelming despondence, he sat down on the grass beside her. 'Why is this doctor concerned with stopping you?' he asked suddenly.

Lucy's brow furrowed, but she didn't look back at him or offer a reply.

Merrick swallowed. 'Jim didn't give you away to the policeman,' he said, waiting for some sign of relief or even thankfulness. He saw neither. 'But I'm not altogether sure if I'm doing the right thing here,' he went on. 'What aren't you telling me, Lucy?'

She pursed her lips, still staring wordlessly out to sea.

He groaned, beginning to feel angry. 'If you want me to help get you out of here, you have to give me a story,' he said. 'And right about now Jim and Myrtle will be looking for one too.'

As he spoke, the sound of footsteps behind them made him turn around. Myrtle and Jim were, indeed, making their way towards them.

'What do I tell them?' he hissed.

When no reply was forthcoming, Merrick stood up and turned Lucy around in her chair to face the couple. 'I was telling Lucy about the policeman calling you,' he said to Jim as they approached.

'I can't imagine what he might want with you,' Myrtle said, frowning at Lucy. She looked more concerned than accusing, to Merrick's relief. 'It sounds serious,' she continued. 'Are you alright, lass?'

'No,' Lucy replied, not looking at Merrick. 'The truth is I'm not alright at all. It's true. I'm dying.'

There was a gasp from Myrtle, who immediately covered her mouth with her hands.

'I have a rare disease, a kind of brain cancer,' Lucy said. She tugged her headscarf away to reveal a flock of very short, wispy, purple hair. 'No one knows what causes it and there are only three hundred cases a year. And here I am, one of the three hundred. Aren't I lucky?'

Although Merrick had no idea what 'brain cancer was, he felt as though someone had punched him in the stomach. He understood dying, and hadn't been prepared to hear anything like this.

'Oh, you poor thing,' Myrtle said.

'Ah, what are you going to do?' Lucy shrugged. 'You can win the lottery or you can be the one in three hundred people that get an incurable brain disease. Either way, I've become one of a chosen few. Yay!' She raised her arms in faux celebration. The other three stood in stunned silence. Undeterred, she went on, 'And yes, I've had treatment and undergone more tests than I could begin to count. But there will be no magic cure. The light of my life is on its way out; there is nothing anyone can do. I'm going to die.'

Myrtle took her hand from her mouth to speak. 'Do you know how long you have?' she asked quietly.

Merrick held his breath, as Lucy shook her head. 'No,' she replied. 'Perhaps six weeks, perhaps six months.' She pulled her headscarf back on and smiled weakly at them. 'But that six weeks or months will be agony. The last year of my life since diagnosis has been terrible. I get raging headaches, I'm sick all the time. I've endured countless admissions to hospital for radiotherapy. And after all of that, who knows how long I have? How long will I have to sit waiting for a slow, undignified and horribly excruciating death?'

Merrick's life had been forever until he'd fallen back to earth. So facing death wasn't something he'd had experience of in more than three centuries. He knew he could now, yet even after all this time, he wouldn't be ready. How could this woman, only midway through a normal human life span, simply accept it? Even bringing the day forward by choice?

Jim broke the silence that followed Lucy's sad speech. 'What a brave lady,' he said. 'This is a bit of a journey for someone so sick, though. What brings you here in particular, Lucy?'

She sighed. 'I'm here because I got tired of waiting for that very thing that is coming for me whatever I do. I came to meet it and get it over with.'

'I'm sorry?' Myrtle said, looking puzzled. 'What is it that you came to meet?'

'Death,' Merrick said, finding his voice at last. 'You came to meet death, didn't you?'

'Oh you brave, brave woman,' Myrtle cried out, reaching for Lucy's hand and taking it in her own.

'It's okay,' Lucy told her. 'I've had a lot of time to come to terms with things and today is one of a string of good days I've been having lately. I'm at peace, you know.' She looked up at

Merrick for the first time, unblinking. 'Both with the cancer and with myself. I'm ready to die.'

Merrick closed his eyes and felt his world spinning as it once had whenever he took to the air in his days as a goose. Only this was no pleasure flight. It was from searing, out-of-control anguish, for a woman he had only just met. He wanted to cry out. His instincts had been right all along, Lucy did want to die; she hadn't wanted him to save her. 'Did you have medicines with you on that ferry?' he asked, opening his eyes again. A sudden realisation that she might be in pain hit him harder than her proclamation of pending death. Was she also so formidable as to be able to hide well the fact that she was in agony?

'That's what I am trying to explain to you,' she replied. 'I haven't had any lately. And it's because I stopped all that invasive, vomit-inducing treatment and decided to let it be, I know it is. This is the right thing for me. I'm done with it all.'

'Then why does your doctor want you detained?' Jim asked her.

'Yes,' Myrtle added. 'Why would they do that?'

'In the United Kingdom there are no rights for the dying,' Lucy explained. 'If a person is suffering and going to die anyway, they can't make up their mind to have it all done with. They have to go on, coping with the indignity of it all.'

She paused, and Merrick saw her look at the couple, her eyes imploring them to understand. It made his heart feel fit to burst.

'I don't want that,' Lucy went on. I've had enough.'

'So you came here to die?' said Myrtle.

'Not here, no. I was heading for Scarba. 'But I made the mistake of leaving a note for my doctor. I thought I'd be there by now. I didn't expect to find myself holed up here for so long, no offence.'

Jim nodded. 'What exactly are you planning to do over there?' he asked.

'Go,' she said quietly.

He looked at his wife, who shrugged. 'Go where? How?' he asked Lucy.

'Into the sea,' said Merrick. 'That's it, isn't it?' He stared at her, willing her to meet his gaze but she didn't.

'I remember someone from Islay did that before.' Myrtle said sadly, rubbing Lucy's hand. She turned to her husband again. 'It was years ago, do you remember it, Jim? It was that old woman's daughter, her that stayed in Scotchin Cottage. What was that lass's name?'

'Olive,' said Lucy.

Myrtle shook her head. 'No, it wasn't Olive. At least, I don't think it was.'

'The old lady at Scotchin Cottage was called Irma,' Jim told her.

Lucy nodded. 'That's right. It was Irma's cottage, and the daughter that killed herself on Scarba was called Olive.'

'That's it, I remember now,' said Myrtle. She looked at Lucy. 'How did you know that?'

Merrick watched as emotion finally got the better of Lucy, and she blinked back tears. 'Because,' she replied stoically, 'Olive was my mum.'

Chapter 40: Lucy

'Jim, Myrtle, could you please leave us alone for a while?'

At Merrick's request, the pair stepped away behind Lucy, both giving her a last look of concern as they retreated.

'We'll be inside when you need us,' Jim said. 'You come right in when you're ready, Merrick.'

Lucy saw Merrick nod to the couple, and waited for him to speak, but only silence followed. He bowed his head and took a few steps forward to sit on a rock, looking, not at her but out to sea.

'There's nothing you can say to change my mind,' she told him. 'I don't want to prolong this any more than I have to. Please, can we leave now?'

He didn't answer, choosing instead to pick up a stick and start poking angrily at the sand with it. He was cross, and it worried her.

'You will still help me, won't you?' she asked him.

He heaved a heavy sigh, and jabbed all the harder at the sand. When at last he spoke, she was surprised to find his voice full of tenderness rather than anger. 'Lucy, I have been alive for longer than you can even begin to imagine,' he said, without turning round. As she opened her mouth to speak, he stopped her. 'And I know you don't believe that, but you don't have to. It's true, all the same. And what's also true is in all this time I've been looking for someone I left behind. That woman you described on Scarba -'

'The witch?'

He ignored her and went on, 'She's someone I have to get to, more than ever now. Until I plucked you out of the sea yesterday, it was all I was intent on doing.' He turned to face her. There was real anguish in his expression.

'But she isn't real -'

'To you,' he replied. 'She isn't real to you. But to me -' He paused, his eyes beseeching. 'It doesn't matter that you don't believe me, none of that matters. This is my journey and you have yours. So yes, I will take you to Scarba. Not because I want you to take something that I don't believe is yours to take, but because I need to go too.'

'What do you mean I'm taking something that isn't mine to take?'

'Your life,' he told her. 'It isn't yours to take.'

'I'm not the one taking it, it's being taken anyway,' she snapped. 'I'm simply fast forwarding to the main event. I won't thank you for your own thoughts and beliefs in the matter, but I will thank you for agreeing to take me to Scarba.'

'Don't thank me,' he bit back. 'I have no money, no possessions in this entire world of humans. I needed help and help came. But you -' He hesitated, catching his breath. 'You need help too. And I think it could come from the same person I'm looking for.'

Lucy scrunched up her nose, puzzled. 'Eh?' she said.

Merrick turned fully about in his sitting place and glared at her, his expression solemn. 'She can help you too,' he said.

Lucy shook her head. 'Nobody can help me,' she told him, wishing with all her heart that this caring, odd character could be normal. Why was there always a weird side to every seemingly nice person she came across? She paused, heaving a heavy, despondent sigh. 'Don't do this to me, Merrick. Not now,' she pleaded. 'This is serious stuff, not one of your fantasy trips to La La Land. I'm dying, and it's not like I had anything to live for anyway.'

'Who says you have nothing to live for?' he barked, the sudden angry outburst startling her. 'Don't you have people that need you? People who will miss you?'

She swallowed, gathering her composure before shaking her head. 'The only person I had that gave me a reason to live was my daughter, Nicola, and she's gone too.'

'Gone?'

'Dead. She died, in the same car wreck that put me in this chair. I survived, she died. Isn't life and all its twists and turns bloody fantastic?'

'There must be something worth living for,' he replied.

'I'm dying, Merrick. As people have died before me of this stupid, incurable disease. It is taking two to three hundred lives a year, and this year, mine is on the list,' she said. 'Do you know I have one friend in the entire world? Her name is Roisin.' Lucy began to cry. 'She's a beautiful, optimistic and incredible lady,' she went on, more weakly. 'She's a widow with three daughters and no family. And she's dying too! That smiley, happy, wonderful woman with everything to live for. So, if your weird magic can actually save someone, save her.'

'Roisin?'

'Roisin,' she repeated. 'Not me. That wonderful woman with three, young daughters who need a mother in their lives. That is the epitome of unfair. Not my disease, hers!'

'Why just Roisin?' he asked. 'Why was she your only friend?'

'Because I don't have the time for friends,' Lucy said sharply. 'What would be the point of that?'

'There's always a point to everything,' Merrick said matter-of-factly. 'Every life touches another life; if you let them in.'

'What the hell is that supposed to mean?'

'That we're all making this journey together,' he said. 'Everything you do, everything you think of, everything you wish for is all part of a wider, bigger story. And everything you achieve becomes the story of us all. There is a point to your life, Lucy. I'm willing to bet that somebody, somewhere is going to miss you. Whether you know it or not.'

'Like who?'

'Like me,' he said. 'I will miss you.'

She swallowed, feeling her cheeks burn. 'But you don't even know me,' she replied.

'Yes, but I like to think we are becoming friends,' he said. 'And you can never have enough of those.'

'I expect barnacle geese have thousands of them,' she said, with a hint of irony.

'Not friends,' he said seriously. 'Family.'

'All of them?'

He nodded. 'Every last goose that I travel with,' he said. 'We're all related.'

Lucy blew out her cheeks and raised her eyebrows, her earlier annoyance at him returning. 'This is utter nonsense,' she said curtly.

'I'm telling you the truth!' Merrick replied, raising his hands to his forehead in exasperation. He stood up. 'Up until two days ago I was a goose on my way to a gathering here,' he explained. 'And I couldn't die.'

Lucy shook her head, still unbelieving, but feeling a sense of sympathy for him. Poor, deluded, Merrick. The man was ill, even though he seemed lucid; sensible even. The rest of his actions didn't add up to the way she expected someone in a confused state of mind to be. Was there so much she didn't know?

'I'm not lying,' he said again.

She stared back at him, tight-lipped.

'I'm not!' he retorted. 'I want you to listen to me. The woman on Scarba is called Gladys, and she has a certain kind of magic. I

196

don't know exactly what it is, but I do know that she can save you. She has a way -'

'Don't you get it? Don't you hear me?' Lucy shouted at last. 'I don't want to be saved, even if what you say is true! There is nothing for me here, nothing! I have nobody, nothing in my life. My husband took off with another woman and my daughter -' she stopped, unable to go on. She wasn't going to cry, not now, not in front of him. Lucy couldn't show any weakness, because if she did, she felt sure that then he definitely wouldn't help her.

'You want to be with your daughter?' he said.

Lucy nodded.

She saw the corners of Merrick's mouth turning momentarily downwards before he replied with a single, 'Oh.'

He turned his attention back to scoring the sand. After the brief silence that followed, she said, 'So you see, I don't want to be saved by this friend of yours.'

He stopped scribbling and straightened. 'Her name is Gladys and she's more than a friend,' he said, without looking round. 'Much, much more.'

In the middle of everything, of all the emotions she was going through, Lucy was surprised to find she felt stung. So, Merrick thought he was in love with this fabricated person? But then, why the hell did she care anyway? 'Thank you, God,' she said aloud.

'What was that?' Merrick said, looking over his shoulder at her.

Lucy bit her lip. I'm going to die, she told herself. This is enough of an impossible circumstance for anyone to cope with. 'I mean,' she said, thinking of a lie to cover any trace of her caring about anything, and fast. 'I'm glad you have someone to find.'

Merrick's brow furrowed and he turned to throw the stick aside. 'Don't you have anyone?' he asked her. 'Anyone at all?'

She frowned. 'The only two people in the entire world who will even realise I'm out of here are my doctor and Brian from FDG.'

'FDG?'

'The gas company,' she replied. 'Who by now have made what I hope will have been about twenty calls a day to the premium rate phone number I left them with.'

He looked puzzled. 'I don't understand.'

'You don't have to,' she said with a wry smile. 'Why would a goose ever need to worry about gas bills?' As she said the words, 'why would a goose', Lucy felt a sense of déjà vu. It sent prickles up the back of her neck. 'That is odd,' she said, more to herself than to Merrick.

'What is?'

She blinked at him. 'What kind of goose did you say you were again?'

He raised an eyebrow in surprise. 'So you believe me now?' he said.

Lucy frowned at him. 'Answer the question,' she barked.

'I don't know,' he admitted, scratching his head. 'A black and white one.'

'Did you come to Islay a lot?'

'Yes, every year for the gathering.'

'On Loch Gruinart?'

'They don't give you a map, you know,' he replied, looking irritated. 'When you're a goose you go with the wind. You follow familiar sights, smells and the rush of spirit. It carries you to the same place, same time, every year. It's innate.'

'Of course,' she said, realising at last what had brought to her that sudden sense of déjà vu. Crazy or not, in thinking he was a barnacle goose, Merrick kept triggering a memory. It came from the depths of her own, quite unique childhood. Lucy was experiencing a sad longing for her grandmother. She knew it had been there since she arrived, but it was positively eating away at her now. 'I want to go somewhere,' she told him at last.

'I know,' he said, unsurprised. 'And so do I, but I think we should talk about things a little more -'

'No, I mean somewhere here on Islay,' she cut in, wondering why on earth she hadn't thought of this before. Perhaps, at least, the rush of spirit thing was as true and real as he'd described it. 'Merrick,' she said. 'I want to go to where my mum died. But first, I want to go see my grandmother.'

'Is she still alive?'

'No.' Lucy replied, feeling a pang of sad regret. 'But I want to go visit her anyway,' she told him resolutely. 'Can we go? Now?'

Chapter 41: Dr Britten

Dr Britten was furious. He had almost reached Islay and now this. He stood over the unfortunate woman who lay unconscious on the deck. An air ambulanceman stood with folded arms and pursed lips, watching the doctor.

'I'm sorry to have called you across,' Dr Britten explained. 'But the crew said you'd be nearby. And I thought it best to get a second opinion.' In truth, he'd hoped they would take the case entirely out of his hands. A risky call; and a terrible waste of resources, but necessary all the same. These people had no idea how important his journey was. 'Pulse seems fine,' he went on. 'A little on the fast side, but steady. Airway is clear and she's breathing. But I can't get a response from her.'

'Do we know a name?' the paramedic asked, kneeling down and leaning in to take a closer look at the patient.

'It's Cathy,' Dr Britten replied. He looked around for her companions, still puzzled about where they might be.

'Cathy?' The other man spoke softly to the woman on the ground, waiting for a response but getting none. He looked up at Dr Britten. 'Who's here with her? Anyone? We could do with getting a medical history at least.'

'She was with two other women,' he replied. 'But I don't know where they've gone to. It's all very odd. They seemed very good friends and yet -'

'Ah well,' the man went on, taking the bag from his back and placing it on the ground next to Cathy. 'Let's get her some extra oxygen first, as a precautionary measure. See if we can't coax her round.'

'Perhaps she's fainted?'

'Perhaps,' the man replied, looking doubtful. 'Or a little too much to drink?' he added quietly, so that the watching crowd wouldn't hear. He raised his eyebrows to Dr Britten before putting his face back near to the patient. 'Cathy,' he said again. 'Can you hear me? I'm going to give you a little oxygen, okay, honey?'

His female companion passed him a case, and he opened it to take out a small oxygen cylinder and mask.

Dr Britten asked, 'How long is this all likely to take? I mean, will you be taking her straight off to hospital?'

The woman nodded. 'I should think so,' she said. 'We're here now and she's not responding, so we have to take her back for a thorough check up, Doctor. But I'm not a qualified paramedic myself.'

Startled, Dr Britten said, 'You're not?'

'No,' she replied. 'I'm in training.'

Dr Britten gasped. 'You're in training; the only medic on the boat has been vomiting all the way here. What have I come to?'

'The medic on the boat is sick?'

'Pregnant,' Dr Britten replied.

'There have been a few incidents recently. It's normally so bloody quiet,' the male paramedic piped up. He slipped the oxygen mask over Cathy's head and felt her pulse. 'We have everyone out today, believe it or not. Ooh you're right,' he added. 'Fast, but steady. I'd say she's had a few too many.' He looked up from his watch at Dr Britten again. 'Were you in a hurry today, Doc?'

'Yes, well, I have an emergency of my own to be honest,' Dr Britten replied. 'It's a matter of life and death, so I could do with getting on my way as soon as possible. I have another boat to catch after this one.'

'Where are you headed?' the air ambulanceman asked.

'Scarba.'

'Hmm, okay,' he replied. Looking at his companion, he said, 'Can you let Arron know we'll be winching Cathy up on the stretcher?'

'Urrrrmmmm murrrmmmm,' Cathy said, opening her eyes.

The paramedic leaned in. 'Are you back with us, love?' he said.

Her eyes flickered and she began to fidget before trying to sit up. Dr Britten and the other man knelt down to gently restrain her.

'It's okay, Cathy, you're in good hands,' Dr Britten told her, as they laid her head back down on the deck.

'Yes, I think you fainted or had a bad turn at least,' the paramedic said. 'So we're going to take you on a short flight to get you checked out at the hospital on the mainland.'

Cathy's eyes widened. 'No,' she said, tugging at the mask to try and take it off.

The paramedic reached down to hook it back in place and held it there. 'Now don't worry, Cathy,' he told her. 'We'll take good care of you, I promise. You're going to be alright.'

Cathy's eyes darted from his to Dr Britten's. He felt a stab of pity at her terrified expression, yet still in the back of his mind, he was thinking of how he had to get away. 'I wonder what happened to her friends,' he said. 'They'll be worried. I must try and tell them what's happened. One of them might want to go with her.' He looked at the paramedic, who shook his head. 'Or maybe we can let them know what hospital she's heading to,' Dr Britten added. He looked around again, spotting a member of the crew watching them. 'Can you put out a message on the tannoy for this lady's friends to come forward?' he asked her. The woman nodded and hurried away.

'Try to relax and keep still,' the paramedic was saying to Cathy, who was fighting to sit up again. 'We need to move her, now,' he said to his colleague, getting to his feet. 'Are we set?'

She nodded and the pair turned to get the stretcher together. But the crew were stopped in their tracks, as Fleur came charging towards them. She was waving something in the air.

'It's alright! It's alright!'

Dr Britten heard another shout and noticed Joanna-Rose running behind her. She was carrying Fleur's very wet bag. 'No, no, stop! Stop!' she yelled, turning back to the doctor before pleading, 'Don't let them take her!'

Cathy sat up again, shouting, 'I'm alright! I'm alright!'

'What on earth?' Dr Britten exclaimed.

'She's alright, Doctor,' Joanna-Rose told him breathily.

'I know.' he said, putting a reassuring hand on her arm. 'She's going to be fine. There's no need for you to panic.'

'But Cathy's not sick, see?' Fleur cried out. 'She passed out… from… from…'

'The drink,' Joanna-Rose finished for her. 'We only… went… to get her a -' she stammered, fiddling nervously with the handle of the bag.

As the astonished crowd watched, Dr Britten signalled for the air ambulance crew to wait. He took Joanna-Rose by the arm and led her away from them. 'Now, I want the truth, and I want it fast,' he told her sternly. 'What is all this about?'

'It… it was all…Fl… Fleur's fault,' she stammered, as Fleur rushed up to join them.

'Tell me you didn't get Cathy to fake a heart attack,' he roared.

The women looked at each other, before Fleur spoke.

'She threw my bag in the water,' she sobbed. 'We only meant to stall the ship's crew for a few minutes so I could fish it out.'

'We never expected you to call the Air, Sea and Rescue!' Joanna-Rose added.

Chapter 42: Gladys

Gladys didn't venture out to Cille Mhoire an Caibel often; only when she was sure not a soul was staying at the only habitable property on the island, Kilmory Lodge, on the eastern shore of Scarba. Every moment spent here was a meditative one; often rueing the day she accepted the spells from Angus. It was a memory she didn't enjoy recalling; that moment when her natural life ended and a new, immortal one began. Her task was first and foremost to hold two spells, and she had taken them eagerly, not knowing that with them came eternal life – or at least, a life as long as the time it took for her to complete the second task.

'Which was what?' her young, naïve, former self had asked Angus.

'To preserve the good of mankind,' had been the reply. And her fate was sealed as not long afterwards, he'd left her alone in the world. And what of the spells? Despair had forced her to hide the second one; she never wanted to see it again. To reverse that which she had made could be worse than being forced to walk the earth for hundreds of years alone. Death; Merrick's death. She didn't want him to fall. There was no way of knowing how many hundreds of feet from the earth he might be when it happened.

What was it about the geese, she often wondered, that could be for the good of mankind?

Feeling inside her pocket she took out another of Olive's notes and held it to her lips a moment. 'My only friend,' she said, picturing again the woman that had come into her life so briefly, yet changed it forever. 'What have you to tell me today?'

She unravelled the note and blinked away the moisture in her eyes to read it:

The quality of life is everything, not the quantity. Fill every chapter you leaf through in the book of you with the entire world's light.

Folding the piece of paper carefully up, she placed it back in her pocket. Her finger joints moved easily, she noted. She was pain free again today. Nothing filled her with rage more than the feeling she'd almost made it to her last chapter.

What the hell was happening out there in the world? Who was meddling in the book of Gladys?

Chapter 43: Merrick

The house was much bigger than Merrick had imagined from the description Lucy had given. Across from a beautiful beach, hidden by fencing and a line of tall trees, he felt sure he'd passed over this area before; it all looked very familiar. To see it from the air would have confirmed or dispelled the thought in an instant. Merrick knew many areas of Islay only from the sky. At the gathering each year, he and his flock of thousands would rest at the same, watery haven: Loch Gruinart. Rarely would they venture away from the central gathering place; this was the calling, year upon year, and he loved it so. He felt a familiar pull to the place even now as he stood, only a couple of miles away, a man again.

Barnacle geese never left behind the wounded or abandoned weaker members of the group. Migration was a spiritual thing which involved the synchronicity of minds, not sounds or smells. When one goose fell behind, two would fall back to accompany it. It was an intrinsic thing, and here he was as a man, feeling the same drive to help a wounded soul. Of course he would take Lucy wherever she needed to go, it was never in question. Even as it slowed his own journey's progress.

'My, it's some house,' he said to James, their driver for the afternoon, who nodded in agreement.

James was Myrtle's eldest son and only too happy to help once he'd heard of Lucy's most desperate of situations. Merrick was astounded by the hearts and generosity of everyone they had met so far on the island, so much sympathy and understanding had they for Lucy – one of their own, as Myrtle had put it upon learning who her grandmother had been. People were not always so unlike geese after all, he thought.

As it transpired, the house was known to the family and the couple had informed them that it was now a holiday let. It appeared to be empty today, with the holidaymakers out for the day or no one staying there this week. Either way, it was ideal for Lucy to at least get a little look about if the neighbours in the single, attached property weren't alerted to them wandering around.

From the back seat of the car, he could see the reflection of Lucy's face in the visor mirror. A single tear ran down her cheek as she looked first at the property and then across the road, through the trees to the bay. Turning her face back, she caught him watching her, and, wiping her eyes, said, 'I used to play on that beach.'

He nodded. 'It's beautiful, as is the whole island. I've always loved it here.'

'Did you grow up here?' she asked.

'Near here, yes,' he replied, before turning to James. 'Do you think it will be okay for me to take Lucy into the garden?'

James nodded towards the house next door. 'The couple in there are ancient,' he said with a smile. 'Friends of the owner. I'm trying to think what their name is because for one thing, they may have the keys if no one is staying here, and for another, they might have known your grandmother, Lucy. I think Dad said they've been here for years and years.'

Merrick saw Lucy's expression brighten. 'I remember them!'

'You do?' James and Merrick said at the same time.

'Yes! Mr and Mrs Toe. The name always made me giggle as a child. Mr Toe used to tend my grannie's garden for her, when she was unable to do it herself anymore.'

'That's it; I remember now,' James said, 'How could I forget? Mr and Mrs Toe.' He turned to grin at her. 'Would you like to come to the door with me?'

She tipped her chin to her chest, and Merrick saw her expression darken. 'Well, I, erm -'

Sensing her unease, he opened his door and started to get out of the car, telling James, 'Why don't you and I go and see them first, eh?'

'Sure thing,' he answered, getting out of the car to follow without argument.

Lucy gave Merrick a silent look of thanks and he nodded to her, before following James through the front gate. As they walked up the path, James turned to Merrick. 'I suppose she feels a bit strange about facing them, what with her illness and all?'

'I suppose so,' Merrick said, 'Let's see if they're in first and then try to approach the subject of her speaking to them.'

'It can't hurt to tell them who she is, can it?'

Merrick would have liked to agree, but felt doubtful. 'We could just say she's the relative of someone who used to live here, if we have to.'

Reaching the door, James stepped up to ring the bell and waited. When no one answered, he tried again.

'Not in after all then?' Merrick said.

'Wait another few moments,' James told him. 'They are a very elderly couple.'

Sure enough, within another minute the door slowly opened and a stooping, wizened gent in a flat, tweed cap appeared.

'Hi there, Mr Toe, isn't it?' James said, putting out a hand, which the old man shook.

'Yes, indeed. How can I help you, young man?'

'I'm James Carron,' he replied. 'My parents run the B&B and holiday cottages at Kilnaughton Bay.'

The old man's face brightened in recognition. 'Ah, yes,' he said, grinning. 'Myrtle and Jim. Lovely couple. How are they doing?'

'Just grand, Mr Toe,' he said with a smile. 'They send their regards to you, of course. But I'm here on a mission. I wonder, is anyone staying in the house next door at the moment?'

Mr Toe raised his eyebrows. 'Gone and overbooked yourselves, have you?' he said, his eyes twinkling with kind delight. 'Well, I'm sorry, I can't help you there. There's a young couple with their teenage daughter in it this week, and they're set to stay next week too.'

'Oh, right,' James replied, looking across at Merrick in silent query.

Merrick took his cue. 'We aren't looking for a place to stay, Mr Toe,' he said to the old man. 'I'm here with an old acquaintance of yours. Do you remember the old lady that used to live here before it was a holiday cottage?'

'Oh, yes I do,' he said with a nod. 'But she died a long, long time ago. I hope you weren't here to find her. I'd hate to be the bearer of bad news.'

'Oh no, no,' Merrick reassured him. 'It's her granddaughter, Lucy, I have with me in the car. She was hoping for a little look about her grandmother's old house.'

At this, the old man opened the door fully and turned to look behind him, shouting, 'Here, Jeanie, remember little Lucy? She's here! Come to see us!'

From behind him, a small, bespectacled lady in a bright, flowery pinafore appeared, looking puzzled. 'Who'd ye say?' she said, putting a hand on her husband's shoulder as though needing it for support.

'Lucy,' he said. Irma's wee granddaughter, do you remember?' He turned to Merrick and James. 'Her memory's not what it used to be, bless her soul.'

'Julie, you say?' the old lady said, her brow furrowed.

'Lucy,' Mr Toe corrected. He looked back at Merrick. 'I doubt she will remember,' he told him sadly, before patting her hand on his shoulder. 'Why don't you go and sit back next to the fire where it's warm,' he said, indicating indoors. 'It's a bitter day out here; you don't want to get poorly again.' Coaxing her back inside, he leaned over to take a key from a shelf and stepped out onto the step to speak more quietly, pulling the door closed behind him. 'Where is she?' he asked, 'I'll come and see her myself, if that's okay? There's no point upsetting her or Jeanie, what with her condition and all.'

'Sure,' Merrick said with a smile. 'I'll bet she'll be thrilled. But on the point of condition, I must tell you, Lucy'll no doubt be a bit changed herself from when you last saw her.'

'Oh?' he said almost absentmindedly, as he led the way down the path towards the gate.

'She's in a wheelchair,' he replied, following him as he shuffled out of the gate towards the car, where Lucy sat, looking startled to see Mr Toe heading her way. For a moment, Merrick thought he might have done the wrong thing, until the old boy finally reached her passenger door and flung it open.

'Lucy, my love!' he exclaimed, leaning in to give her a hug which she accepted immediately. 'Where have you been, my girl?'

'Uncle Albie!' Lucy replied, with a voice so full of delight Merrick felt his neck prickle with pleasure and surprise. 'How lovely to see you again. I can't believe it,' she exclaimed, pulling back from his embrace to regard him more fully again. 'You look exactly how I remember you.'

'Ach, you're a wee flatterer,' the old man said, keeping a hold of her hand and grinning like a proud father at her. 'I'm older and a hell of a lot slower these days,' he laughed. 'I don't look after my own garden very well now, never mind your grannie's.'

Merrick stepped off the kerb to stand in front of the car, peering in the windscreen at Lucy to watch the happy exchange between the pair. As he thought of the few days she had left, and whether she might let the old boy know or not, it tore at his heart so hard, he had to stoop to hold on to the bonnet of the car.

Noticing him watching her for the first time, Lucy looked back at Mr Toe and said, more uncertainly, 'How's Auntie Jeanie?'

'She's still with us, my love,' came the soft reply. 'But only in body these days, I'm sad to say. Her mind's lost, you see. She has dementia.'

'Oh no!'

Merrick saw Lucy's eyes brim with tears again, and in that moment he knew bringing her here had been the absolute right thing to do. Whether she realised it or not, Mr and Mrs Toe were family; one of her group - that much was obvious. Even if not in blood, here was a couple Lucy would be leaving behind forever and who would be stricken to hear news of her diagnosis. She didn't have nobody, he thought, feeling very satisfied with himself.

'I'm sure the old Jeanie would have loved to see you,' said Mr Toe, looking uncertain.

'And I her,' Lucy said.

'Why don't you try?' Merrick said. 'What harm can it do? We can get your chair from the boot and take you in to spend some time with your aunty and uncle.' He put emphasis on the 'aunty and uncle' part, which didn't go unnoticed by Lucy. He pursed his lips as their eyes met but what he saw in them was acknowledgement, as though she was reading his mind.

'Oh no, I really should be -' she started, but Merrick was quick to interject, signalling for James to get her chair.

'Yes, you should!' he told her, with a kind smile. 'That will be alright, won't it Mr Toe? Do you think your wife would be upset at seeing Lucy?'

'Perhaps not,' Mr Toe replied. 'In fact, now that I think of it, it might do the old girl some good.' He turned to Lucy. 'Yes, yes, you should come. Jeanie might not know you, but she'll be pleased to see you anyways. She's pleased to see anyone these days; we never have any visitors you know. They're all gone; the family I mean.'

Merrick smiled kindly at Lucy. 'I have places I want to see myself,' he told her. 'So why don't you? It'll give us both a little breather before our trip.'

Before she could offer a reply, James was already wheeling the chair around the car to beside the passenger seat for her. 'Come on,' he said cheerily. 'Let's have you in here.'

From his place in the back seat of the car, Merrick watched James deliver Lucy and then return to the driver's side and jump in.

'I think we did a nice thing there,' the young man said with a grin. 'She seemed happy.'

'She did,' Merrick agreed. 'At last' he thought to himself.

'Do you think she'll tell them?'

'No.'

James ran both hands across the top of the steering wheel in a sweeping motion, looking deep in thought, before reaching for the ignition key. 'Where to now?' he said finally, starting the car.

'How long have we got?'

'I said we'd be back in forty minutes or so,' he said.

Merrick smiled to himself, and without further hesitation, replied, 'You know, I'm dying to see the barnacle geese at Loch Gruinart. Do you think we could make that and back in forty minutes?'

213

Chapter 44: Lucy

Lucy's childhood memories were sketchy, but Mr and Mrs Toe looked just the way she remembered them. To a younger Lucy the pair had always seemed elderly. There were some differences, she noted. Mr Toe had been a strong, robust character in the past. It seemed he was able to move or fix anything. Now, she noted, he trudged around with a stooped, almost genteel posture. Yet it made him more endearing than ever to her. And even though she wasn't able to visit her grandmother's house today, this one was special too. She'd realised as soon as James had guided her chair over the threshold, that it held equally fond memories for her. The furniture was exactly the same, as though preserved in time. Nothing appeared to be changed in the décor, even the familiar, homely scents remained in the air. The gentle hints of ointment, violets and cotton towels. She even felt excited butterflies in her stomach as she had as a girl, in being here. Mrs Toe had always given her baked treats. It was strange that even as an adult, she still felt the same childish prickle of excitement of those visits now. What would the treat be today? A slice of cinnamon-infused clootie dumpling? Some buttery-soft tablet? A crumbly empire biscuit? Lucy could almost smell Jeanie's baking hanging in the air. It was a sensual memory that still made her taste buds tingle. Sometimes Mr Toe used to press a finger to his lips while reaching into his pocket for a ten pence piece to give to her. She would save it for her next trip to the shops. The thrill she got in spending that precious coin on a poke of sweeties was still fresh in her mind. How had she forgotten all this?

'You used to sit there.'

She sipped her tea and glanced over to the place that Jeanie Toe was referring to. It was a window seat padded out with faded, green, floral cushions. They were the same cushions she would sit

215

on to read her favourite Enid Blyton books. She peered questioningly at Mr Toe.

'Sometimes she remembers,' he told her with a kind smile.

'Do you know who I am, Aunty Jeanie?' Lucy asked the old lady. Mrs Toes turned her attention back to the television. It was switched off, yet she nodded as though watching something.

'Get him, Big Daddy,' she shouted suddenly, making Lucy jump.

'Hit him with your handbag,' Mr Toe cheered, giving Lucy a reassuring wink. 'It's the Saturday afternoon wrestling,' he explained, with a wide grin. He patted his wife on the arm, adding, 'Giant Haystacks versus Big Daddy, isn't it, Jin?'

'He's holding him! They're not allowed to hold people!' she grumbled, snapping a digestive biscuit in half. She dunked it angrily into her tea.

Memories of long lost Saturdays with Mr and Mrs Toe were flooding back thick and fast. The times when the couple would watch her whenever her grandmother had to go out. The steaming-hot toast Mrs Toe would make for her that was so juicy with butter it would run down her chin as she ate it. Sometimes she would dip it in her tea so that little butter bubbles would sit on top. And the freshly picked blackberries from the garden that Mrs Toe put in a cereal bowl for her with milk and sugar. Every piece of fruit or vegetable the couple ate had been grown in their garden. Or, from a patch in her grandmother's back garden, which the old lady would let Mr Toe use.

Mr Toe nodded at the television. 'World of Sport was always on when you were here,' he said. 'Funny that's what she's watching now. Not that you'd remember too much about it as you forever had your nose in a wee book or comic.'

The Bunty, Lucy remembered. It was a favourite comic that her grandmother used to have delivered along with the papers. It made the little girl feel very important and grown up indeed to have her own post. The Bunty had paper dollies you could cut out, along with a set of interchangeable clothes. She would create a world of imagination, mothering the little dolls. It was a place of great solace for her in after the death of her mother. 'I remember,' she said, almost absentmindedly. 'I remember everything. I used to love coming here, Uncle Albie.'

He nodded. 'Yes you did.'

'Uncle Albie -'

'You don't have to call me that anymore, you know. You're a grown woman now,' Mr Toe chuckled.

Lucy smiled. 'But you know what?' she replied. 'I like calling you that. It's the only thing that feels, I don't know, right.'

'Uncle Albie it is then,' he agreed.

'Uncle Albie, do you remember the geese that used to appear in grannie's back yard?'

'Irma didn't like cheese,' Mrs Toe mumbled.

'Irma was lovely, wasn't she, my sweetie?' the old man said to his wife, before turning back to Lucy. 'She's better than usual today,' he said. 'It must be your influence. Will you come and see us again?'

She swallowed. 'I'll try,' she lied, feeling terrible for it. 'About the geese?'

'Do you mean the barnacle geese?' he asked. 'They're all over the island at this time of year.'

'So it was a barnacle goose,' she said aloud, not meaning to.

'But I don't remember your grannie saying anything about them visiting the garden,' he went on. 'They flock to Loch Indaal every year in their thousands. You don't normally get strays in the garden though. They travel with the crowd, if you see what I mean.'

She nodded. 'Yes, I do. But I remember there was one that used to appear in the back garden, all by itself. A black and white one. That's a barnacle goose, right?'

'In these parts it will likely be, yes,' he agreed. 'But if your old grannie was seeing one on its own in the back yard, that's very unusual. They don't go about by themselves, as I said. Are you sure it was just the one?'

She nodded. 'Yes, I'm sure.'

'And why is it significant?'

Lucy took another sip of her tea and cupped it in her hands again, enjoying the warmth of the mug in her palms. She thought of Merrick and exhaled slowly, her mind awash with pieces of a puzzle she didn't know how to assemble.

'I'm not entirely sure that it is,' she told him in earnest. 'But Lord knows why, I have a feeling that it might be.'

'Easy! Easy! Easy!' Mrs Toe shouted at the television.

'Oh, I wish it was,' Lucy sighed.

Chapter 45: Gladys

Gladys was grateful for the headphones Joe MacNeish had given her, especially today. Since the pain had vanished and another friend left her life, so had her enthusiasm for anything. Music was the only thing that helped her escape this tiny, island prison. She could turn away from loneliness, close her eyes and lose herself in beautiful memory. Each song took her away to another place. Joe had introduced her to music via a selection of CDs that ranged from the very old to the ultra-modern. By far her favourite artist of all was the late, great Freddie Mercury. Such power and intensity came forth from his music, yet even he had passed on. These days she envied anyone who died. It was something she could only look forward to as much as a Scarba heatwave. But Freddie was a genius. His writing; his inimitable and extraordinary voice. In particular, the song she was listening to now, which seemed to speak both to and for her. *'Who Wants To Live Forever?'*

As she listened on this particular morning, she lamented her body's return to the status quo. She wasn't dying, but something had shifted. After all these years, she must be on the way to completing whatever she had been left here to do, but what was that? Something very much about the geese, that much she did know. One of the spells was to turn someone into an immortal barnacle goose. The other was to turn a barnacle goose into a human. She'd kept her promise with a slight variation: the second was hidden away.

She had dispensed with that spell and life in Islay many, many years ago and for the same cause. She had never been sure whether Merrick had the power, or mental capacity now that he was changed, to remember her. If he did, he would hate her for what she'd done. But even more crucially, she hadn't wanted his life to end even as she wished it for herself. But then, was he now as miserable as she with the longevity of it all? She may never know now, she supposed. After all, he would have long forgotten her. Yet she knew the numbers of barnacle geese that landed annually on Islay had increased. Joe MacNeish, and all the MacNeish men before him, would recount news of the numbers every year as per her wishes. A part of her task was to bring to completion the perpetuation of the propagation of the species; that was clear.

The legend of the barnacle goose's beginnings was one Gladys believed to be true. The rest of the world had labelled it as folklore, but what did the rest of the world know for certain of the past? Their origins were not animal, but vegetable. Or, to be more specific, they were born from goose barnacles. They were the black and white barnacles that first floated to shore on pieces of driftwood. The barnacles were the fruit that, when ripe, gave birth to the geese. Thus the genesis of the barnacle goose had been born. This was no legend, it was fact. It was said that when a goose fell on sea it would live. But the most horrifying part for Gladys was that if it should fall on earth, this would mean death. After changing Merrick to save his young, mortal life, she had to accept that she would be unable to bring him back. She would never see him again.

Angus had brought her to hide on Scarba, and it was only now and again she felt a deep remorse for leaving Islay. Merrick could have found and visited with her over the years, but she might never know.

She had completed her pennance now, surely? The number of barnacle geese had risen from mere hundreds in the beginning to thousands now. The propagation of the species seemed set. Why wasn't she being allowed to breathe her last breath now?

Who dares to love forever, when love must die?

220

She pressed the earphones deeper into her ears with both hands to increase the volume. Exhaling, she endured a familiar agony that was almost as old as she was. 'Freddie,' she whispered inside her mind. 'You were wrang when ye said love must die.'

Chapter 46: Merrick

'Do you believe in love that lasts forever?' Merrick asked.

'Hah.' James laughed, before changing his expression to serious as he caught sight of Merrick's more solemn countenance. 'It's not much a men-who-just-met kind of question, but yes I do. I became a dad last year and the way I love that little boy, well, it's incredible that's all I'm saying. I've never known anything like it.'

'Congratulations,' Merrick said, meaning it. He stared up at the cloud-filled sky. 'There's nothing of greater excellence than love.'

James nodded, taking his eyes off the road for a moment to offer Merrick a wide grin. 'So,' he said. 'You want to see the geese?'

'Yes.'

'Have you seen them here before? They're quite spectacular.'

'Oh, yes.'

Turning the car into a long lane Merrick recognised, James pointed over to the right. 'We're coming into the place where they normally start to gather now,' he told him. 'See the dark patches all over the fields over there?'

'The geese, you mean?'

'The geese, yes,' he said. 'I haven't got my glasses on so they look like lines to me. I shouldn't really be driving without them, I guess.'

Merrick neither knew what glasses were, nor cared to worry about such things at this moment in time. He was here. Taking a deep, long inward breath, he scanned the expanse of the vast area before them, which he had never seen from this perspective before. As a boy growing up on Islay, he recalled that there had been no barnacle goose gathering here. For all he knew, there had been no geese at all on the island three hundred years ago. Who was to say?

James pulled the car up at the side of the road and pressed a button to lower the windows, and the sound of thousands of familiar voices filled the air. All around them, the fields were occupied by his flock, as well as the glittering loch over on the right, where thousands more swam and ate. They'd done well this year. These, Merrick thought with pride, were record numbers.

'Are you one of those twitcher types then?' he heard James ask.

'Twitcher types?' The pull to jump out of the car and escape was beginning to feel overwhelming; Merrick could hardly contain the intensity with which he wanted to join his kind. He was home, yet he couldn't quite get there. 'I'm grounded,' he murmured, more to himself, the realisation sending so many conflicting emotions through his body he could hardly breathe. He heard them, felt the call, knew each and every scent. They were all as one.

'Eh?'

'Home,' he replied, still ensconced in the glorious hum of familiarity. 'Can we wait here for a wee while?'

'Sure,' the other man replied, turning the key that shut off the engine, which made the hum from Merrick's family louder. 'Do you want to get out for a closer look?'

'No,' Merrick told him quickly. 'That will upset... erm... everything.' It might send the whole flock into the air, he remembered. Panic at the nearness of man; *him*. This was the only way they would see him now, his own kin. Except, he thought, with a pang of conscience, they weren't the entirety of him, were they?

'They won't all take off if you're quiet,' James said, confirming what Merrick already knew, far more than the young man could ever realise.

He was right of course; the gaggle would always fly at the sight of people. Unless those people were quiet and unobtrusive, like the watchers that stood there for days on end, pointing dark objects at the geese; objects that neither made a sound nor served to hunt them. Not all men were dangerous to them and Islay was one of the places where they felt safest. He could step outside, but for now, he needed to sit and observe. To think.

'Incredible phenomenon isn't it?' said James, watching in awe, though for different reasons to Merrick's. 'When I was a kid, my mum and dad would bring me here to watch them. I was amazed then and I'm still amazed now. Reckon I'll bring Todd here too when he's a bit bigger.'

'Your son?'

'Yeah, our Todd. Little so and so is only starting to find his wee feet at the moment though. He couldn't appreciate the wonder of this yet, not really. It took me a while. I mean, when I was a boy I always enjoyed looking at them but I never wondered why they were all here, you know?' Still staring out of his window on the passenger side, Merrick felt James stop to look at him, and he nodded back in agreement but didn't turn to him. He was mesmerized by this new perspective – the view of what to him was everything, from the eyes of man. He needed more, but James's talking was becoming too much of a distraction. 'I think I will take a little walk out there,' he told him.

James started to open his own door but Merrick stopped him. 'Do you mind if I go alone?' he said.

Looking slightly embarrassed, James said, 'Oh no, no, of course! On you go,' and waved him on.

Merrick got out of the car and walked over to the edge of the field on the left hand side of the road to where he could see both fields and water. The sky was grey and overcast and there was a biting chill in the air which he was becoming accustomed to noticing more again now, and he hugged his jacket to himself to keep warm. It was there on the grassy verge, as he watched the rows upon rows of birds for almost as far as his eyes could see, that the realisation hit him as hard as the very ground had only a few days earlier. He was utterly, completely human. His skills as leader of the group would be gone. As he looked over the land at the pecking and gawking crowds of geese, he recognised nobody just as they didn't know him. All the creatures looked the same. Magnificent, majestic; marvellous. As he observed this array of black and white stirrings, not one of the geese seemed to be individual or recognisable. This was no gradual transition, he realised with a jolt. This was it; he was back in the body he'd been born to occupy. Back to stay, and yet he felt conflicted; a soul caught between two alternative worlds, both of which he belonged to. After all of this time and all of his experiences of life, on land, on sea, and in the air, he knew where his true place in the universe was and he had for some time. It was only now, as he'd come to look for that someone he'd left behind, and with this choice before him at last, that the answer had arrived. He was born to be with her. There was nothing of greater excellence than love.

Closing his eyes, Merrick felt waves of nauseous urgency rise from his belly into his chest, the tight knot that encased his desire to get to Scarba exploding, intensifying his need right there in the moment.

'This can't go on,' he said quietly into the breeze, and he hugged himself tighter; the sense that he was so close and yet at the same time so far almost bringing him to his knees as he pondered for the first time, 'What if I'm too late?'

Chapter 47: Dr Britten

'This really is good of you, to take me all the way,' Dr Britten shouted to the helicopter pilot who nodded a response, his attention firmly on the island ahead of them. He seemed to the doctor to be frowning.

'The trouble is, it looks as though I won't be able to land,' the pilot shouted back over the noise of whirring and chucking blades.

'Why?' Dr Britten called back.

'It's the wind,' came the reply. 'It's a little stronger than it should be and there isn't much clear space on Scarba.'

The doctor felt panic rise in his throat. 'But as I have explained, this is a very urgent, highly unusual matter. And nobody knows better than you how a very urgent situation requires you to pull out all of the stops.' He looked down at the female medic who was sat in front of him. 'I need to get there right away,' he said to her. 'I might already be too late.'

The pilot and the woman exchanged brief, concerned glances.

'This is highly unethical,' the woman told him. 'And could be dangerous too.'

'What?'

'We can send you down on the rope ladder,' the woman said quietly.

'What was that?' Dr Britten shouted.

'I SAID WE CAN SEND YOU DOWN ON THE ROPE LADDER!' she repeated.

The pilot twisted to face them both. 'Oh no,' he said to her. 'That's not happening.'

'But the woman might die,' his colleague said, getting up and placing a hand on his shoulder. 'We can't just leave her out here. This involves all of us, really. We wouldn't leave anyone, would we? We'd find a way to get there wherever there was one.'

'It's ridiculously dangerous,' the pilot replied, his expression grim. 'Madness!'

'I'll do whatever it takes,' Dr Britten said, aware he was asking a lot of all of them in the circumstances. He turned to the woman again. 'There are extraordinary factors involved in this particular case,' he explained. 'Whatever happens, you have my word that I won't hold you to account. I'll do it.'

Her brow furrowed. 'At your own risk?' she asked.

'DON'T BE STUPID!' the pilot shouted back.

'I'll take the rap, Dougie,' the woman shouted back. She looked at Dr Britten and bit her lip.

He offered her a weak smile.

'We'd take you down, but I don't think it's possible today,' she explained. 'It's never easy for us to land on Scarba.'

'As I said, I'll do it on my own head,' Dr Britten replied.

She nodded, before looking doubtfully at her colleague, who was back to concentrating on his flying.

'She's going to end her life,' the doctor reminded the woman. 'I don't have any choice but to try and stop her.'

'ARE YOU SURE YOU KNOW WHAT YOU'RE DOING?' the pilot shouted.

Dr Britten nodded. 'I'm sure,' he said.

'As long as you're sure, Doc,' the pilot said, turning to pat him on the shoulder. 'Because we're needed at sea as we still have a man missing. And we don't need another casualty.'

'We're almost over,' his colleague shouted. 'Are you ready, Dr Britten?'

'Ready as I'll ever be,' he said.

She patted his chest, and made her way to the door to roll out the ladder. This was it.

'How's the patient doing?' the pilot asked, distracting Dr Britten from his uncertainties a moment longer.

The doctor looked down at Cathy, still out cold on the stretcher beside them. Her fringe was almost glued to her forehead from damp sea-spray, yet she grinned like someone who was enjoying the most intense and satisfying dream.

The woman medic gave her a gentle, probing nudge.

'Fire!' Cathy shouted, before letting out a loud snore, turning over onto her side and hugging the edge of the blanket.

'Okay,' the doctor said to the medic. 'As you're all set here with this patient, I'll go and save another.'

Chapter 48: Lucy

The knock at the door came far too soon, Lucy wasn't ready to say goodbye. There had been no recent goodbye's that made her feel as sad as this one. The only other one was to Doctor Britten. But it had served to express gratitude as well as a final perfunctory nod of farewell. It was business-like, almost. A 'Thank you for trying, but now, I must leave you,' message. It wasn't one of love or loss.

'You will come again, won't you, Lucy?' Mr Toe held on to her hand for a while longer. James paused on the doorstep, allowing Lucy a last hug with her old neighbour.

She didn't want to lie, yet, as she peered into his kind, grey, pleading eyes it hurt her heart to do anything but nod. From over Mr Toe's shoulder, she saw his wife stood in the doorway. She had been watching them with a vacant, uncertain expression.

'Oh,' she said to her, 'you've come out, Aunt Jeanie.'

To Lucy's astonishment, the old woman's eyes filled with tears as she said, 'Ta-ta, Goose.'

Mr Toe stood up straight and turned around to reach for her hand. 'That's right,' he soothed. 'That's right my love. It's Goose. She's come back to see us. Wasn't that nice?'

Prickles ran down Lucy's spine, a sense of déjà vu enveloping her. She'd forgotten they used to call her that when she was small, both the Toes and her grandmother. Lucy Goosey. The Goose.

'See the goose, Lucy, over there in the bushes? I think it's here for you.'

Swallowing the painful sting of her memories, she held out a hand to Mrs Toe. But the old woman only shied further back into the house. Lucy looked from her back to her Uncle Albie. 'It has been lovely to see you both after all this time. Really lovely.'

'Don't make it so long next time,' he replied. 'She's only come back to us for a moment or two today, but she rarely does it at all these days. You don't know how happy that has made me.'

Seeing that his eyes were now wet with tears too, Lucy felt a constriction in her throat, making it hard to breathe in. This pain was more unbearable than the months of gruelling treatment. It was even worse than all the crippling headaches, nausea and lack of sleep. More than the knowledge she was dying. A pain almost as raw as losing Nicola. Yet she wasn't saying goodbye to her real family, only a couple she had once lived next door to. As she opened her arms to accept another hug from Mr Toe, she saw at last what had made the gates of her heart open up. This was like saying a last goodbye to her grandparents. How could she have pushed this wonderful, welcoming couple to the back of her mind for so many years?

'We'd better be getting on our way then, I guess,' she said, leaning back.

Mr Toe released her and straightened up to standing again. 'Yes, I suppose you'd better,' he told her kindly, with a wave of his hand. 'Now don't forget your promise,' he added.

Lucy nodded, feeling awkward. Yet she hadn't actually made any promises. How could she? 'I'll be seeing you,' she told him.

And that at least, she imagined, would be true in some sense.

'How was it?' Merrick asked her, as he stepped out of the front passenger seat to help her into it. He opened the back door and shuffled himself onto the seat behind her.

'It was nice,' she replied, only half telling the truth. The visit had been nice, the parting, more agonising than she'd anticipated. She looked across at her grandmother's house. That sting of deep regret, something she'd aimed to avoid at all costs on this journey to the end of her days, was there now. No looking back. No reminiscing on what might have been. None of this had been on the imagined itinerary. As James jumped back into the driving seat and fired up the car, she caught sight of Mr Toe in an upstairs window. She waved.

Merrick dipped his head to spy him and also waved. 'Nice old couple,' he said.

'Yes they are,' she agreed. 'The best.'

'What do you suppose he'll do without her?' James said.

Merrick and Lucy turned to look at him together. 'Why do you think he'll be the one to go first?' Merrick asked him.

'Oh, I'm sorry, that was insensitive of me,' James said, looking at Lucy with an expression of woe.

'Why did you say it?' Lucy asked him.

James blew out his cheeks, turning his attention to the road ahead and switching on the engine. He fiddled with the gears, replying, 'I thought, well, old Mrs Toe can't be long for this world. She's pretty ill, what with the dementia and all, according to my mum, anyways.'

As James they pulled away, Lucy waved for as long as she could to Albert Toe until he was out of sight. 'Oh who knows with these things,' she said finally. 'Aunty Jeanie always was a hardy old lady. I'll bet she's got a few years to go yet.'

James shrugged as response, but Merrick's was a more reassuring, 'I'm sure she has.'

The three travelled in silence for a time. Merrick eyed Lucy in the mirror on her sun visor. She knew he was trying to guess what she was thinking.

'If you don't mind my asking,' James went on, 'did you tell him about your... situation?'

Merrick waited for her response, and seeing none forthcoming, replied, 'No, I'm going to guess not.'

Lucy remained silent, facing the road ahead, giving away nothing in her expression.

James cleared his throat, breaking the uncomfortable silence. 'It must be so hard for you,' he said. 'I can't even -'

'Thank you,' Lucy replied, not looking at him.

'I mean, does it hurt right now?'

'No,' she said shortly.

'You aren't in any pain at all?' Merrick asked, leaning forward in his seat. This was the question he'd been meaning to ask her for a while. He was glad James had broached it now.

She shifted in her seat and looked up at the mirror to meet Merrick's curious gaze. 'Not since I left for Islay,' she told him. 'I made my decision and since then my whole being has accepted it. Truth be told, I've never felt better.'

'Really?' James said, eyeing her in amazement.

Merrick wondered at the brute honesty and straight forwardness of the young. James was asking Lucy everything he wished he'd had the courage to ask himself.

'Really,' she said. 'I think my mind has reached a state of acceptance, so my body has too. I feel fine, if a little tired from time to time. This time last year I couldn't have held a coherent, thought-fuelled conversation. Some days dragged like I was squeezing through a tunnel without being able to see the other side. I was praying for death so that I could sleep at last.'

'And you have none of this going on right now?' Merrick asked.

'None of it, no,' she replied. 'Which is why I know this is the right thing for me.'

'I think you're very brave,' James cut in, as Merrick and Lucy exchanged glances.

'Don't do this,' his eyes told her.

'I have to,' hers said back.

'I mean,' James continued, 'if it was me, I couldn't leave my family. I'd have to of course, because, well, you do, don't you?

The Big Man has taken the decision out of your hands, so to speak. But I couldn't do it myself,' he said, scratching his beard. 'When it came down to it, I know I wouldn't have your courage. I admire you, I really do. And if there's nobody to leave behind, then why not? Why suffer? They should change the law.'

'But what if this life isn't yours to take?' Merrick responded, looking at James instead of Lucy's annoyed stare. 'What if it was never supposed to be your decision? What if, say, you're going to go to hell for doing it? Not suggesting that you will because none of us know, after all, but what if you are?'

'I don't believe in things like that,' Lucy snapped back. 'I respect everyone else's right to have those thoughts and opinions, but I, for one, do not. This is my life, my body, my journey. And I choose not to suffer or be a burden anymore.'

'But you said you weren't suffering,' Merrick observed.

'At the moment,' Lucy said stiffly. 'But this is my rollercoaster and both the scenery and the ride changes from day to day.'

Merrick turned to look out of the window, offering no response.

'I want to get off the rollercoaster,' Lucy went on. 'It's time.'

'You said you had no one to leave behind,' Merrick replied.

'That's right.'

'But you do,' he said softly.

'No I don't,' she replied. 'There is absolutely nobody. Everything I ever loved is right there where I'm headed.'

'And the Toes?'

Lucy's lip quivered and she pressed them together to prevent giving any emotion away.

'We're almost there,' James announced suddenly, pointing to a sign at the side of the road. He slowed down to show to let them read it. 'Are you sure you want to go? Last chance to turn around, as they say?'

235

'I'm sure,' Lucy responded, reaching to take off her seat belt as the car slowed to pull into a parking space. Before them was a jetty with a single, small fishing boat waiting at it. The final part of the trip lay ahead, she thought, wistfully.

Merrick patted James on the shoulder. 'Thanks for the ride, buddy, and the trip to see the geese. That was outstanding.'

'I know, right?' James responded, taking the keys from the ignition and jingling them as he spoke. 'It's a shame about the planned cull though.'

'What's that?'

'The cull,' James replied, shaking his head.

'Cull of the geese?' Lucy asked, stunned.

'Yep. There's a plan to humanely destroy some to keep the numbers down. The wildlife watching community are furious.'

'I don't know what that means,' Merrick said to Lucy. 'Destroy, as in, kill?'

'Ah huh,' James answered for her. 'Bloody terrible shame if you ask me. A lot of local farmers and businesses have been screaming for it for a few years now. They say the geese are out of control and destroying the land.'

'They can't!' Merrick cried out, so loud it made James visibly flinch.

Lucy's eyes widened. She felt immediate sympathy for Merrick, even though she hadn't believed his story. He believed it, that much she knew. 'That's horrendous,' she said to James. 'Why on earth would they even consider such a terrible, destructive thing? Curse this damn world,' she added,' I'm glad I'm getting out of it.'

Her last few words were lost on Merrick, who sat staring disbelieving at the back of James's head. 'That can't happen,' he said quietly. 'It can't.'

'I'm afraid it's already set to start this year,' James told him. 'Bastards, they are.'

'How many will go?' asked Lucy.

'Perhaps ten, maybe twenty thousand,' came the reply.

'Come on, Lucy,' Merrick said, his expression so angry and determined it startled her. He opened the car door to get out. 'We need to get going, and fast.'

Chapter 49: Gladys

Despite her extraordinary history, Gladys was a humble soul who liked to wallow in the simple pleasures, like making fresh, chicken soup loaded with fresh vegetables and laced with a generous cup of thick cream. Today, as she lost herself in the gentle motion of stirring the soup, she thought to add sprigs of fresh thyme, until remembering her plant had died during the cold, harsh winter, as though mocking her with its ability to do so. Even more annoying, she'd forgotten to freeze some and was no longer able to order supplies of anything from the mainland. Poor Joe. And poor Gladys, she realised, as it looked like the pain she'd been experiencing was indeed well and truly gone. This was not her year to expire. Curses. No more fresh thyme, no Labrador puppy, and no more chicken after the few she had in the freezer were eaten.

Gladys could have kept chickens, were it not for the fact that her hideaway risked being discovered more often were it to be surrounded by clucking and pecking hens. It was going to be a huge problem, Joe MacNeish having neither had a son nor told a soul about her. He was the first MacNeish to ever let her down, but she supposed his excuse was an acceptable one. Judging by the continued chug chug of helicopters in and around Scarba recently, it seemed they still hadn't found him. If only she'd had the power to bring him back to shore herself; but immortal she may be, blessed with inordinate amounts of super-strength, she was not.

It was unfortunate to have become used to the sounds of those helicopter things overhead. However, when the sound of yet another caught Gladys's attention, as she poured hot chicken soup into a mug ready for demolishing, it dawned on her that there was something a bit different about this one. She cocked her head and listened. Was this one louder? Nearer? Putting down the mug, she strode over to the window and peered outside, in time to see a chopper disappearing over the trees, with what appeared to be a man dangling from a long rope ladder under it. 'Hmmm,' she said to herself. 'Louder *and* nearer.'

Wondering what the blazes this latest hero adventurer was up to, she scratched her head, thinking. There was no Joe. No fresh thyme, no Labrador puppy and no more chickens. And here a man was being dropped off on Scarba alone. He'd be one of those survival experts no doubt; a lone wolf. She needed to find somebody to keep her in home comforts. She didn't want to live the next hundred years without those and, despite the island having a few sheep and cows, she had never been any kind of butcher. She could fish, but more than anything else, Gladys liked chicken. And company. She needed a dog.

Reaching for her coat, she swung it around her shoulders and stepped outside into the windy, dank afternoon air. The no doubt, delicious soup would have to wait.

Guessing that the chopper must be headed for high ground, she took the path that led to Cruach Scarba, the island's highest hill, following the sound of the helicopter. After a few yards, it came into sight again and Gladys had to draw back into the cover of some bushes as she realised it was no longer travelling, but hovering. For the first time she noticed that it was an emergency helicopter, which was strange. Why were they dropping one person alone instead of picking someone up? From her hiding place, she observed the awkward-looking character that held on to the long rope ladder, looking down at the ground. Was he going to jump? Looking up, her eyes straining to see as they streamed from the dust that was being blown into her face, Gladys could see two heads poking out of the open side of the helicopter, a couple of paramedics, who appeared to be shouting down to the man.

Whatever they were saying, it wasn't helping. Gladys thought perhaps he either had his foot or arm entangled in the rope, either way he was hugging the thing, unwilling and afraid to let go. 'Training,' she thought. 'That's whit this is.'

'Yarrrrgggghhh!'

The yell from the man made her chuckle to herself; this exercise was not going well. The helicopter rose higher again and the rope ladder swept over the top of a tree, dragging him with it.

There was not enough clear ground for this, she realised, as the chopper lowered again to leave the man a few feet from the floor and she jostled with a notion to help him. She'd be seen, but the rest of the helicopter crew weren't going to land here today. Before she could consider this a moment longer, the wind swept the rope ladder over towards a clump of bushes, as the man finally let go of the ladder and made a gigantic leap of faith into them, sending a wild deer thundering out of its hiding place in the thicket. Gladys winced. Sure, she hadn't felt pain in a good many years, but she knew that a mortal man crashing down from a ladder in mid-air was going to need urgent help. There was a brief pause, and then to her enormous relief and astonishment, the man appeared from the bushes and ran out into the small clearing, waving at the people in the chopper. He was okay. They could go.

Good, Gladys thought.

Seeming happy that all was well, the helicopter began to circle and then swivelled around to retreat back to wherever it came from. Staying undercover, Gladys watched the man from her safe distance, curious to see what his plan was from here. As he staggered around, looking about, there was a definite air of uncertainty about him. He had only a small backpack, and didn't appear to be kitted out in the kind of hiking attire she was used to seeing folks wear when they visited Scarba. He wore a reflective, waterproof coat, but something about his footwear wasn't right.

241

She couldn't quite make out his shoes, but she was sure they weren't the kind of heavy boots he would need for exploring the jaggy, rough terrain of the island. It was all a bit odd. What was he going to do now?

Before she could consider this a moment more, the man appeared to keel over, sending Gladys off on her heels, out of her hiding spot and running towards him. As she neared the stranger who, she realised too late, had not collapsed but was bending over tying a shoelace, she stopped and stared when he turned his face to her and their eyes met.

'What in the name o'… Angus, is that you?'

Dr Britten stood up tall and twisted to face her full on. 'Gladys?' he said.

She blinked and began to look about her, aware of a sense of the unreal as a sudden spinning sensation in her head made her feel as though she was the one who had fallen from a great height. 'Angus… Angus…,' she stammered, her heart racing as she struggled to believe her own eyes. 'I… I…'

As her knees gave way, the man raced over to catch her by the arm and, letting him hold her up, she stared at his face, touching it with her free hand to be sure it was real. 'Angus,' she said finally, her breaths coming faster now. 'I thought ye were long dead!'

Chapter 50: Merrick

Merrick had been watching Lucy for the past ten minutes. She was staring out to sea from her seat at the bow of the fishing boat Jim and Myrtle had chartered for them. It had been an emotional farewell, as the pair wished her Godspeed, feeling no need to interfere. He wondered at their ability to let go like that; Merrick had to be able to do this too, somehow.

'Why are you so bitter?' he asked her.

He saw her stiffen at the question, but she didn't turn round. 'Have you ever lost a child, Merrick?' she said.

'Yes,' he replied. 'Hundreds of them. It may be about to change to tens of thousands, if the farmers on Islay are allowed to have their way.'

'What?'

From her profile, he saw her brow furrow, perhaps more from anger than bewilderment.

'They are planning a cull of the geese,' he said.

'What geese?'

'The barnacle geese that winter on Loch Gruinart each year, remember? That's where I was headed when I fell. They say the geese, my birds, are ruining the land. James told me they blame us for devouring a lot of the good grass and making it difficult to farm.'

She turned to look at him now, her eyes flashing with fury. 'Merrick, I am talking about my dead daughter, did you hear that? Did it register in that crazy, disillusioned mind of yours? She was here, I brought her into the world! A beautiful, intelligent, funny young woman with a bright future. A future that should have gone on for years. She had a life! And now she's dead. Can't you put aside your peculiar fantasies for one moment to pay attention to what's real?'

'I'm sorry, I -'

'You asked me why I was bitter, this is why! I lived and she died. I don't care that I can't use my legs anymore, or that I'm dying now. She deserved to live! I should have died that day.' Lucy put her head down and wept out loud. Her shoulders shook, her anguish contorting her features until she was almost unrecognisable.

Merrick had never seen a person break down so completely before. He didn't know what to say. He looked toward the Skipper of the boat. He still faced straight ahead, focused on steering them to their destination.

'I watched her die, Merrick,' Lucy raged on. 'I watched my baby girl crying in agony and begging for me to help her. But there was nothing I could do. I was her mother! I was supposed to take care of her. When my child was born I wrapped her in my arms and told her I'd never let anyone hurt her!'

Merrick swallowed, resisting the urge to rush forward and hug her, knowing she would push him away. 'It wasn't your fault,' he said.

'I know,' she sobbed. 'I know it wasn't! But I can't stop feeling responsible all the same. It eats me alive. It has done every day since the accident. I can't stop seeing her face in those last moments; her broken body. She was looking at me, pleading with me, but she couldn't move. I can't switch that memory off.'

'You have to,' Merrick replied. 'She's your daughter. You have to try to turn those awful, vivid memories into the good stuff, don't you see? Do you want to spend the rest of your days thinking of her only in that way? As someone she wasn't, instead of the wonderful, loving, alive person she was?'

'The rest of my days,' Lucy spat. 'I have this one left.'

'Fine!' he snapped back. 'Then use this day to remember your daughter the way she deserves to be remembered.'

Lucy sniffled and she stared at him in disbelief.

'I'm sorry,' he said, immediately regretting his outburst. 'It's hard, I know it is. But Nicola deserves that from you. It's about time someone dragged you kicking and screaming out of this sea of self-pity you've decided to take a swim in. I know how you feel, you're not the only one who's had loved ones ripped away from you without warning.'

'Oh for heaven's -'

'I'm trying to tell you that you're not the only person who has suffered,' he said. 'I've had to let those I love go too, more times than you this past three hundred -'

'Stop it!' she shouted back. 'Stop telling that ridiculous story, I can't bear it anymore!'

Aware that the skipper was trying to listen to everything, Merrick spoke more quietly. 'Are you so arrogant as to think you know all there is to know about the world?' he asked. 'Not that I can claim to have never thought the same, but my view has changed. I was given a gift. I've been allowed a different perspective from yours. I've seen things, felt things. I've lived two lives.'

She glared at him, her lips tightly closed.

'I know what this sounds like but 'm not lying, Lucy. I swear it.'

Merrick wished he knew what she was thinking, as was his power when leading the geese. What she was feeling - this woman who couldn't accept that she had a life, even if it was God's will that this one would be brief. He wasn't going to get through to Lucy, she was dead already. In spite of the disease that had ravaged her body and the disability she'd never let hold her back, she was lost. She had been since Nicola's tragic demise. As her face turned away toward Scarba again, he watched her intently, feeling helpless. He'd always taken care of his family, watching

245

over every being that came into his skein. Whether Lucy realised it or not, she was within his skein now; he was responsible for her. To end her life, she needed him. No matter how determined Lucy was she couldn't do what she had planned without his help. He didn't know how he was going to live with himself after that, even if she was terminally ill. He'd never helped a member of his flock - or another human being - to die.

The boat was drawing closer; Merrick saw the blurry lines of the land become clearer and more defined. He could make out a shoreline. Staring at the rich, densely forested edges of the tiny island he wondered if he'd ever flown over it before. Had he come this way in the countless years when he had tried and failed to find Gladys? He'd always believed she must be somewhere on Islay. Why hadn't he at least looked here, only an ocean crossing away?

Lucy had turned her whole body away, her intention to ignore him for the last part of the journey obvious. Sighing, he let his mind leave her problems a while for his own. He recalled the beginning, when it had been the most difficult for him. The day Merrick found his wings and flew back to Gladys after his metamorphosis. The shock had been immeasurable when he'd arrived to find the witch hunters hauling her away to burn. He had swooped and dived at them, only to be batted, chased and jabbed at. The people cheered and dragged her, bound by ropes, to the pyre, screaming, 'Burn the witch! And her familiar!'

The 'familiar' they spoke of had been him. Unaware that he could no longer be harmed, he'd escaped the baying crowd and flown for safety. There he could only watch as they took her. She whose love was so true she'd revealed her magic and sacrificed herself to save him. His desperate bark had filled the air as they tied her to a post in the middle of a bonfire and set their torches upon it.

Amid the terrible screams, he'd taken to the sky and flown solo for months thereafter, devastated. In the following spring, he found a few more of his kind and resigned himself to join them. As a gaggle of twenty, they returned to the place where Merrick had lived as a man. This was when he learned the incredible truth: that Gladys didn't burn on that fateful night. She had been taken to Finlaggan on Islay. The witch-hunters had her imprisoned away from the mainland to keep them all safe from evil.

So began the gathering at Loch Gruinard, over three centuries ago. Merrick unwittingly became leader of the geese. He took to the waters of Islay to watch jailers attend to Gladys in her cell, followed by the flock. The group would watch and wait as he flew to the window whenever she was left alone, calling to her through the bars. She must have known it was him, yet, he recollected with a deep sense of remembered pain, she paid no heed. He continued to visit day after day, night after agonising night. Yet food was ample on Islay, where it had become scarce in their former land. As time passed, the migration was one for continued survival. It was no longer a needless search. All his intrinsic needs had changed. And they followed, their numbers growing stronger all the time.

Before long he began to feel the pull of the wild, smell the change of the wind. He heard the voices of his companions as a whole. Merrick was no longer a man; no change was coming that would return him to her. Another land began to call to him, in the whispered scatterings of the earth. He had to break away, and the other geese felt it too, somehow he knew this. Or perhaps, he heard it. As he and the original twenty took to the air and left Islay one spring, the innate need to breed arrived within him. Later, his heart told him to return the following winter, and they did, as forty. By then Gladys was gone. And for all the winters that followed, as his family continued to grow, year upon year, he never found her again.

Until now.

Chapter 51: Dr Britten

Dr Britten hadn't anticipated that he might come across Gladys this easily whilst looking for Lucy. He expected her, a three-hundred-year-old woman, to be deep in hiding. She wouldn't want to draw attention to herself. Yet there she was in front of him, only minutes after he'd landed with a pain-free thud on the ground. Falling out of trees was a cinch, it was drowning he hated the most. Water in the lungs until they were almost fit to burst was extremely uncomfortable. He hated boats and now he knew helicopters weren't his favourite thing either. They made him dizzy.

'I've got tae sit doon a minute,' he told Gladys, reassured that she was going to be alright. He let go of her arm and she stretched up for a better look at him.

'It is you,' she murmured, staring intently at him. 'I cannae believe it. I thought I wis alone.' She shook her head, sitting down on the soggy ground beside him, looking dazed. 'All these years, I thought there wis no one else.'

'I can and I will explain everything,' he told her. 'But first I have an important question to ask.'

'Whit is it, Angus?'

'It's Dr Britten,' he corrected her. 'I stopped calling myself that name a long time ago.'

'You're calling yersel' doctor, now?'

'Yes,' he said, nodding. 'I'm a medicine man; I've always been a medicine man.'

She nodded. 'Aye, that's right,' she said. 'That's what ye were.' She clasped her hands together in front of her mouth and began rocking back and forth, deep in thought. 'It's been such a long time, Angu… I mean, Dr Britten,' she said after a moment. 'Where have ye been? Why didn't ye let me know you were alive?'

The doctor took a deep, slow breath in and rubbed his temples. There was too much to say, so much lost time to make up. 'Okay,' he said finally. 'Let's cut to the most important part of my being here first. Is Lucy here?'

'Lucy?'

'Has a woman in a wheelchair come here?' he elaborated. 'Her name's Lucy.'

She shook her head, puzzled. 'I dinnae see everyone that comes and goes,' she replied. 'But whit with the weather and the regular boat service going doon, there's been no visitors of late. If that helps ye.'

He heaved a sigh of relief. 'That does help,' he replied. 'Very, very much.'

'Who is the lass?'

'She's a patient of mine.'

Gladys's eyes widened. 'A patient, is she?'

'Yes.'

'So you're a real doctor?'

'I've lived five lifetimes, Gladys. In the past two centuries I've earned my doctorate no less than three times,' he explained. 'I'm a universal healer.'

The woman's eyes widened. 'You?' she said. 'A healer? Oh my jings!'

He nodded. 'Yes, and I've lived on the mainland.

'With the people?'

'Yes,' he confirmed. 'I've studied, I've treated the dying and I've saved lives.'

She blinked at him uncertainly. 'What happens when people see that you don't age or die?' she said, after a moment.

He regarded her seriously. 'I told you, I've lived five lifetimes. I simply faked my own death, disappeared for a while and then took on a new identity.'

She sat up straight. 'You can do that?'

He grinned, patting her on the back. 'It wasn't easy, but it was necessary. And I'm going to be able to tell you why,' he said. 'I can explain everything, as soon as Lucy gets here.'

'Who's Lucy?'

Dr Britten sighed, idly scratching an itch on his knee. 'Do you remember Olive?' he said.

Her expression brightened. 'Yes! How do ye know Olive?'

'I sent her to you.'

'It was you?' she exclaimed. 'You're the one that telt Joe to bring Olive here?'

'Yes,' he replied. 'Because I knew you would help her. But this time, I need to make sure you don't do the same for Lucy.'

'Why would I? Is she dying too?'

'Yes,' he said. 'Well, she was. But now she isn't.'

'So ye sent Olive here and then ye sent this Lucy lass?'

'No, I didn't send Lucy, she's decided to come of her own accord.'

'Odd,' Gladys said, 'Scarba isnae whit ye might call a popular destination for the masses.'

'Ah, but she has a specific reason for coming here.'

'Which is?'

'Lucy is Olive's daughter.'

Gladys looked puzzled. 'But Olive isnae here,' she said.

'I know she isn't,' he replied. 'I know what you did for her, but all Lucy knows is that her mother came here to die, and that's what she wants to do, too.'

'She wants tae die?'

'Yes,' he said. 'But only because she thinks she's dying already, as Olive was.'

Gladys's eyes widened, as she stared at him, beseechingly. 'Olive didnae die,' she told him. 'I-'

'I know where she is, Gladys,' Dr Britten said, 'I sent her here because I knew you would help her. But Lucy isn't dying. She thinks she is, but she isn't. She's cured.'

'Well then, you need tae tell her that,' Gladys replied.

'When she gets here, and this will be soon. So, I have to get to her before she takes matters into her own hands, for both our sakes,' he said.

'What do ye mean, "for both our sakes"? I dinnae get it.'

'All will be explained, Gladys,' he told her. 'What I need right now is for you to take me right away to the place that boats most frequently come to shore on this island. We can talk more when we get there. I'm ready to tell you everything.'

Chapter 52: Lucy

Lucy remembered the day she'd left Islay. Determined not to look back to where the sorrows of a lonely, difficult past lived, she'd made her move. The island of Islay signified childhood; the mainland, a new beginning. Her journey to womanhood had begun the moment her coach rolled from the ferry and out onto the open road. She'd pressed her cheek against the window, watching hedges and trees pass by in a blur as the bus gathered speed. Before long she'd noticed a roaring sound inside her ear as, at the same time, windblown trees waved at her. As an adult, she knew the sound was the whir of rubber tyres on asphalt. Yet, at seventeen, it was as though nature was cheering; crying out a fond, yet sad farewell to her.

Now, the isle of Scarba watched them arrive, cutting itself from the sky as they approached. The island had few trees thanks to centuries of being battered by the wind, but they waved a welcome all the same. By the time their boat reached the shore, the weather had decided to be a friend at last. The clouds parted and the sun appeared above the horizon – honey spilled over a sheet of glass. It was as though summer had arrived for a second glance at the year.

'Looks like there's been some excitement here.'

The skipper pointed to a helicopter that flew overhead as they neared the jetty.

'I'm not going to stop,' the skipper went on. 'These waters have been a bit unpredictable of late, so I'll be dropping you both off as instructed. Are you sure you don't need me to come back?' He eyed them both, clearly wondering why they had no supplies along for the trip. 'It can get pretty wild out here,' he added.

Lucy shook her head.

'Well, if you're sure,' he replied, turning off the engine. He walked to the bow, picked up the anchor and threw it over the side before glancing back at her. She saw what he was thinking; it was written all over his face. Why would anyone come to this wild, rugged place with no baggage? No waterproofs? No maps? And in a bloody wheelchair? She wanted to say what she always said in response to the Are You Okay Brigade:

'I'm fine.'

'I can cope.'

'Do I look like I need a nursemaid?'

Seeing her scowl, Merrick saved her. 'It'll be magic, thanks. I can take it from here,' he said to the skipper, taking away the need for her to say anymore. He allowed the man to help him lift the wheelchair out on to the jetty and thanked him. Then he turned around to face Lucy, opening his arms toward her. 'Are you willing to accept another lift from me, my lady?' he asked.

'Absolutely.' Lucy smiled as he lifted her gently from the bow of the boat. Any last doubts about why she was here now left her as he swung around to show her the beautiful landscape. This was the view that would have been the last place her mother saw. As he placed her into the opened out chair, she found herself facing out to sea again. Yet it was all so captivating, this hidden, forgotten corner of Scotland. She looked at the calm, untroubled waters from where they'd come. And then, out over the great whirlpool, to the right of the land. The skipper had avoided sailing through it and she was glad. With the sun illuminating the water, she observed the vast swirling, twisting current. It drew huge figures of eight on the surface of the sea, between Scarba and the isle of Jura at the other side.

'I didn't notice the whirlpool from the boat,' she remarked to Merrick, who had paused to look at it too.

'No, me neither,' he agreed. 'It's a wonder, isn't it?'

'It should be the eighth wonder of the world,' she said.

The skipper lifted anchor and took his place behind the wheel. As he steered away towards Islay, the pair watched the boat leave. Lucy marvelled at the skill of the people that sailed these waters. It was amazing how they knew exactly how to navigate the Corryvreckan. She imagined it as a huge hole under the sea where someone had let the plug out. At its base the water swirled around, making its way out of the depths. Nobody may ever know all that was lost to it. Perhaps she would be too.

'Lucy, I am surprised at you,' Merrick said and she turned to look up at him. 'You struck me as someone who had resigned herself to stop caring about the wonders of this world.'

She shrugged. 'I'm dying, but I'm not dead yet.'

'And what if I told you that you don't have to?'

'I'd say you were a kind man, but absolutely and unequivocally bonkers,' she told him.

He sighed, disappearing behind as she felt him taking the brake off the wheelchair.

'But despite this, I like you, Merrick, I really do,' she continued. 'I want you to go and get some help after I'm gone, please. I don't have long left, and when life-altering things happen to you it gives you rare insight. I fear there's so little time to say everything about... well... stuff. I hadn't thought of any of this before, but then I saw Mr and Mrs Toe and some things I'd been trying to block out came back.'

Merrick walked back round to face her and frowned. 'What are you going on about?' he asked.

'Like how important they were... are to me.'

His expression brightened. 'And can you see your own life in those terms now, Lucy? Do you want to live?'

She shook her head. 'Don't you see, Merrick? Don't you believe me? I've accepted death; I know that I'm dying. But you were right when you said that I wasn't on my own. That's what's changed me, the knowledge that there are still people who care. It's forced me to see things with my heart much, much sooner. I've seen my mistakes now, and the people I'd forgotten I cared about. I pushed them out of my mind because I felt they were somehow attached to my bad memories of my mother.'

Merrick blew out his cheeks and she saw him look uphill before he disappeared behind her again.

'And I know... I just know there isn't any more time for games or play-acting,' she continued. 'I can't pretend I haven't noticed, Merrick. That you may be... I don't know... ill? Get some counselling. Because I don't mind saying, now that I'm so close to leaving this life behind, that I've been very fond of it all. That, in fact, I'm very fond of -'

'She's here!'

Interrupted by this shout from Merrick, Lucy tried to turn far enough in her chair to see what he could see. 'Who?' she asked. 'Who's here?'

But her answer came only in the sound of feet – Merrick's feet – trudging through sand and jagged pebbles. They got further and further away as he ran, she imagined, up the hillside somewhere behind her. He was rushing to meet the love of his life, someone Lucy knew wasn't real. Poor, disillusioned man.

Chapter 53: Gladys

Gladys felt her knees give way once more, as her brain struggled to believe the vision before her eyes. Wis that...? Could it be...? 'Merrick?' she said, as Angus rushed forward to steady her, stopping her from falling down in shock.

The man was scrambling up the craggy hillside, his rust-red hair glistening brightly. It was redder than she remembered. Of course, her senses were heightened now, all thanks to Olive. It was him, right then she knew it, even before he had gotten to within three feet of them.

'I have tae sit down,' she said, doing so as Merrick finally reached her.

He stood over her, breathless from exertion. 'I've found you!' he cried between breaths, 'I've found you at last! I can't believe you were here all this time!'

'Merrick?'

It was Angus that had spoken, and Gladys put a hand on his thigh, nodding her head to him. 'It's true,' she said, 'It's him, Angus!'

'He's alive?'

She nodded. 'The spell,' she said simply. 'I gave it tae him.' Turning from Angus to Merrick, she searched his expression for anger but found none. He was home again; back down to earth. Did he hate her as she'd feared he would? 'Come here, laddie,' she beckoned to him. 'I need tae see your face. I need to touch it; tae know you're real.'

Smiling, Merrick knelt down in front of her and she reached out, placing a hand on his cheek. Hurt, confusion and bitterness was what she'd expected to find were they ever to meet again. But all she saw in his expression was love, still there, in spite of everything. Then, at last, after three hundred years apart from each other, they embraced. Feeling his arms around her and sensing a joy that matched hers, Gladys thought her heart might burst. She had never been so happy. 'After all... all this... time,' she stammered, hardly able to believe the moment was real.

'I looked for you,' he told her through tears. 'I promise, I did.'

'I know,' she soothed, patting his back. 'It's not your fault, it's mine. I hid from ye, I thought... I thought -'

'But how did you find her?' she heard Angus say.

Gladys pulled back from Merrick's embrace to see Angus indicating, not to her, but toward the seashore. There, a woman in a wheelchair sat with her back to them, trying desperately, it seemed, to turn the chair around.

'How did you find Lucy?' Angus asked Merrick again.

Still breathing hard, Merrick wiped tears from his eyes and got to his feet. 'How do you know Lucy?' he asked, looking perplexed.

'I'm her doctor.'

There was a pause as both men studied each other, neither speaking.

'This is ma friend, Angus,' Gladys explained. 'He's the one wae the magic that made ye a goose, Merrick. That saved yer life.'

Merrick's eyes widened, but as he opened his mouth to speak, the woman at the shore called to him.

'Merrick! Where are you?'

'You have to come, come with me,' he said quickly, pulling Gladys up by her hands. 'I need you to see Lucy.' He peered at Angus. 'I think... I think I need you both to see her.'

Allowing him to drag her up to standing, Gladys had a flash of recognition. A memory; something about this name: Lucy. She looked again at the woman on the jetty below and then at Angus. 'Is that her?' she asked him. 'Is that Olive's wee girl?'

Angus nodded slowly, but he wasn't looking at Gladys. He was watching Lucy, deep in thought. 'Merrick is the immortal gander,' he said, as if to himself.

'She's someone I need you to help,' Merrick said to Gladys.

'No!' Angus shouted, so loudly it startled them both. 'You're not to help her. You can't, and you don't have to.'

'What the -' Merrick began. 'Hey, wait! Who are you anyway?' He looked at Gladys. 'Who or what is this man?'

Angus kept his gaze fixed on Gladys. 'She isn't dying,' he told her. 'Not like Olive was. She's cured. She's the reason we're here. The reason we will soon be ready to die ourselves.'

Gladys felt her stomach drop. 'We will?'

'What does he mean?' Merrick insisted. He tugged at her arm but she couldn't look at him. A mixture of emotions overcame her and she closed her eyes, feeling like she couldn't breathe. Looking forward to death was all her yesterdays, only now she had Merrick back. The world was no longer as bleak as it had been. They'd lost so much time. How could she deal with finding then losing him again all in the same day?

'I dinnae want the pain,' she said at last, realising that the knuckles on the hands she held in Merrick's had begun to ache again. It was subtle, dull ache, yet there. She hadn't noticed it until now. Opening her eyes, she turned to Angus. 'Make it go away again,' she begged him. 'Please! I dinnae want to die the day.'

He put his hands on his hips, still studying Lucy. 'It won't be today,' he said. 'Things are shifting at last. They started, I suspect, when Lucy left the mainland. Perhaps they stopped when Merrick fell back to ground. I assume you fell, right?' He turned to Merrick, who squinted uncertainly back and nodded. 'And now, by some miraculous game of chance, the two have arrived here together. It's extraordinary,' Angus added, his mouth curving into a smile.

'Merrick!' The shout had come from the woman again, still sat facing out to sea where Merrick had left her.

'We should go to her,' Angus said. He started downhill, until Merrick jumped in front of him.

'I'll be there in a minute!' Merrick called back to Lucy, signalling for Angus to stop. 'You say you're her doctor?' he said, his lower lip quivering.

'Yes, Lucy knows me.'

'And she's cured?

'By you,' he replied.

'Me?'

'Merrick,' Angus said, putting a hand on his shoulder. 'Did you have a permanent mate?'

The corners of Merrick's eyes crinkled. 'What?'

'Did you find one, constant companion when you were a barnacle goose?' he insisted. 'One that lived for years, like you?'

'No,' he replied, sadness clouding his features. 'I had several mates, of course. But none that lived as long as me.'

'Have you one that has lived for twice as long as all the rest?' Angus cut in. He looked back at Gladys and she met his gaze, uncertain about where his questions were leading.

Merrick scratched his head and then he looked up, eyes wide with astonishment. 'Yes,' he said. 'The mate I have now. How did you know that?'

Gladys stared again at the woman waiting in the chair, and then back at Angus, who smiled warmly at her. And, recognition dawning on her face, she knew, the whole story – all of it. She knew.

Noticing her eyes light up, Merrick gave her a questioning glance. 'What?' he asked.

'Your mate,' she replied quietly. 'It's Olive, isn't it?' she added, addressing the question to Angus, who dipped his chin in wordless confirmation. Her eyes glistened.

'They had the same disease,' Angus said, his brows snapping together. 'The one I was destined to cure. I'm a healer, Gladys. A universal healer, do you understand now?'

Gladys's eyes went round. 'Of course!' she exclaimed.

'A healer?' Merrick mumbled. 'What's that?'

'They're related and both afflicted,' Angus went on, ignoring him. 'Although I'm not sure how that's possible yet. It's a first, for sure. But I knew it was the geese all along, I felt it! I've waited for this day! All my instincts were leading me to this place in time; all my work. But never, ever did I know how or what it was about them.'

Gladys covered her mouth with her hand, feeling a surge of both relief and amazement. 'This is whit it was all for? The two spells?' she asked him.

He smiled. 'Yes,' he replied. 'I thought I only needed the species to propagate through time, but something was missing. Even after Olive, when two immortal geese of opposing genders were together, I couldn't find the key to it all.' He looked at Gladys now and she saw that he too had tears in his eyes. 'It was Lucy,' he said, pointing to her. 'She was the key. Somehow, between her and her mother, they've brought about a reversal of symptoms. Now all I have to do is work out why.' Angus stepped to one side of Merrick, who took his hand away, allowing him to go to Lucy.

Elated, Gladys walked behind Merrick and placed a hand briefly on his shoulder.

So it was over after all, the beginning of the end. She squeezed the aching knuckles of one hand with the other. Then, remembering her fate, her heart felt heavy. Yet somewhere ahead of time she sensed it would all become lighter. The weight of her long life was about to be lifted at last. She walked round beside Merrick and reached for his hand, he who was the long-time keeper of her heart. 'Ye have to return to her, Merrick,' she told him gently. 'Ye have to go back tae Olive.'

Merrick pursed his lips. 'That's what I came here to do,' he replied. 'But no matter what happens I can't leave Lucy behind like this, I can't!'

She saw in his glossy-wet eyes now that like her, he too was conflicted in his emotions. 'But she disnae need us,' Gladys said. 'Lucy's cured. Angus knows, Merrick; he's a universal healer. He may not know why the now, but he'll find out. Healer's know; their minds are attuned to an authentic, guiding spiritual truth.'

'I didn't know such people existed,' he said. 'You never told me any of this.'

'I couldnae dae that to ye,' Gladys replied. 'Ye already knew too much to make it in those terrible, witch-hunting times. But I had no idea Angus wis one o' them healers until now. I hadn't believed the things he told me. I thought he was a wee bit glaiket.'

'But you used the spell.'

'To try and save ye from burning, I'd have done anything! I didnae know whether it would work or no until ye flew from that room.'

His eyes swam with tears. 'You did it to save me?'

'I had tae protect you. And now we have tae protect life; all life.'

Merrick sighed, his eyelids drooping. 'But it doesn't matter that Lucy is cured,' he told her. 'She wants to die.'

Gladys watched Angus reach Lucy and lean in to speak to her. 'She willnae when she kens everything,' she said to Merrick.

'She won't believe us,' he said. 'She won't believe any of this, I know it. I know her. You have to help me change her mind.'

'Change her mind about whit?'

'About dying,' he said. And then, he added something which almost tore out Gladys's very soul. 'Lucy came here to be helped to die because she's all alone in the world. She feels she has nothing to live for. You have to make her see that she has a life; something worth holding on to.'

His beautiful eyes pleaded with her, melting her heart as they had done before. She recalled the day he came screaming into her life, changing everything – the years of solitude she had come to accept as her lot. She had fallen in love once, and from that love, came Merrick.

'Please,' he pleaded. 'Please, you can't leave until we've saved her, mother.'

Chapter 54: Merrick

Merrick looked at the jaggy, muddy slopes and knew there was only one way to get Lucy to the bothy to hear what Angus had to say. They had to carry her. He looked over at the doctor, noting he seemed so out of place here in his suit, shiny shoes and over-sized luminous jacket. 'I think I might need your help,' he told him.

Dr Britten nodded. 'Okay,' he agreed. 'It is turning a little colder in the wind, despite all this sunshine.'

'That's Scarba for you,' Gladys remarked. 'Four seasons in a day, every day.'

As Gladys and Merrick stooped to collect her, Lucy said, 'Wait! Don't I get a say in all of this?'

Merrick knelt down in front of her, tears misting his eyes. 'Do you trust me, Lucy?' he asked.

She blinked, touching his chin with her palm. 'I don't want you to be sad,' she told him.

'Then come, please. At least listen to us.'

'But this is where I wanted -'

'Please, Lucy,' Merrick pleaded.

She stared gloomily back at him and heaved a despondent outbreath. 'Okay,' she relented. 'I'll come, but only because Dr Britten here is probably arranging to have me sectioned as we speak.'

'I can confirm that I have absolutely no signal right at this moment,' the doctor responded, offering her a weak smile.

'Good,' Lucy snapped back.

'Shall we go then?' Merrick asked her.

She dipped her chin, murmuring, 'Yes,' under her breath.

Merrick looked up at Gladys. 'And what about you, are you fit to help?'

She rubbed her hands uncertainly before nodding.

'Good,' he said stoically, 'because I need your help too. We have to carry Lucy here to shelter, and this chair will never make it over this boggy ground. Where are you living?'

'Not far from here,' she said.

'It's just a quarter of a mile up the hill,' Angus added.

'Then come and help me carry her, and you,' Merrick looked at Angus, 'you carry her wheelchair.'

'You promised to help me,' Lucy hissed at Merrick, as he and Gladys heaved her out of her chair. 'Why won't you leave me alone!'

'It's okay,' he said to Gladys, as he saw she was struggling to take the weight. 'I'll take her myself.' Gathering Lucy fully into his arms, he peered down at her sombre face. Her cheeks were still damp from tears she was trying hard to keep in. 'I never left anybody alone in my life,' he told her firmly. 'And I'm not about to start now.'

266

Chapter 55: Dr Britten

'The first thing I have to tell you, Lucy is that my name is not Britten. It's Campbell. Angus Campbell.'

'Angus Campbell?' Lucy repeated, staring at the doctor in disbelief.

He nodded.

'But you are a real doctor, right?'

'Yes, of course,' Angus confirmed. 'I have earned my doctorate more than once. You see, Lucy, I've been alive for four centuries. First I was a medicine man. Later I came to realise that I was a universal healer. The qualification had to come in more modern times.'

Lucy blinked at the doctor, then looked from him to Merrick and finally, to Gladys. 'Are you all out of your actual minds?' she asked, her eyes flashing. 'I mean, you are all in this together, right?'

'Just listen to him,' Merrick said softly. 'I know this is a lot to digest.'

'Well, you've got that much right,' Lucy snapped.

Angus sighed. 'Lucy, there are a lot of things in this world that can't be properly explained by anyone,' he went on. 'Like when several members of the same family, both alive and dead, share the same birth date. Like women who live together beginning to ovulate at the same time. Why do you think these things happen, Lucy? Do you – does anybody – have answers for everything?'

Lucy shrugged. 'Because coincidences happen?'

'Because there is a higher order,' Angus said. 'There's a place between this world and the next that very few can truly access. Universal healers can, and so can geese.'

'Hah,' she scoffed, turning to Merrick. 'You're a member of this order too, then?'

He stared blankly back, but didn't speak.

'Universal healers are vital to all life,' Angus explained. 'Over the last 200 years, the average human life expectancy has doubled. We have helped this process.'

'It's because somebody discovered penicillin,' Lucy remarked, the corners of her mouth curving into a wry smile.

Angus nodded enthusiastically. 'Yes, yes!' he exclaimed. 'But there were prerequisites for that discovery. Things that had to fall into place at a specific time in order to allow it to happen. In each case of a cure, there has been a single soul involved in creating, shall we say, opportunities? Working out the higher order of things; how man and nature work to coexist. That person was a universal healer,' he told her.

Lucy nodded. 'Oh… kay…' she said, still smirking.

'Okay, so, you must have questions. Do you?' he asked her.

'I have a question,' Gladys said. 'Why didn't you tell me all this all those years ago? We could have solved this much earlier by working together.'

'Would you have believed me if I had?' he replied. 'I gave you the spells and at first you lost them.'

'You did?' Merrick said, his eyes widening.

'It's true,' she confirmed, her face flushing. 'I did think you were a little… err… misguided. I didn't ask for this eternal life curse, though. You could have at least warned me about that part.'

'I needed you to protect the spells.'

'You have spells?' Lucy shot back. 'Then hallelujah, we're all cured!'

Angus shook his head and looked at the ground. 'If only it was that simple,' he said. 'I don't have all the answers, I've never claimed to. I simply have a gift that allows me to see further than the average human. I can concoct, deduce, create, do a little magic, but I can't heal the world. My task is to cure what I now know to be Morsley's Pholblastoma. That is all I am put here to do.'

'But why barnacle geese?' Gladys asked. 'Whit has that tae dae wi' a higher order?'

'I always believed that the tree geese had the power to heal,' he explained. 'But I wasn't ready to tell anyone until my work was complete.'

'How is it now?' she said.

'Because the cure is in the blood of the geese,' he replied simply.

'Oh,' Lucy said, her eyes flashing in anger as she glared from the doctor back to Merrick. 'So you are much more than a man,' she said to him. 'You are, or were in fact, an immortal barnacle goose. And you,' she turned back to Angus, 'are much more than my doctor. You're a universal healer, sent to ensure the longevity of man, am I getting this so far?'

Even though he guessed from her tone she was being sarcastic, Angus nodded. 'It's true,' he told her in earnest. 'There have been many of us. All destined to stay on earth until our given task is complete.'

'And you're a healer too? A person who can't die?' she said to Gladys, who didn't reply.

'Well, that part isn't technically true,' Angus said. 'Because now we're all here and the cure is ready to be revealed to the world, Gladys should, as has been her wish from the beginning, begin to expire at last.'

'Expire?' said Merrick, screwing up his nose and looking perplexed.

'Die,' the doctor confirmed.

'But whit have we solved?' Gladys asked. 'Was it that Lucy isnae gonnae die?'

'I'm not?'

269

'No, you're not,' Angus told Lucy. He knelt down in front of her chair, took her hand in his and looked into her eyes. 'Lucy,' he said. 'I want you to listen to me, and listen well.'

'Okay,' she said, looking more unsettled.

'Those tests we ran, the ones that were sent to the doctors in Japan,' he said. 'They came good at last, you're cured.' He waited for her response, a shocked expression, excitement, joy – but she simply stared back, her expression laced with scepticism.

'I know you're only here to stop me going through with this,' she announced finally. 'But you're not going to change my mind. I have nothing to live for. Can't you all leave me alone?'

He sighed, putting a hand to his temples. The action gave him an idea. 'Lucy, have you had any headaches lately?' he asked. 'Any dizziness? A dry mouth? Bouts of vomiting?'

'That was the medication doing that,' she said, matter-of-factly. 'And in case you didn't know, I'm not taking any of it anymore.'

'It was the disease in your brain that gave you the headaches,' he told her. 'And the occasional memory loss, have you had any of that?'

'She's been fine,' Merrick cut in. 'I've been with her for two days. You've been fine,' he said to her.

'I told you, my body is ready to accept the inevitable,' she said. 'I'm not fighting it. It's over. The disease has won. I'm only sorry that you came this far to try and change everything. Come to think of it,' she added, 'how did you know I was here? I never told a soul.'

'Because this is where your mother went.'

'How do you know that?'

'Because it was I that sent Olive here.'

'This is ridiculous,' Lucy groaned, her eyes misting up.

'I sent her here to save her life,' the doctor said. 'She didn't leave you, Lucy, she was dying of the same thing you have - *had*. You're the missing link in all of our research. You and your mother, who I never realised you were related to until I got your note and set out to try and find you. I had no idea her case and yours were related, it's never happened before. As far as we're aware, there are no other hereditary cases, yours is somehow, miraculously unique. You're the reason the cure works, Lucy. Your genetic make-up must carry exactly the right mix. You are a product of your mother, who had the disease, and her blood now, which carries the cure.'

'What do you mean, her blood now?' Lucy said, her bemused expression of earlier turning to anger. 'My mother drowned here in these waters. She died.'

'Now I'm confused too,' Merrick said. 'Who brought me back then, if the blood of my kin is so needed?'

'Somebody had to have read the reversal spell,' Angus said, looking questioningly at Gladys.

'I hid it,' Gladys explained quickly. 'I didnae want Merrick tae fall from the sky; tae be hurt. I didnae ken where he might be, how high up! I -'

'Where did you hide it?' Merrick and Angus said together.

Gladys swallowed. 'It wis my pal, Joe that took it for me. I asked him tae press it into the wishing tree at Finlaggan.'

Lucy's eyes went round. 'I know that tree!' she announced. 'The one with coins pushed into the bark!'

'Aye, that's it,' Gladys said, nodding.

Angus stared at Lucy, noting the change in her eyes from disbelief to recognition.

'But I went there,' she cried. 'On my mother's last day; the day she left. I was hiding in the back of the truck and I heard her talking to the boatman. She said she was taking a note to

271

the tree!'

'So it wis Olive that hid the spell,' Gladys said, her eyebrows knitting. 'But she wis so confused.' She looked at Angus. 'Maybes she didnae dae it right and someone found it.'

'Oh yes she did do it right,' Lucy said.

Gladys looked at her. 'How do ye know?'

'Because after she died I went and fetched it,' she replied. Her eyelids drooped and Angus saw the tears come all at once. 'I mean, she didn't get it exactly right because the paper was just poking out, fluttering in the wind behind the coin. But I thought it was for me; a note for my Advice Bucket.'

'Your what?' said Merrick.

Gladys blew out her cheeks, her astonished face flushing crimson. 'They both had the same disease,' she said quietly, silencing them all. 'It's in the goose blood ye said, isn't it?' She looked at Angus, who nodded.

'Then I ken whit happened,' she explained. Her forehead creased and she picked up the poker from the fireplace and stabbed at the floor with it. 'I ken why Lucy's ill. It's the wishing tree.'

Angus raised his eyebrows. 'Oh heavens!' he exclaimed. 'You don't think -?'

'What?' Lucy said.

The doctor stood up, walked to the window and looked outside, shaking his head.

'People who are sick go tae the wishing tree to press a coin intae the bark,' Gladys went on. 'This is supposed to put whatever ails them in the tree and leave it there, the idea being that they get better.'

'Which doesn't always happen, I might add,' Angus remarked.

'But the legend goes that anyone who takes oot that coin will transfer the illness to themselves,' Gladys explained. 'And on this occasion, who knows?' She looked at the doctor. 'Maybe Lucy took her mother's sickness. It could be true.'

Angus nodded. 'Well, like I said,' he replied. 'Nobody knows everything in this world.'

'But where is the spell?' Merrick cut in. He stared at Lucy. 'Where is it now? Did you read it?'

She frowned. 'Yes, I did,' she admitted. 'I kept it in my grandmother's bucket and read it from time to time. I always wanted to believe it was some kind of final goodbye or advice note from my mother to me, but it was gibberish. Then, on the day before I left for Islay -'

'You read it aloud,' Angus finished for her.

He turned around to see Lucy and Merrick, eyes wide, staring at each other. Merrick was the first to speak:

'Lucy,' he cried. 'It was you! You brought me back!'

Chapter 56: Lucy

'Do any of you have any idea how incredible this all sounds?' Lucy said, peering up at the other three in utter disbelief.

'But you said it yourself, you read out the spell,' Merrick said.

'I said I read a load of gibberish from a note,' she bit back. 'I don't remember what it said and, in case you haven't noticed, I'm no witch.'

'Lucy, ye turned Merrick intae a man again,' Gladys explained, placing a hand on her arm.

Lucy pulled away from her. 'Oh, nonsense!' she roared, anger rising in her throat.

'Do you believe that you're cured?' Angus asked her.

'I believe nothing any of you crazy people have to say,' she snapped back. 'This is ludicrous. And using my own, dead mother to get to me too!'

'She isn't dead,' Gladys said quietly. 'She's alive and well. She's the cure. It's your mother that has saved your life, Lucy.'

'I don't understand,' Merrick said. 'Are you telling me my mate is Lucy's mother?'

Angus nodded. 'And the cure is now in your blood as well as the blood of all your kin to come,' he said. 'That's what I have been testing ever since Olive came here. I started to study the barnacle geese, their migration habits, and the populace. Ever since Gladys changed Olive and the Greenland genus's population began to rise on a more consistent basis. After years of the figures crawling up, then falling off. It was because there were two mortal geese now, instead of one. I don't know why I didn't think of it before Olive -'

'Before Olive what?' Lucy demanded. 'What are you all talking about, Dr Britten – or whatever your bloody name is? This is madness!'

Angus bit his lip. 'Before Olive was changed into an immortal barnacle goose,' he said at last.

Lucy threw her hands into the air in exasperation.

'Like me?' Merrick said quietly.

'We've done it,' Dr Britten said to Gladys, ignoring him in his excitement. 'We've done what we're supposed to do, albeit in a roundabout, three hundred year way, but it's over.' He looked at Lucy. 'You have to come back with me. You have to care again about your life, because you're about to help me save thousands of lives.'

'Sure I am.'

'Yes!' he cried, taking her by the shoulders and giving her a shake, which did nothing to remove the scowl from her face. 'Maybe more than thousands, we may never know the true figure in our own lifetimes.'

'Extraordinary,' Lucy exclaimed, the incredulity in her voice still evident. 'Well, it's good to know I might have such an impact on the world. And now I expect you'd all like me to go with the good doctor back to my place of pain, misery and a certain, undignified slow death.'

Gladys's eyes narrowed. 'You think I, trapped for eternity on an obscure island in the Hebrides, could collude with anyone to make up this story for you?' She sniffed, stooping to pick up a thin piece of wood beside the fire before tossing it angrily in. 'One small action creates reactions,' she said, pointing to crackling wood as it slowly began to burn. 'Do you see that? But if you choose to give credence to all of these "coincidences" instead, then I suppose I could have guessed your mother's name, couldn't I?'

'I'm sorry to have to tell you this, lady,' Lucy went on, her irate expression unchanged. 'But my mother is dead. She didn't even have the decency to leave me a bucket!'

'What the hell is this bucket all about?' Merrick asked sullenly.

'Oh, *that*,' Gladys said at once, rising up from her seat and turning her back on Lucy. She walked over towards the door.

'Look, Lucy, I came here to tell you that your life has in no way been for nothing; that there are things to live for,' the doctor continued. 'You're not going to die! Now please, I implore you,' he held out his hand to her. 'Come back home with me.'

'You don't understand,' she said, her eyes begin to tear up. 'None of this grand act of yours matters, even if it's true and I *am* cured, I don't have anything to live for anyway. I mean, forget Morsley's Pholblastoma. So I may be in remission and thank you so much for going to all this trouble to find me and tell me. But I don't want to be alone anymore. I've wanted to die ever since...' she hesitated, drawing in breath that felt more like thick, heavy soup than air. 'I want to be with Nicola,' she went on. 'Screw everything else. Screw my life. I don't want it anymore.'

Gladys grunted as she rattled a tin bucket on the windowsill.

'Lucy,' Angus went on, 'you don't get to give back a gift like your own life, you can't. Do you know how many people would wish to have what you have today?'

'Don't put all that on me,' Lucy shot back. 'I'm not everyone else. This is my life and I want the right to end it my way, when I choose and in the way of my choosing. Just like my mum.'

From the corner of her eye, Lucy saw Gladys take a piece of paper from the tin bucket and unravel it.

'Your mum didn't leave you,' the doctor said to Lucy, 'Olive was dying. She felt, in order to shield you from everything she was about to go through, it was the quickest, cleanest way out.'

'And she was a very confused lady at the end,' Gladys added, turning around to face her with the bucket in her hand. 'She couldn't recall the most recent memories. She wasn't aware she was leaving you without a word. Sometimes she thought you were here with us.'

Lucy didn't speak. Her eyes were fixed upon the bucket. 'Don't!' she barked. 'Don't you play your games with me, especially when it concerns my mother!'

'She isn't dead,' Gladys insisted. 'This is hers.' She shook the bucket. 'You recognise it, don't you?'

'I -' Lucy's mouth fell open.

'She isn't dead. And I can prove it, right now in fact.'

Lucy began to cry. 'My mother died right here, on this island. She came here to drown herself.'

'Yes, she did,' Gladys agreed with a nod. 'Just like you. But she didn't die here, no, no, no! She went on.'

'You have to listen to this,' the doctor implored Lucy.

'She went on,' Gladys insisted more quietly, seeming to be speaking to herself now.

'To some idea of the other side, I suppose is what I'm supposed to take from this?' Lucy snapped back. 'Do you think I'm insane like you? And you.' She turned to glare at Merrick, who bit his lip in wordless answer to her. 'And you, you can go home too,' she said to him. 'Please. Just leave me alone.'

'She went on,' Gladys mumbled. She put down the bucket and took a seat before flattening out the crumpled paper on her knee. 'Olive lived. Do you think you could recognise her writing or her thoughts, my girl?' She pointed to the tin bucket. 'This bit o' paper,' she went on, waving it at Lucy. 'Do you want to know what it says?'

The others fell silent, and a flood of tears slipped down Lucy's cheek, as Gladys read out the note.

'It says, "Before I die, this is for The Goose. My beautiful, Lucy-Goosey."'

Chapter 57: Dr Britten

The doctor observed the three, curious-looking faces that watched him as he stood over the fire, prodding at the flaming wood with a poker. 'This will take a lot of explaining,' he told them all. 'But I will do my best.'

Placing the poker back on its hook, he sat down on a chair, placing both hands on his knees. 'I, and hundreds of universal healers before me, have been consistently working to keep fresh the theory that there is something in nature that will cure every human ill,' he explained. 'We keep it fresh because it is the truth. For humankind to be allowed to forget would be the beginning of the end of everything.

There are those who have worked to bring about certain dependencies on a massive scale to counteract this – to make us forget - all in the name of profit. Profit against nature; greed and self-interest before the human lives. It is an age-old concern. We have seen it in the discovery of previously denied public health hazards, such as tobacco and sugar. There have been cover ups on a global scale for the protection of continued financial gain. All all the while, people have suffered. Medicine men have come and gone over the centuries, but we are tested by this new enemy in modern times: industry working to hasten humankind's demise. We have been forced to stay longer; our healing work disadvantaged by these human dependencies.

Hippocrates said, "First do no harm". He meant that before prescribing medication we should try good food and exercise. What you eat becomes your body and what you drink becomes your blood. Industry has poured poisons into our bodies and our blood and while it remains true that we are what we eat, we are closer to extinction each time we chose industrial over natural resources.

For my own efforts, I had been testing a treatment that involved the blood of geese. I'd been studying it for three hundred years in my efforts to cure a multitude of ills. It was I that created the first barnacle goose. You may remember the story that they came from nature – specifically, the trees; and fell upon the land. This is true. It was a creature born of phytonutrients of the natural world. Yet, after creating it, I only saw depletion, not propagation, of the species. They started small, numbers steadily grew and then, by a process of natural selection, culling and environmental issues, these numbers declined again.

I was flummoxed. I was so close to a medical miracle, yet so far. How could I keep the momentum going? I needed to be able to keep testing them.

And so I created the spells. I adapted them from my originals; the ones I used for the creation of the geese from barnacles. I simply had to alter it to create an immortal goose from man himself. And later, much later, when this single, immortal male failed to produce the numbers or the cure, I had the idea to send a female. Only this one was predisposed to Morsley's Pholblastoma. It was a hunch based on a study of the genetic markers of the disease. Little did I know that her daughter would contract the disease to complete the cycle of events that would lead me to this day.

We have a cure, after years and years of research. My initial hunch has at last been proven. The barnacle geese have the potential for so much more, thanks to the healing power and soul wisdom of the trees they evolved from.'

'But I still don't understand what trees have to do with geese? Why did you put these two completely different things together?' Merrick asked.

Lucy scowled at Merrick, groaning loudly. 'This is bunkum,' she complained.

Ignoring her, Dr Britten went on, 'As I said, it was a hunch. I realised that trees channel energy vibrations from the earth. It seemed logical to me to combine this energy - this healing power - from the fruit of a tree with the synchronistic power of a goose.'

Merrick's eyebrows knitted. 'Synchronistic power?'

Dr Britten nodded. 'Yes, Merrick. You must have been aware of the higher energy that led you?'

Merrick stared blankly back.

'Okay,' Dr Britten continued. 'Let me explain. In flight, a goose has to synchronise itself with the communal mind of the entire flock to survive. It's one of the greatest powers bestowed upon them. They have the power to tap into the Universal mind, something all who believe in this higher power wish they could do. It is the reason Merrick saw your struggle early on, Lucy.' He nodded to her, but she pressed her lips shut and looked away angrily. 'And it's his community spirit that wouldn't allow him to leave your side when he could sense you were in trouble,' he went on. 'His higher power was listening to yours. That is a thing that geese do, which no human being ever can. Although no longer able to fly, Merrick hasn't lost this, because once the Universal mind is opened, you cannot close it again.'

'So he took me under his wing?' Lucy scoffed.

'Indeed,' he said. 'My work has, of course, been highly experimental. But this is the very nature of medicine men. We work to challenge convention. We study, we observe, we employ logical thinking and we treat. It might not seem logical to you to combine the characteristics of a goose with the healing power of trees. How would anyone come up with that? But that is what sets me apart from others. I think of myself like Beethoven – I cannot hear, yet I feel the notes. My intuition guided me to put together these two seemingly unrelated things and I was right.'

'Yet you have the power to create magic spells?' Merrick asked.

'Yes. It was I that gave Gladys the spell that saved you. And it was I that sent Olive to Gladys, not knowing she was leaving anyone behind. It formed part of my search for a cure. This was the product of years of medical research and a part of my study of the genetic markers of the disease. The answer was always in there somewhere, but something was missing. It's been eating me up for all the days of my life, lately.'

He turned again to Lucy. 'Lucy, *you* were that missing link. Who would have thought that after all my years of study and testing, the answer would come as a result of an accident? A coincidence? It was synchronicity, the power of the geese.'

Lucy shook her head. 'This is just plain ridiculous.'

Despite her sardonic tone, the doctor smiled at her. 'You know it was your Mother that wrote that note, don't you, Lucy?'

She breathed in, the corners of her lips twitching.

'I know you know it,' he said. 'I can see it in your eyes.'

'I was too young to know her writing,' she snapped back. 'And Goosey is a very common nickname for the Lucy's of the world.'

Merrick got to his feet and clasped his hands to his mouth. 'It's useless,' he uttered. 'Useless.'

Gladys cleared her throat, making everyone turn to look at her. 'Olive adored you,' she said to Lucy. 'You were the only thing she kept recalling again and again. She mentioned your name almost every day she wis here.' She got up from her seat and walked over to the Advice Bucket on the windowsill, stopping to pick it up. 'This is yours,' she said, holding it out to her. 'In her more lucid days, Olive would beg me tae make sure ye got it.'

Lucy's eyes went round as she stared at the bucket.

'Take it,' Gladys insisted, walking over to place it in her lap. 'If ye won't believe me, read her. Read yer Mammie's own words. They were all intended for you.'

Chapter 58: Lucy

It was what everyone had called her when she was a girl. Her mother, her grandmother, the Toes. To everyone she'd loved as a child, she was The Goose; their little Lucy-Goosey. These last few days had been incredible. It was like she'd stepped out of the pages of her regular, fast-disappearing life and into another world. She could hardly believe it.

First, she'd been saved from the sea by a man who claimed to have fallen from the sky. He'd been an immortal goose, on his way to roost at Islay. Together, the pair had travelled to Scarba to find that a 300-year-old, Scottish Cailleach of legend who, it turns out, actually exists. And now, the final, fantastic truth: she was free of the terminal, incurable disease that brought her here with the express purpose of ending her life.

She looked at the Advice Bucket, still in her lap where Gladys had placed it. How was it all possible? Lucy thought she might have slipped from reality to a parallel universe. That she'd been lifted from the boat to this mystical island so far from civilisation. Had she stepped off a boat and into The Twilight Zone? Was she dead already? It was all too much.

'I need to get some air,' was all she said to the two men and one extraordinary woman who stood watching her in this tiny cabin in the woods. Like it was something a lady in a wheelchair could do by herself through wild, Scottish wood and moorland.

It was Gladys that had responded. 'Let me take ye.'

They sat outside together, the two women with nothing in common except for Olive.

'She wis lost, but it wis obvious she loved ye so much,' Gladys told her, without turning her gaze away from the sinking sun. 'She talked about ye, but she couldnae tell me where you were. The bucket was for her wee girl, she said. I was to take it to ye.'

'But why did she bring it in the first place?'

'Lord knows,' Gladys replied. 'But I tried tae coax it out o' her; to find out where ye lived.'

Unable to shake of a sense of the surreal, Lucy blinked, staring ahead at the hazy, astonishing view over the isle of Jura ahead. The island's inky-blue form only served to confirm her fears; that she must surely be in the midst of a dream. 'I understand,' was all she could say.

She heard Gladys sigh. 'If ahm honest,' she said to Lucy, 'I have tae tell ye I've been ever so glad o' those wee notes.'

Lucy smiled. 'Well, that pleases me,' she said, not really knowing why it did. She'd never read one, after all.

'Aye,' Gladys continued. 'Yer mammie had an outlook on this world o' ours that I have yet to see, but you have, Lucy. You've been given that rare gift.'

As Lucy found herself staring with interest at her now, Gladys nodded, repeating, 'Ye have.'

'What do you mean? What gift?'

'Ye've seen the very jaws of death, and she saw it too.'

'I don't know what could be so enriching about that,' Lucy said, sounding a little more sardonic than she meant to.

'You know, I have had this gift too,' Gladys went on. 'And it came right from the words on yer mammies pages. I see things in bright, fantastic detail, like ye might expect tae get from a shot o' the old magic mushrooms these hippy types seem tae enjoy.' She chuckled at herself and, despite the madness of the situation, Lucy found herself smiling too.

'I mean, it wis never going tae happen to me once I took the spells from Angus. I held out my hand to take them, like an eejit.

I was doomed tae live, just as you've felt doomed tae die. Ye start to feel like that once yir over two hundred, you know.'

Lucy nodded, but she didn't.

'All Angus said wis that for every ill there's a remedy in nature. And that wis that. I was never ill again and they witch-hunting folk couldnae burn me, so I guessed he must have been right. But I wanted tae know death, Lucy. So, so bad. Once Merrick wis gone I had nobody and nothing until the day I met your mammie. The intense detail, the brightness; that arrived with her.'

'Just like that?'

'Och no,' Gladys replied with a wry smile. 'But she taught it tae me.'

'So you can't die?' Lucy asked.

'Well, for a long time I couldnae, no.'

'And what does this have to do with my mother's notes? Oh wait,' Lucy replied. 'You told me. My mother knew death.'

'That's right. Olive saw bright detail too, don't you?'

Lucy shook her head. 'But I'm not dying,' she said.

'Aye, but for a while there ye thought ye were.'

'I haven't cared enough,' Lucy admitted, her eyes dropping to the floor.

'Ahh,' Gladys said. 'Well, even though yer mammie was mair than a wee bit confused, she could still show me a thing or two. She could tell me how the world looked in her last days. She's continued tae tell me ever since, through the Advice Bucket.'

'Her notes are about dying?'

'Many are, yes. But the majority are about knowing ye're alive. I mean, really knowing. Do you know ye're alive, Lucy? Can you see the braw, bright detail now?'

Lucy was reminded of her note to her doctor, drawing an astonishing parallel. She had spoken of the detail Gladys was now

287

describing. She had confessed to never, ever knowing it was there. 'Did Dr Britten – I mean, Angus - show you my letter?' she said.

'Your letter?'

'Yes,' she replied, feeling unexpectedly irritated. 'The one I left, telling him my final plans. Are you all in this together?'

Gladys stood up to leave. 'I meant what I said in there, Lucy,' she said. 'Yer mammie isnae deed. And, for the record, neither are you.'

'Please,' Lucy said, reaching up to offer her hand, which the other woman didn't accept. 'Please don't leave. I want to hear more about my mother. It's just... it's just... this is all a bit much to take in. What happened to her? What did you do to help her?'

Gladys frowned and looked over Lucy's head to the sky beyond. 'Like Amgus told ye, I sent her to be with Merrick,' she replied simply, before sitting back down beside her.

'So, I guess Merrick will be staying here with you now, while I make up my mind whether I want to go back with my doctor or finish this thing once and for all.'

'Whit thing?'

'My useless, pitiful life,' replied Lucy.

'You had a pitiful life?' Gladys was staring intently at Lucy, but her tone was, nonetheless, mirthful.

Lucy nodded.

Gladys chuckled. 'Was it three hundred years long and without love nor company?'

'But you had Merrick, and he's back now,' Lucy told her. 'Doesn't that change things for the better?'

'Aye, but as ye know he cannae stay.'

Lucy felt stung, from a place she didn't know or recognise. 'Why not?' she asked.

'As a goose he cannae die. But as a man, he'll die like everyone else on earth.'

'Okay, well…' Lucy said, mulling over the detail with what she hoped was a level of optimism. 'Perhaps that's good enough now,' she continued. 'All he talked about on our journey was getting back to you.'

Gladys's eyes crinkled. 'He did?'

Lucy blinked. 'I'm surprised you're surprised,' she said.

To her further astonishment, Gladys laughed. 'Well, I hoped he'd want tae see me, but as we all want for our weans, I'd rather hoped he'd carved out a better, much more extraordinary life for himself than wanting to spend it wae his mammie.'

Lucy's eyes widened.

Gladys grinned back at her. 'Yes,' she said. 'I'm his mammie. What did you think I… oh, wait -'

'But you're the same age,' Lucy gasped. 'I thought… I thought…'

'When you've lived hundreds of years, you lose count a bit, you know, Lucy. Do we look the same age? Aye, we do. That's why I changed him. It wis tae save him from the witch hunters back in the day. They all knew there wis something not right aboot him, only it wasnae him, it was me. I was the one Angus gave immortality to. I was the strange one. The trouble was Merrick thought he had magic too for some reason. He was always a wee bit special like that. He thought he could save people, like he heard they healers could do. Only he was less quiet about it than I wis. So they cried for him to burn too, only I couldnae let them do that. So I did what any mother would do, I saved him. I let him go, and take to the skies.'

'And you haven't seen each other since?' Lucy asked. 'He didn't visit you? You didn't look for him?'

She thought she saw the woman's eyes mist up as she replied, 'I ignored him for years until he quit following me and I could disappear. I thought he wis gonnae hate me for whit ah'd done tae him.' Gladys stopped to offer Lucy a grave look. 'He cannae stay here like this,' she went on. 'He has to go back now, to his own kind. He has to live; to keep the barnacle geese alive.'

'I don't understand?'

'The cure for your illness is in their blood, you heard me tell you that.' It was the doctor that had spoken, appearing from behind.

'So that's it?' Gladys said. 'That's why I had the spell to keep for all this time?'

'I don't get it,' Lucy said. 'How am I cured by Merrick's blood? I only just met him.'

'Because our blood – mine and Olive's - now flows through the veins of all the barnacle geese.' Merrick stepped out of the thicket as he spoke, and stood before them all, smiling kindly at Lucy, who felt a momentary awkwardness at his appearance.

'The early population kept growing then depleting, because of a mixture of natural selection and being hunted by man,' Angus told her. 'The group never seemed to get any bigger for years, until Gladys and I unwittingly colluded to perform the final act.'

'Which was?' Lucy asked.

'I added another goose who was immortal.'

'And of the opposite sex,' Gladys said, clapping her hands. 'It's brilliant, when ye think of it. Ye should have done that at the start'

'But not just any other goose,' said the doctor. 'One who had the disease herself as a human, so her genes and the goose blood combined, and the cure was created. It was an accident, nothing short of a miracle! I never thought of this.'

'Do you mean to say -' Lucy began.

'That it's all true,' said Merrick.

'That your mum is a barnacle goose too?' Angus added. 'You can believe it, Lucy.'

Lucy looked at Gladys, who nodded her confirmation. She swallowed hard, taking a moment to digest everything she'd heard, and as the pieces knitted together, so, it seemed, did her insides. 'Are you telling me,' she said, turning to Merrick. 'You're my mother's... what...?' She felt her face flush crimson, not wanting him to answer but wanting him to all at the same time.

'Goose,' he replied, without a hint of irony.

She swallowed. 'And that would make you my, what?'

'Goose,' Merrick repeated.

'Step-goose,' Angus added, with a grin that wasn't entirely welcomed by Lucy.

She glared at the doctor. 'This isn't funny.'

'I'm not laughing,' he told her, his expression turning serious. 'Look, above all, you need to start to believe that you're cured -'

'And want to live,' Merrick cut in.

'Start to live,' added Gladys.

'Of course,' Angus went on, nodding enthusiastically. 'Lucy, it may well turn out to be because of your mother and some intervention from Gladys -'

'That we've found the magic cure to my illness and I have a couple of anatine parents I didn't know I had.'

'It's all incredible, I grant you,' he replied. 'But it's also true.'

She tutted, yet underneath, she was beginning to believe them. Perhaps, she realised, it was because she wanted to. 'This goes from the surreal to the outlandish,' she shot back regardless. 'You expect me to believe that my mother didn't die all those years ago and has, in fact, been living a fabulous life of migrating and procreating as a barnacle goose without once thinking of... of...' She paused, as a memory from long ago that had materialised again in her recent visit to the Toes house, sprang to mind. 'She came to see me,' Lucy gushed, feeling the hairs on her arms stand on end.

Merrick put a hand on her shoulder.

'Who?' asked Angus.

'She visited my grandmother's garden every year,' Lucy heard herself say, her voice almost indiscernible, because deep down, she couldn't believe her own words. Yet the pieces of the puzzle of her younger life kept on clicking into place. 'She was coming to see me.'

'She went to watch over ye,' Gladys said with a knowing smile. 'Because she loved ye.'

Lucy stared at the floor and then, in a moment of inexplicable realisation, she turned to face the now darkened sky over the horizon. 'How many times did my mother and I watch the same sky, when I thought she was in heaven?' she murmured, feeling like her heart might break.

'Oh, she was in heaven,' Merrick told her. 'That is what's I think it's like up there, Lucy. We've had a fantastic life.'

'My mother is a goose,' Lucy said. 'That sounds like a line straight out of *Monty Python's Holy Grail.*'

'Your mother was a hamster, and your father smelled of elderberries,' Angus said, with an awkward laugh.

'I told you, it's not funny,' Lucy snapped back. 'It's…' She paused, struggling for a single word that could possibly describe receiving the news that your mother has been turned into a goose and the man you just met and had begun to feel fond of was her goose boyfriend. And they'd made babies together – thousands of them. She had hundreds, maybe even *thousands* of goose brothers, sisters, aunts, uncles and cousins too. 'It's weird,' she added, finally.

And then, for what seemed like the first time in forever, she began to laugh. It was a gut-aching, cannot breathe, oh-my-God-I'm-going-to-fart giggling fit of the century.

Chapter 59: Merrick

'Don't think this is the end of a life where you weren't loved, Lucy,' Merrick said. 'You were always loved. It isn't your destiny to die today, this isn't your time.'

'He's right,' Angus added. 'The medical world needs you. I need you. Thousands of men, women and children who might be set to die of Morsley's Pholblastoma need you. Lucy -' He knelt down before her, taking her hands in his. 'It isn't the rare disease you think it is. I've been researching it for many, many years before it was formerly recognised. And the numbers are rising. And now I've realised who your mother is, there might be genetic implications to explore too. Please, I beg you, come back to the mainland with me.'

Merrick saw Lucy's eyes dart towards Gladys, who was rubbing her wrist with a pained expression.

'But aren't you going to die now, like Gladys?' Lucy asked Angus.

'No, I will never die,' he said. 'There's still a lot of work for us. For both of us.'

'It's funny the way you and Merrick ended up coming here together though,' Gladys remarked. 'It's like the stars aligned for us, so it is.'

'That's because Lucy inadvertently told me you were here,' Merrick explained.

'How did ye know I wis here?' Gladys said, staring wide-eyed at Lucy.

'Because you became the stuff of Scottish legend,' Lucy told her. 'Have you ever looked at the internet, Gladys? You are all over it in the history of Scarba.'

Gladys stopped rubbing her wrist and gasped aloud; her eyes wide with astonishment. 'I am?' she said.

Lucy laughed.

'Why didn't they all come tae get me then?'

'Because nobody believed in you,' Angus replied, laughing now too.

Amongst all the merriment, Merrick had begun silently watching Lucy. Her eyes were brimming with tears, and just as he'd begun to wonder what she was thinking, she announced, 'I'll do it,' at last. 'At the very least, I'll do it for Roisin.'

Angus stopped laughing and his brow furrowed. 'Roisin?' he said. 'Who's Roisin?'

'Roisin Blake,' came the reply. 'She's one of your patients too, you must know her.'

The very air between them all seemed to change, as the doctor's forehead puckered and his gaze fell to the floor.

'What?' Lucy asked. 'What is it?'

Angus sighed heavily, before giving an answer. 'She died,' he said. As Lucy opened her mouth to speak, he answered the question that Merrick knew had been on her wordless lips. 'It was last week.'

Lucy covered her mouth with her hands, screwing her eyes tightly shut. 'Oh no, no, no,' she wept. 'That isn't fair. Not Roisin, not Roisin! She had everything to live for! Why not me?'

'You *have* something to live for,' Merrick said, almost to the wind, almost as an instruction from him to himself as he watched Lucy collapse into misery again, unable to hear him. He looked at the doctor, who shook his head sadly.

'Lucy, you have to hear me,' he insisted. 'You have to let this be the first day of the rest of your life. Don't lose focus.'

'But I couldn't save Roisin,' she cried. 'It's too late. Those poor girls, her poor children!'

Feeling what little progress they'd made with Lucy slipping away from them, Merrick put his head in his hands.

'You have the chance to save lots of children,' Gladys said. 'Don't you see that?'

'The cure is already there!' Lucy shouted out, startling them all. 'You don't need me. I don't want this miserable existence anymore. Everyone I've ever cared about has left me!'

'No -' Merrick began.

'YES! You're leaving too, Merrick. You have my mother. What do I have?'

He looked helplessly from Angus to his mother and threw up his hands. He had come so far. He had made it here to be reunited with Olive; his one, true love. But first, he had to make Lucy see that not only was she cured, but that she had a life.

Chapter 60: Gladys

'Here,' Gladys said, offering Merrick the mobile phone that had been given to her by Joe MacNeish with a shaky hand. The group were stood at the freshly dug out grave of the 130-year-old woman on Scarba. 'I've opened the music app there. I want you to play this tune after you've put me in the ground,' she explained.

Merrick stared blankly back at her, but took the phone, saying, 'I don't know how to use this.'

'I do,' Lucy cut in, holding her hand up to receive it. 'Give it to me. Which song is it?'

'It's called "*Who Wants to Live Forever*",' Gladys replied.

Angus gave her an approving nod. 'It's perfect.'

'This is all so... odd,' Lucy said, peering down at the phone.

'It's whit I want,' Gladys said. 'Ma wee hole in the ground that they dug for me over a century ago.'

'And put you in already,' said Angus.

'Aye they did that, Angus... I mean, Dr Britten,' she agreed. 'But I'm ready to stay asleep this time. I was thinking of having "*I'm On My Way*" if ahm being honest. But Freddie says it better.'

'I prefer *Highland Cathedral* myself,' said the doctor.

Merrick eyed Gladys with an expression that almost broke her cheerful determination. 'Why don't you come with me, Mother?' he asked.

'I cannae cast a spell on masel', you nugget,' she said with a smile that didn't reach her eyes. 'And even if I could, I've had enough. We've been around a lot longer than you, Angus and I. I'm ready to go now. I'm so cold.'

'Oh, Gladys,' Lucy said to her. 'Take my coat, please.'

'I cannae do that!'

'It won't be for long, Mother,' Merrick soothed, reaching for the coat Lucy had tugged off her arms. He held it out for Gladys, who accepted it around her gratefully.

'I have to say, I've not felt cold like this for years and years,' Gladys told him. 'But there's something I want to say to you before I go, son.'

Eyes glistening, he said, 'What?'

'That I'm sorry for all the time we've missed together. I wis always here, always missing ye, always loving ye. I've been so proud and so lucky to have ye in ma life. You're the best thing I've done wae it all. You're the best bit o' me.'

Merrick nodded, and she knew he was ready too. Ready to continue the human life-saving barnacle goose line forever and a day, sharing the joy of every season with the love of his life, Olive. Not only did the knowledge that he was happy make her happy, but it also made her now fast-aging heart swell. Knowing what it had all been for was the sweetest parting gift she could have wished for. She turned to the doctor. 'What I don't understand is why the pain went away and then came back,' she said, scratching her chin. 'Even though he'd fallen out of the sky, he was on his way here.'

'I'm not quite sure,' Angus said. 'It would seem that the future of the population is quite secure once he returns.'

Merrick put his hands to his temples, as he remembered something.

'What is it, Merrick?' Gladys asked him.

'It was when I was in the car after getting you from Mr and Mrs Toe's house,' he said to Lucy. 'James told us something about the islanders plans for the geese, do you remember?'

'They are going to have a cull,' replied Lucy. 'Yes, I do remember.'

'A cull? Are you sure? Why would they do that?' Angus asked.

'Because the geese affect the land, which is already sparse for farming,' Lucy replied. 'They eat all the good grass. They plan to kill thousands of them.'

'Oh my, oh my!' Merrick cried. 'That's it, how could I have forgotten about the cull?'

'Which won't be happening now,' the doctor reassured him.

He stopped and looked at him. 'It won't?'

'Err, no,' he replied. 'The geese carry the key to saving thousands of lives the world over. There will be no cull on Islay this year or any other year for that matter. That's why your mother can go now, Merrick. Everything has neatly slotted into place. Her job here is done, as soon as we have you back to where you're supposed to be.' He turned to Gladys and Lucy, his expression serious. 'Are we all ready now?'

'I want to say yes, but, Merrick, I need to thank you first,' said Lucy, holding out a hand for him, which he stepped forward to take in his.

'What for?' he said. 'You were coming here yourself, you'd have found out all of this on your own.'

'But it was you that got me here,' she said. 'And I'd have drowned out there,' she pointed towards the ocean, 'if it hadn't been for you.'

'Well, Lucy, it has been a mighty privilege to sail with you and an even mightier pleasure to meet you,' he told her with a smile. 'You're probably my twenty-seven thousandth dau-'

'Don't even go there!' she barked, her eyes twinkling. 'I refuse to call a goose, Daddy, no matter how much I like you.'

'I'm half-man, half-goose, half-daddy,' he replied, patting his free hand over hers. 'Hey, we can visit in the holidays, if you come over to Islay.'

'I sold my grandmother's house,' Lucy told him, her eyes lowering.

'Yes, but you can visit with the Toes, can't you?'

She looked back at Merrick, and Angus coughed.

'They need ye for the trials,' Gladys said to her.

'Yes, we do,' Angus agreed.

'Well then, it's a given, isn't it?' said Lucy, although the deep isolation she felt failed to convince even her that she meant it.

'You're not alone any more, Lucy,' Gladys told her. 'Ye have your mammie, Merrick and, by the sound of whit my boy here is saying, yer toes are pretty important to ye.' She nodded towards Lucy's feet.

'The Toes,' Merrick corrected her. 'They're her aunt and uncle on Islay.'

Gladys rolled her eyes and gave a relieved sigh. 'Ahh!'

'We're not actually related,' Lucy said to Merrick.

'But you still have them,' he said. 'It was obvious they care for you very much.'

'Merrick, I really think it is time we got all of this work in motion. Sorry to be the mission man in this party,' Angus said, 'but time's marching on and we have a boat ordered to collect us in an hour.'

Merrick nodded his head. 'You're right,' he said, looking at Gladys. 'It's time for me to be on my way.'

Gladys took a long, deep breath inwards. So it was time to say goodbye to her son again, only this time, it was forever. It was goodbye to everything forever. 'Are ye ready?' she asked, as he released Lucy's hand and walked over to give her the longest hug she had ever had.

'I'm ready,' he said over her shoulder. 'Thank you, Mother. For my life, for saving me.'

She heard him start to cry softly and pulled herself gently away from his grasp to look at him again. 'Now away and make me proud,' she told him.

'And for saving Lucy,' he added, looking over at her.

'Well,' Lucy replied through sniffles. 'Are you going to give me a hug too?'

As Merrick went over to her and kissed her on the forehead before kneeling down to hug her, Gladys said, 'I think she meant me.'

Noticing him whisper something in Lucy's ear, Gladys felt a warm rush to her ailing heart; her breaths seemed to be coming slower now. Yet she was grateful. Her stretch was almost up; there was no time left to delay. With each step towards Merrick's departure to the skies, she was fading herself. It was a pivotal moment, filled with an intoxicating mix of joy and sorrow. This is the end, she thought, and this is the beginning. My boy is going to save this woman; she's going to be alright. She fumbled around in her pocket, searching for the spell.

'Right, it's time for both of us to leave,' she announced. 'Please ensure my home and everything in it gets destroyed, just like we said, okay, Angus?'

He nodded. 'Okay, Gladys,' he said. 'God speed, my lovely.'

Taking the paper from her pocket, Gladys read out the words that were scribbled upon it as Merrick stood up, making himself ready:

'Fortanium barnaculous talamh.'

There was an awkward silence.

'Oh,' she said, hastily throwing the note from Lucy's coat down and reaching into her own pocket. 'It's not that one.'

'That's mine,' Lucy cried, holding out her hands as Angus stooped to pick it up. 'It's the note from the wishing tree!'

'Oh jings! The one that changes the goose...' Gladys began, and then stopped. 'We've done it again,' she said to Lucy.

'What?' said Lucy, taken aback.

'Is this the one – the exact one - you read out recently?' Angus asked her.

'Yes,' she replied, feeling suddenly uncomfortable. 'But it's just jibberish.'

'It's no jibberish,' said Gladys. 'It's the spell that brought Merrick down.'

'It is?' Lucy said, her eyes widening. 'It really is?'

Gladys and Angus nodded together.

Merrick gasped, and everyone turned to look at him. He was holding his hand over his mouth.

'What?' Lucy said to him.

'What happens on the second reading?' Gladys asked the doctor.

'What you think might happen,' he said, his brows knitting.

'Oh jings,' Gladys said again, turning to Merrick.

Taking his hand off his mouth, Merrick screwed his eyes tightly shut and yelled:

'OLIVE!'

Chapter 61: Dr Britten

Dr Britten drove them from the ferry at Islay for three quarters of an hour, everyone in complete silence. The sun over Loch Gruinart retreated behind clouds, adorning the sky with bursts of blood orange and apricot. It was a colour explosion worthy of Monet. As he finally pulled the car into a stopping place, the doctor blew out his cheeks and patted the steering wheel. He turned to Lucy, his voice full of concern. 'We can do the reversal now,' he said.

'No,' she shot back. 'I want to see her. I need to know she's okay, don't you?'

Beside him, Merrick nodded his own agreement, turning to look out of the window into fields full of geese. 'Well, let's go,' he said to the doctor, opening his car door and going round to get Lucy's chair out of the boot.

'Can't I just sit here and wait?' she protested, making a show of shivering from the cold.

Dr Britten got out of the car, rushing to help heave the wheelchair out of the boot. As soon as its wheels hit the ground, Merrick opened it out and pushed it to the passenger side door. The doctor followed behind. 'Are you going to come find her, or not?' Merrick asked Lucy, banging on her window.

She rolled it down. 'You said she could be naked,' she replied. 'And what if she's hurt? I couldn't bear that.' She put her hands to both cheeks, her eyes pleading. 'I don't want to see.'

'Okay, I can understand that,' Merrick said, nodding. 'But we roost here. She is, I imagine, very likely to be sat on the ground somewhere nearby, perhaps freezing.'

'Take my coat,' Lucy said, slipping it from her shoulders and offering it up for the second time that day.

Merrick sighed, but held out his hands to take the coat. 'Okay, I tell you what. I have to go, and I have to go now. Olive is somewhere lost and she needs me.' He looked back at the doctor. 'How long do we have until my Mother reads the spell?' he asked him.

Dr Britten looked at his watch. 'One hour,' he said.

'Will you wait here with Lucy for me?'

The doctor nodded his agreement and returned to the driver's seat. 'Alright, but you have to hurry,' he said. 'Lucy's Mother is suffering and goodness knows what sort of condition shes in. Make haste, my friend.'

Without another word, Merrick jumped over a nearby fence and began to run across the field. Seas of chuntering geese parted as he passed, making his way toward the loch beyond.

'It'll be fine, you'll see,' Dr Britten reassured Lucy, patting her arm as she watched Merrick go.

She rolled up her window and continued to look out of it.

'Gladys was dying when we found her,' the doctor continued. 'Which would suggest to me that your mother lives.'

Lucy drew in a breath, holding it for a second. 'I still can't get a handle on all this,' she admitted after a moment.

The doctor gazed intently at her, noting that her eyes were glossy. Some of this was getting through, he knew it. Despite all that she said, he felt she believed. She had to now; just as she had to want to live. He turned away to the thousands of barnacle geese that roosted in the fields all around them. 'Lucy,' he said, after a moment.

'What do you think your life has been for?'

'Judgment,' she replied without hesitation.

'What?'

'Come on, Dr Britten, any fool can see I must have done something wrong in a former life. Everyone I've loved is gone. They were all predestined to leave me, I know it.'

'But your mother didn't leave you,' he insisted. 'She was here all along. She's been coming back to this island with the rest of the geese for all the years since she changed. Do you think she had no choice in that matter? That she couldn't have chosen to join a different group to the Greenland one?'

'I suppose -'

'Barnacle geese come from several continents,' he cut in. 'Yet only the Greenland group settle on Islay each year.'

'And I'm supposed to believe that she came here for me?'

'Yes, I-'

'Wouldn't it be the obvious choice, given that this is where she once lived?'

Dr Britten heaved a sigh. 'Okay, you have me on that point,' he agreed. 'But who knows how the geese decide to group once they fly to other continents? Who knows what choices Olive had to make along the way? She stayed, Lucy. She did. And I believe, whether you do or not, that she did it for you.'

'But I wasn't here.'

'True,' he replied with a nod. 'She lost you, for sure. Yet if it was me and you were my child, I know I'd stay in the place that you might be bound to come back to some day.'

Lucy turned to him and blinked. 'Here? Why would I?'

He looked deep into her eyes, offering her a knowing look. 'You're here now, Lucy,' he said finally.

She turned to stare back out of the window, her demeanour giving nothing away. Pursing his lips the doctor sighed, feeling exasperated. He rolled down his window, as the chorus of what he knew to be thirty thousand or more barnacle geese grew louder. 'If you don't mind,' he told her over the din. 'I'm going to go into the field over there.' He pointed to where Merrick had gone and opened his door.

'What for?' Lucy snapped.

'I'm going to cause a bit of a stir,' he replied, getting out of the car.

'What? But where are you going?'

Without answering, he started to climb the fence, his heart beginning to hammer in his chest. He had to make her see; see everything. Perhaps no moment in Dr Britten's life had ever been so pivotal as this one.

'Do you want to come out?' he shouted back at her, wobbling as he fought to keep his balance. 'You can't see anything from there.'

She nodded, and he felt relieved, jumping down to go back for her. He helped her into her chair then pushed her to the fence to let her see the field of geese in all their glory. There was a paused as the pair took it all in: the sights, sounds and smells of this incredible place. Thousands of geese barking and scratching over land and water for as far as the eye could see.

'It's a miracle,' Lucy whispered, almost to herself, but Dr Britten heard her.

She was, as was he, in awe and wonder at the spectacle. It was a start, at least. 'It is that,' he agreed, 'and what's so special about this mass gathering of simple barnacle geese, Lucy Colwyn?'

She stared up at him, her expression grim. He knew she'd already anticipated what he had to say and didn't want to hear it. Turning away, the doctor climbed back onto the fence and hauled himself over it.

'Where are you going now?' he heard her call after him. Ignoring her, he strode forward, wading through the geese. They darted this way and that to get away from him, making him a path. He was heading for the middle of the field. Within a few moments he was in the place he wanted to be, waving back to where Lucy still sat watching him. 'LOOK LUCY!' he shouted. 'LOOK!'

There was the loud hum of thousands of wings as the sky over him darkened. Turning his face to the sky he watched as thirty-thousand geese took to the air at once. Not only from the field, but from all the surrounding fields and from the loch beyond. Every bird spirited upwards as if by a magic, unseen power. 'LOOK!' the doctor shouted. He raised both arms up to a sky that was now black and heavy with barnacle geese flapping to a new place of safety.

Starting back towards Lucy, he saw her face was turned upwards too. Her mouth open in a gasp as the geese flew over her head, filling the air with their gentle thunder as they went.

'This is what your life is for,' Dr Britten shouted as he reached her side. 'This was it, Lucy Colwyn.'

Her eyes sparkled, but her expression revealed a different, more dubious Lucy. 'I don't get it,' she said.

Dr Britten clambered back over the gate to stand beside her, pausing to catch his breath.

'What has this got to do with me?' she said.

He knelt down to take her hand into his. 'Everything,' he told her gently. He pointed up at the still packed sky and beamed at her. 'They're all descended from your mother,' he explained. 'The geese that carry the cure to Morsley's Pholblastoma.'

'You don't know that,' she scoffed.

'It's as good as so,' he went on. 'Barnacle geese mate for life. In the last forty years Merrick found his mate. She's the one who outlived all the others so that the species could go on and on, all the while creating new life. Every year this incredible group has been getting bigger and bigger.'

He stopped to watch Lucy, his eyes boring into her, pleading with her to understand; to know how much he needed her to. And at last, a fat tear spilled from one eye and trickled down Lucy's cheek. He caught his breath, as her eyes widened and she looked from him up to the sky once more, the tears coming faster now. Dr Britten's heart lifted and he felt released. It was as though the wheels of his very life had begun to turn again.

'My mother did all this?' Lucy whispered.

He nodded. 'There's a good chance these geese are all descended from Merrick and your mother, Lucy,' he told her. 'Every cure-carrying, life-giving goose here is related to you.'

'All of them?' she said, her eyes twinkling in renewed amazement.

'All of them,' he repeated. 'Isn't this an astonishing world you want to give up on?' He said, before clasping both her hands in his. 'It needs you so much more than you could ever have realised, Goosey Lucy. I'm begging you, don't leave.'

Chapter 62: Olive

Tiny diamonds danced in front of Olive's eyes and her body quaked with cold. It had been a clear day, she remembered that. Sometimes she could soar right through the clouds, following the scent of the wind. She was sure she'd done that today. Or was it yesterday?

How long had she been here?

A gust of wind caught her where she lay and she sensed every hair on the surface of her skin standing to attention. Her teeth chattered and she tensed, pulling her knees to her chest; curving her body into a tight ball in the grass. There were sounds she recognised. Small dogs barking. No, that wasn't it.

I love you, Mummy.

'Mum?' Lifting her face from the ground she peered around, blinking in the light. There was nobody there, only the ocean. Miles and miles of ocean, tranquil and glassy under a blazing sky.

You were going there to die.

She sat up, sure now that somebody was there. Where were the voices coming from? She breathed in crisp, clean air, and above its biting iciness she felt remembered bliss. The sky; she loved the sky. Where was everybody?

'Lucy?' she said, trying to recall something else. Why was this word important? A fluttering sound made her start and she turned to find a field of black and white behind her. Some kind of bird for as far as her eyes could see. Then they lifted as one, filling the sky over her. Where was she?

You're dying.

Olive cried out, afraid of the voice. 'Please,' she cried. 'Please tell me where you are?' There was no reply. What did it say? She was dying? Her moment of panic passed, warm relief washing it away almost as soon as it came. That's right, Olive was dying. She was going to the sea to get away.

Run. Sink. Never be found.

She stood up and felt her toes curl into sand. Striding forwards, she shuffled towards the shore, every bone in her body aching. Yes, she was dying; it was decided for her. All she needed to do was disappear.

Chapter 63: Merrick

Merrick knew where she would be, the roosting site on the tidal mudflats of the loch. The geese gathered there daily at dusk, and she would have waited for him each evening. She always waited, never leaving until he joined her on the land. They were only ever separated by tailwind in the skies, or when she was on the nest and he, foraging for food. On this land, they were as one; a team. A family.

He ran on and on, through damp grass and peat bog, sending geese flapping away in all directions to safety. As he neared the water his eyes searched the area, until he spied something. It was floating a short way off shore. A lump or mass of some kind. He stopped and stared, his eyes straining to make it out. It was larger than a log, paler than seaweed. Throwing Lucy's coat to the ground, he ran on until he noticed arms outstretched.

'OLIVE!'

Instinctively, Merrick stretched out his own arms, feeling the wind under them. He waited for it to carry him, but it was useless. He had only human limbs that carried him far slower than he needed them to. Cursing the sky he pressed on, heart pounding in his chest, until he reached the water and tore through it. Reaching the icy depths at last, he plunged in. 'OLIVE!' he shouted, swallowing water as he went under again. His arms and legs flailed, cutting through the water as fast as he could make them. His mind screamed, 'Don't die. Don't die. Don't die!'

Finding himself at last within reach of her face down body, he stretched out and caught her in his arms. 'No!' he screamed, turning her over. 'NO!'

Chapter 64: Lucy

Envy consumed Lucy for a time as she watched the barnacle geese return to settle in the fields. They had taken the moments she should have had with her mother away from her, so it seemed. Yet, in truth, she knew they hadn't. It was all the fault of the cursed disease. She hugged the Advice Bucket Gladys had given her tightly, overwhelmed with emotion. At least she had this - at last. 'But I can never get the time back,' she murmured into it.

'What?' Dr Britten said. He was sat on the bonnet of the car, watching the field they'd seen Merrick disappear into, waiting on his return.

'Nothing,' she said, aware of her pulse beginning to race. She was becoming anxious and excited in equal measure. Lucy believed the doctor now. She believed Merrick. 'How long do we have left now?' she asked the doctor, feeling her neck prickle.

Twisting to face her, Dr Britten looked at his watch and she saw him frown. 'Twenty, maybe thirty minutes if Gladys takes her time,' he replied. He turned back towards the field.

'What if he doesn't find her?' Lucy said.

'They'll change anyway.'

'And I won't see her?'

'No.'

Lucy looked up to the sky before closing her eyes. Feeling the breeze on her face she took a deep breath in, tasting the air. 'It must be amazing to be able to fly,' she said.

'They're here!'

Snapping her eyes open, Lucy's heart jumped into her mouth at the shout from Dr Britten. 'Both of them?'

'Yes!'

She turned her attention back to the field and squinted, unable to see well without her glasses. At the far end she could make out a figure. It moved nearer to them until at last she could make out Merrick, carrying what appeared to be a cloaked figure. She gasped. 'Is that her?' she said to Dr Britten. 'Is that my Mother?'

The doctor stepped in front of her and started climbing the gate. 'I'm going to help him, wait here!' he commanded, jumping over.

Lucy craned her neck, hearing her heartbeat thumping inside her ears now. It was true. She was moments from Olive, after a lifetime of thinking she was dead. At once she felt weak as a child again, anxious to see her mother. She held her breath, watching Dr Britten run across the field. As he finally reached them, Lucy's view of Merrick and her mother was blocked by his back.

'MUM!' Lucy found herself shouting. It wasn't a sound she recognised as her own voice. It was a child's cry. A five-year-old girl, watching her beloved mother disappear on a boat. Witnessing the only parent she had leaving her far behind. The tears came thick and fast. How much time did they have left now? Twenty minutes? Ten? She hugged herself, anguish rising in her throat as she gave a final, wretched cry:

'MUM!'

Chapter 65: Merrick

'She... doesn't... know who I am,' Merrick told the doctor between wheezes and coughs. He felt like his lungs might burst at any moment.

'Of course she doesn't,' Dr Britten replied. 'She's never seen you before. Not like... like this, anyway. Can she walk?' He leaned in to look into Olive's dazed, bloodshot eyes and frowned. 'Can you walk, Olive?'

Letting the doctor help her to her feet, Merrick replied, 'She's a bit wobbly. That's why I had to carry her.' Free from the weight of her, he brushed Olive's wet hair away from her face. 'Are you alright?' he asked her tenderly.

'I... I think so,' she stammered, her lip quivering.

'Oh, you're freezing Olive! Here,' the Dr Britten said, taking off his huge coat to put it on her over Lucy's. He smiled kindly at her as he studied her face. 'Do you know who I am?' he asked.

She gazed back, her eyes searching his features. 'No,' she told him finally.

'I found her floating in the water,' Merrick said, fighting back tears. 'I thought I'd lost her.' He bit his lip to stop it trembling, before adding, 'I don't what I'd have done.'

'I'm your doctor,' the other man told Olive. 'You don't remember me?'

She shook her head.

Dr Britten put an arm around her shoulder with Merrick and glanced at his watch. 'We'd better hurry this up,' he said. 'Let's get her to the car.'

The pair started walking with her to the gate. As they neared her, Merrick could see Lucy craning her neck, watching them with an anxious expression. 'Do you remember Lucy?' he asked Olive.

'Lucy,' she said, hobbling along awkwardly, her doleful expression unchanged.

Olive was managing to walk better than Merrick had first anticipated and within moments they had reached the gate. He let her go and she stood a while unsupported as he waited to catch her should she tumble again. As Dr Britten opened the gate, he turned to look back at Olive, eyes wide, as she instantly strode out towards her daughter.

'Mum!' Lucy cried, her face soaked with tears. She held up her arms and Olive stopped in front of her. 'Mum!' Lucy let out a heart-wrenching sob. 'It's you. I can't… I can't believe it!'

Noticing Olive's pause, Merrick walked up and took her hand. 'This is your daughter, Olive,' he told her softly, leading her onward. 'This is Lucy, do you remember?'

'Lucy?' Olive repeated, looking from her to him.

Her eyes appeared glazed, but as he nodded a confirmation to her, Merrick thought he saw the briefest flicker of light.

'My Lucy?'

Feeling like his heart might break, Merrick put his other hand over hers and nodded. 'It's your little girl,' he said.

Letting go of Merrick's hand, Olive took a step forward then paused, turning back to peer at him again. 'Am I dead?' she asked him. 'Is this heaven?'

'No,' he replied. 'This is home.'

'It's me, Mum,' Lucy cried between sobs. 'It's Lucy Goosey.'

Olive's brows raised and Merrick saw her clouded eyes widen and twinkle. Turning her face away from him, she took another few steps then fell to her knees, embracing her daughter. 'Lucy,' she sobbed. 'It's my Lucy.'

The women hugged for what felt like an age to Merrick, yet he knew the reality was all too brief for them both. Right at that moment he realised something important, something that had been

316

there in the back of his mind since first he'd pulled Lucy from the sea only a day earlier. Merrick cared deeply for both of these women. They were each a part of him now. Before he could consider these thoughts of family any further, Dr Britten coughed.

'It's time,' the doctor said.

Lucy peered up at him over Olive's shoulder, blinking through tears. 'No,' she pleaded. 'I want longer! Can't she stay longer?'

'There's no more time,' the doctor replied, his expression grim.

'But I'm not dying!'

'No, you're not, Lucy,' he agreed. 'But she is.' He nodded to Olive with a sad half-smile. 'You have to let her go back.'

Olive pulled herself away from Lucy and got up to stand, swaying awkwardly as she did so. Merrick rushed forward to steady her. 'I'm dying today,' she said as he caught her, her dewy eyes clouding over again.

'No, my love,' Merrick said, taking her hand to gently press his lips to it. 'We have forever, you and I. That's our today.'

'Merrick,' Lucy said, brushing the tears from her eyes. 'I want to thank you. Before... Before -'

'No,' he told her firmly. 'Don't thank me, Lucy Colwyn. Honour me and honour your mother.'

She blinked, looking taken aback. 'What do you mean?' she asked.

'People have died,' he said. 'People who deserved to live, do you understand?'

Lucy lowered her eyes to the ground.

'They didn't have a choice,' he continued. 'Now you do. Lucy -' Merrick stopped, hugging Olive to him as, at once, the bright haze of orange sky seemed to flash a warning. It really was time, he could feel it. The call of the earth encircled him and his mate, whispering wishes for a brighter tomorrow into their ears. Consumed once more by the song of the hull, he felt his body lift.

The last words Merrick would speak as a man were left in the air as he and Olive took flight:

'You are loved.'

Chapter 66: Lucy

'Lucy, Lucy! Come see! There's two barnacle geese in the garden!'

Lucy looked up from her book in the Toes conservatory and smiled. It was that time again.

'Shall I come with you, dear?' her Auntie Jeanie said.

She smiled back at the old woman, whose days had also been cheered by the appearance of four, new, charming and adorable girls in her life. It made her heart glad to see her aunt look so contented. It would be a long road back to happiness for Roisin's daughters too, but they were getting there. And whilst Jeanie Toe was still most often confused, moments of clarity had kept returning, to the delight of Mr Toe. They had stayed for two summer holidays so far, but there would be more – many more.

She needn't have wondered whether it was okay for a single, disabled woman to adopt not one, but four girls, all hungry for knowledge and ready to go out and make their mark in the world. There had been no one the child services department of her county could think of to do the job better of raising Roisin's children than Lucy. This was the woman who was helping researchers from three continents to work to produce the cure for the disease that took their mother's sadly short life and had once threatened to take hers. And no one had come forward to offer a home to all four, allowing them to stay together, except for Lucy.

Blinking, Lucy wheeled herself out into the sunlight to see the geese. Tall, proud and stomping in the bushes, the mated pair seemed – to her mind - to be smiling. In fact, she knew they were. As one of the girls got too close to them, Lucy beamed as two pairs of wings flapped and rose up out of the bushes. 'Bye Mum, bye Merrick!' she called, looking up to follow them with her eyes as they took to fresh, Islay air; flying free.

Watching them go, she felt an enormous sense of peace. The geese numbers would grow and keep on growing, their future secured by the miracle they carried in their blood. Cases of Morsley's Pholblastoma were now on the decline, with Lucy's story reaching media attention. She thought of her office at home, awash with thank you cards and photographs of the men, women and children whose lives she had saved in agreeing to work with Dr Angus Britten on more trials. She had a new family to treasure now and even, she hoped, the prospect of grandchildren. No other life would ever be more worthwhile than that of Lucy Colwyn. She'd even paid her gas bill.

Feeling inside her pocket, she took out the note that was scribbled in what she now knew to be her mother's handwriting. It said:

You may think the earth is very small. In fact, it is tiny. Strive every day to make the kind of noise only the entire universe will hear.

Lucy lifted her face to the sky, just in time to see the geese disappearing beyond the trees across the road. 'I LOVE YOU, MUM!' she yelled.

Acknowledgments

There have been so many selfless people who have helped me see this project through to the end, it has been a long road, made far easier with their help.

I want to first say a huge thank you to Di Dyke, Carol Hopkins, Michelle Ryles and Simon Leonard, who each gave their time so gracious and selflessly in reading through my first, very rough draft of this novel. Without you, I literally do not know what I would have done to see this work finished. Your kind comments make a terrified author a little less scared and a lot more confident.

A huge and very special mention here for the wonderful, supportive TBC Facebook book club, founded by Tracy Fenton and run with her marvellous team: Helen Boyce, Teresa Nikolic, Sharon Bairden, Helen Claire, Emma Mitchell and Diane Dyke. Words cannot express how much this group has helped me and expanded my miniscule, writerly world. I have so many friends in the group and cheerleaders, all who give their time freely. All TBC's authors are supported above and beyond in this very special place. Words cannot begin to express my gratitude to you or show just how wonderful you are. Thank you, thank you, thank you. I'm so grateful for you.

And to the amazing and super-talented Debi Alper, who again has helped me put my head above my heart to straighten out the thoughts and ideas that went into this very different (for me) book. Your patience, your skill and your honesty had me returned to you after your help with the others. Thank you so much, Debi.

To the fabulous author, Rowan Coleman, whose magnificent books have inspired and tutored me on this journey, further enhanced with the addition of Rowan's amazing writer's course at Ponden Hall in Yorkshire. I achieved more in four days that I had in the eighteen months running up to it, when fear had been holding me back with certain areas of my story. The Advice Bucket has been a different, somewhat unfamiliar direction for me and you helped me release some of the creative thoughts I'd been unknowingly suppressing. With your help I have discovered a new world of ideas to take forward. Thanks also to my fellow students on the course: Anoushka Huggins, Debbie O'Shea, Rob Baldwin, Stephanie W. Scott and Claire Maycock – all great writers I cannot wait to read in future. I had so much fun, laughing until I cried on the course. But I also learned a lot in such a short time, sharing with and feeling supported by this terrific group of people. Great things are to come! I hope we have a reunion one day.

Finally to the lovely Mark Chambers, who was contacted by a frantic woman and asked if she could steal him amazing photo of the barnacle geese at the Caerlaverock Wetland Centre at dusk for her book cover. Thank you for your marvellous gift, Mark. It's a truly beautiful thing – both the cover photo and your act of giving.

Note from the Author

The beautiful barnacle geese that gather on Islay and at Caerlaverock each year are indeed in danger, with Scottish authorities proposing culling more than a quarter of the population. There are around 80,000 Greenland barnacle geese in the world, making them a relatively uncommon bird. Around 40,000 of these overwinter in one place – Islay. You can read more about the complaints raised by the Wildfowl & Wetlands Trust (WWT) and RSPB Scotland to Brussels on the WWT website at wwt.org/wetland-centres/caerlaverock.

About The Author

Heather Hill - comedy writer, author and mum of five (not the band) lives in Scotland and is one of a rare kind; the rare kind being one of the 0.5% of females that is ever-so-slightly colour blind. She is known to have been prevented from leaving the house with blue eyebrows on at least one occasion.

Heather started out writing lines for comedians in the Aberdeen, Glasgow & Edinburgh live comedy circuit, before embarking on a novel writing career. Her debut British comedy eBook, 'The New Mrs D', was an Amazon No1 bestseller before the paperback was published by Fledgling Press, Edinburgh in Spring 2015.

You can connect with Heather online by visiting her blog at www.heatherhillauthor.com. Or catch her on Twitter & Instagram, where she is often found sharing photos of her breakfast. Follow Heather - and her breakfast - @hell4heather or on Instagram @heatherhillauthor

By the same author

The New Mrs D

After Shirley Valentine, after The First Wives Club and hot on the naked heels of Calendar Girls... there was The New Mrs D!

'Wine-spittingly, chocolate-chokingly brilliant! Hill is the Tom Sharpe of her era! Genuinely laugh out loud funny with great writing and a plot to keep you hooked. Buy it, read it - but if like me you are of a certain age, do so with an empty bladder.' – Amanda Prowse, author of the No Greater Love series.

Four days into their honeymoon in Greece, Bernice and David Dando have yet to consummate their marriage and after having accepted his almost non-existent desire for sex throughout the relationship, Bernice finally discovers the reason; he is addicted to porn. Learning that the love of her life chooses the cheap thrill of fantasy over her is devastating but then, 'every man does it; it's just looking, right?' If she leaves the relationship because of virtual adultery, will she be labelled as pathological, overreacting, or even worse, frigid?

When funny, feisty, forty-something Bernice plans the adventure trip of a lifetime, she doesn't expect to be spending it alone. But as it turns out, unintentionally contributing to a Greek fish explosion, nude karaoke and hilarious misadventures with volcanoes are exactly what she needs to stop fretting about errant husbands and really start living. But when Mr D tries to win her back, Bernice has a decision to make: is this a holiday from her humdrum life, or the start of a whole new adventure?

"The New Mrs D is a refreshing, sharp-witted and empowering romp that reflects real life, delves into unspoken about subjects and slaps the reader in the face with honesty." Fleur Ferris, author.

The New Mrs D is a story about one woman's midlife awakening... on her honeymoon alone.

I Hate That You Bloody Left Me

'Totally Bonkers... and Totally Brilliant!'

'Dare to never lose the silly side of yourself.'

When three silver-surfer widows take a road trip to a bewitching island in the Southern Hebrides, kidnapping a world-renowned psychic medium was the last thing on their minds. And the first thing they did...

After three bereaved, elderly ladies meet in an online forum, it soon becomes clear they each have their own, quite specific, senior citizen plan. The first is desperate for a message from her husband, but his sudden death has made him unavailable. The second just wants a hole in the ground to swallow her up, and so it duly does. The third is in search of her true identity, and has all of life's essentials in her over-sized handbag: lipstick, phone, spare pair of knickers, mother...

As a trio of desolate women transitions into a trio of friends, they embark on a mission to track a recently retired, world famous pyschic medium, which takes them on a series of zany and hilarious adventures, where shocking secrets are revealed, relationships are tested, and lobsters are liberated. The women want to know, and they want to know now: Is there life BEFORE death?

Light-hearted, funny and moving, 'I Hate That You Bloody Left Me' is a journey of friendship, whisky-rustling and accidental kidnapping, set on the spectacular Scottish isles of Jura and Islay.

It's a pint full of belly laughs, with a whisky chaser.

'Fizzles with wit and humour... Warm, funny, poignant - I loved this utterly original story!'

- Fiona Gibson, author

'Although on one level the novel may be considered '"light" entertainment, with its elements of slapstick and double entendres, it's also a poignant, touching and life-affirming study on the themes of grief and loss.'

– Debi Alper, author and freelance editor.

'Heather Hill's writing is hilarious, touching and honest. A truly original voice in women's fiction.'

– Jon Rance, author.

'A wonderful blend of comedy and pathos.'

– Bennett Arron, comedian and author

Printed in Great Britain
by Amazon